THE HOTTEST SUMMER IN YEARS

ANURADHA KUMAR

YODA PRESS
79 Gulmohar Enclave
New Delhi 110 049
www.yodapress.co.in

ISBN: 9789382579687

Editors in charge: Arpita Das, Ishita Gupta and Tanya Singh
Typeset by R. Ajith Kumar
Published by Arpita Das for YODA PRESS, New Delhi

'For a long time—and this particular time with greater force than usual—summer has been a season that gives me a sense of emptiness and absence, and takes me back to the past. Is it the too-harsh light, the silence of the streets, those contrasts of the shade and the setting sun, the other evening, on the façades of the buildings in the Boulevard Soult? The past and the present merge in my mind through a phenomenon of superimposition.'

PATRICK MODIANO, Honeymoon

'Our words may seem to you,
eavesdropper, to skip over surfaces,
like today's last dragonfly before it's absorbed by shadow,
and some things may be clearer to you later,
much later, like, as every evening darkened, we imagined
we'd lift off the bench without effort
and sail home as steady as herons.'

ADIL JUSSAWALLA, 'Old Men on a Bench'

For my parents, and all those who go looking for lost loves.

CONTENTS

PROLOGUE

The map, pinned to the wall, was old and yellowing. It flapped gently in the occasional breath of air from the window. Facing it was my table, and to one side, my bed, sparse and uncluttered. I'd torn the map out of the first newspaper I'd read the day I reached Bombay. Rough and quickly sketched, it showed most of the world, apart from Australia and the eastern Pacific. Places I'd never visit now.

My own hand-drawn lines covered the map, curving up from Africa, toward southern France, Italy and then Germany. My first journey away from home. Then other thin, broken lines, faint, like a secret barely disclosed. I had drawn these, as I left Berlin, then Cologne, and headed southward, crossing borders of every kind. Other lines, straggly and jerky, to show someone on the run. Then the extended, sweeping lines of a ship's journey down the Atlantic.

Lines in blue showing my return to Africa, circling around three places before surging out oceanward toward the east. This time headed toward a dot somewhere in India's centre. A dot I had erased, then pencilled in again. For I really hadn't been sure of where I was headed.

That winter of the late 1950s, I had boarded a ship, the first I could find passage on, and sailed to Mombasa, then to Bombay, from where I had taken the most crowded train to Calcutta. I had soon drifted into sleep, as the wheels turned and moved slow, even slower, under me, and it was still night when I felt that nudge on my shoulder. The train had stalled for no apparent reason. I came to, hearing voices from outside, the coolies shouting out the name of the station, and then that tap on my shoulder. It was no accident, for it happened again, and I jerked awake.

Stale breath brushed against me, as someone bent to whisper, 'Here's your stop.' I've never liked voices close to my ear. It's not the feel of stale air against my skin as much as the suggestion of secrecy, even intimacy, this gesture implies.

'That man,' someone had once whispered to me, pointing to someone else just as this man was now. Then the man in my past had placed a gun in my hands. I returned to the present, made out the man's white uniform, his frayed yellowing badge and then he pointed out, 'Raurkela, sahib...your stop?'

'What? Oh yes, yes.' I looked out toward the darkness he pointed into, and already there was the thin reddish glow in the east, greying the dark mane of trees by the road. I spent that night in the waiting room. In the morning, someone from the steel plant came to pick me up. A car I clearly recognized, that I was meant to recognize: the blue Daimler I'd last seen in Berlin. The last year of the Second World War, though at that time, no one could possibly have known this.

1

THE HIGH TEA

The year was 1960, and that summer of May, my first in that hot Indian city. In the west of Africa, my childhood home, the sun had never been so merciless, so very steadfast in its attention. Later, as the drama of Ahmed Ali's murder unfolded, I would learn that it had been one of the hottest summers ever recorded.

I had arrived only some months ago, in a mild winter. The other Germans, the engineers from Krupp, and the maintenance staff had already been there for a year and more. It was a time when the sal forests were still being cut down, and the shouts of the lone crane operator could be heard as the bricklayers, sullen at their work, built the new quarters for the steel plant workers. They were working overtime, and at night their soft conversation could be heard over the buzz of the kerosene lamps in their tents and the unfinished construction site, the moths singeing themselves and falling with the faintest of hisses. You could also hear the clink of glasses and laughter from the new officers' club that I had been officially appointed to manage.

Appointment as Club Manager; and so the letter that had arrived for me in Durban, had begun. After listing in a banal way all that the job entailed: stock-keeping, maintaining logistical control, and setting up an efficient team of local people who would soon learn German, it ended with a pious benediction; *Make it a home away from home for your fellow Germans.*

I'd look often enough at the letter in my early days. I'd kept moving from one place to another before that time, and no place had been home. Nothing in me felt German, though for a time, more than being German, I had been the replica of another German, a hated one. To take on oneself a hatred that was due someone else, to become someone else entirely, is a feeling that is hard to shake off.

Late when all the noise had died, you could hear the jackals come stealthily out of the jungle. I'd wake from my nightmare thinking they had come for my long nebulous, undecided self. I'd almost wish that they had come for the part of me I longed to tear away from. The man I once resembled. The coward in me that hadn't been able to fire in time. When the ship had lurched, I had lost my footing, and I felt the spray on my face, but this time it was the sweat on my cheeks, my clammy palms that woke me.

Then more fully awake, I'd wait for the stray shout or two, or the thud of a stone that would be enough to scare the jackals away. When I emerged from the dark room where I kept my photos, and slept on a low mattress on the wooden floor, all I'd see was that one bright light from the raja sahib's palace, filtering through the trees, fading but never going away.

That meant, as I'd learn in a few days' time, that Lisa was awake, and up late reading. But in the darkness before I knew Lisa, I saw only how the light blinked every time the leaves moved, sighing in the breeze. The shifting moon played with the shadows, the jackals howled, steel fell from the slags. All through that hot summer, as the steel plant came up, and I worked hard to get the club going, Lisa read long into the night, and it made her late for the high tea that afternoon at the palace when I finally met her.

I'd come to think that everything of significance to me occurred in the same ordinary way. Events unwrapped themselves before me, slowly, one after the other, and I witnessed it, like a lone member of the audience, always on the margins. That is how I had felt when I was invited to high tea at the palace. The other guest at the palace that afternoon was Ranjay Das, the district's new superintendent of police. He had arrived in the town only a fortnight before me. But as he had explained to me twice before—once at our first meeting in his office and later in the club—he knew the palace grounds well, not the palace itself. Decorum, he'd said, and his hat had shifted to a jauntier angle. And then he had gone on to say, in a deliberate laconic tone, fingering his bowtie, that his father's position had never allowed him access to privileged spaces. 'No entry into the sanctum sanctorum,' he said, laughing, his teeth a flash of sly white on his swarthy face.

Das's life story changed often, as I'd come to realize soon. His father was variously a lawyer, then a clerk, then an assistant. For Das had spent his childhood here in this town, and had a pile of injustices, to mull over, conjure up, consider and resolve. He was so busy regaling me with them over and over, that I missed the fact that he genuinely wanted to work out a resolution, a complete happy ending for himself. As if that were even possible. But I am getting ahead of my story.

One afternoon some time before the high tea, Das had come by the club; all the district's senior administration officials had honorary memberships. Das knew that of course, and so he came straight to the point, having looked for several minutes out through my window at the makeshift structures all around and the dry hills farther away. He was lean and looked even more so as he stood with his head against the window ledge. His shirt was tucked neatly into his trousers.

He asked why I hadn't formally paid my respects to the king, for I had been here several months already. I must have looked flabbergasted as I replied, 'I meet them at the club.' And Tilo in secret, but I didn't tell him the latter bit. A moment later, I forced a laugh; it occurred to me that it was his suspicions that had made him ask in the first place.

Das made an airy wave with his hand. His way of being dismissive came with a winning informality. 'It's what's done, old chap,' he had said. 'A formal meeting, where you introduce yourself to the raja sahib rather than wait to be introduced. It has been almost a year for you, hasn't it? They expect it too.'

His tone was lighter as he went on, his finger toying with his hat. It whirred between us before he placed it on the table.

'You're lucky, you're not from here. In the days just gone, you might have been....'

But he left the sentence unfinished, and when he made a slicing motion with his hand against his neck, I laughed.

Das was nearly as tall as me, and slender, with a hooked nose, the kind that enabled him on occasion, to appear patrician and condescending. He advised that I must write, ask for an appointment and when he called to check, a day later, he offered to come along as well. He wanted to see the place for himself.

I welcomed his company. No one else sought me out. Tilo did, and she was perhaps as lonely as I was. She sent her poetry out to magazines in Bombay and Calcutta, but there was no one who really read her poetry in this town. She had even stopped writing for a bit, she told me. A block, she said. Sometimes a lack of something can do that to you.

As something of a friendship developed between Das and me, I'd learnt of the deep reservoir of resentment the man carried over the past. I'd also learn over time that this was matched only by his giant ambition that would make him stop at nothing.

He wasn't one of the Adivasis, the original people of the forests I had read about. Keith, my predecessor at the club, had written of them in the notes he had left behind. The Adivasis, whose land

and rights to the forest were now being threatened by the ever-expanding steel mill and the proposed dam project on the river that bordered the town on one side. They had been promised jobs, but it all seemed to be taking time.

Keith had also left behind various other things in the cottage that had once belonged to him and that I occupied now. In his notes, Keith had listed out the castes, his own information supplied by a British-era gazette from a century ago. My eyes had glazed over this part. Just one too many names, just too much history when I was running from my own. He also suggested a couple of places I must see—the pond where Lakshmi the tigress played with her young, that also happened to be a favourite haunt of the elephant herds every summer because it never ran dry. But Keith tantalizingly never left me a map. I did find out more from what Das revealed, that he came from one of the middling castes, the ones that had educated themselves during the British rule, thanks to the missionaries. This group resented the upper castes, traditional holders of privilege, who would do anything in a free India to hold onto their exalted positions, with only a token nod to centuries-old discrimination. Das explained it all with his characteristic elegance but the edge in his tone gave away the antagonism he felt.

Keith Rawson was now somewhere in the north, a town called Dharamshala where he intended to live out his retired life. Write to me at the post office where your letters will reach me, he said on the last page. There's my man Friday, Karma. He really is one, for that's the day he seems sober. For all my curiosity about Keith, I had not had reason yet to write to him. This place, its heat and then its people took up most of my time.

Keith, I'd understood, did not really belong to England. For Anglo-Indians like him, like half and half people everywhere such as I was, it was difficult to belong anywhere. This place, Raurkela, he had written too in his notes, overwhelms you, and you see yourself differently, sometimes that may be a good thing. But it's time for me to leave, so welcome. He had ended his letter with a quiet flourish. I reread those last lines often, wondering always if I should read more into them.

Keith left me his Winchester Long Rifle and so far in my first year here I hadn't had a chance to take it by myself into the forests. The land here was different, the forests dipped and rose suddenly, and one could drown in them, and in the pungent, bitter smell that lay on every tree.

I had indeed written to Tilo about a meeting, I told Das the next time I met him in his office; not telling him that, only the previous afternoon, I had traced the words with my finger on her smooth, fair back, lingering on the spot on her neck.

'Tea then, and you could bring along a guest too,' Tilo had said that afternoon, 'It would make it more official.' That afternoon, her husky laughter added to the sloth that lay everywhere, even in our thoughts. When I told her, I might bring along Ranjay Das, there was a pause before she laughed, somewhat uncertainly. 'He's young, isn't he?'

'Grew up here, he says,' I said.

'Whatever it is, I am sure he isn't as handsome as you are.' Tilo had bent and beat her head on my shoulder as if she hadn't been able to stop herself from saying that. Tilo lived between extremes.

When I was with Das in his office, he had told me more about his past, the past he liked to dwell on and change constantly. I remember his piercing silver eyes and a gaze that pinned one down like an insect. And though it was hot, Das's tie was securely in place, his shirt sleeves buttoned to the wrist. 'It's a habit I picked up in England', he explained. It was then I learnt he was an Oxford man, sent there on a scholarship. Then, having cleared the difficult civil services exams, he was now, eight years later, the district's police superintendent. A man of merit, as the

Indian society would see him, with all doors open for him, at least in a superficial way. His lips twisted cynically as he said this, and I noted his mismatched white socks and black oxfords. Even now, I can remember the cucumber sandwiches his orderly served, they tasted bitter as did my lies about my own past. I had no one, I told him. I was found in a German orphanage after the war, was captured, and served in the Allied war camp for some years. It was there I picked up photography. Then I got sent out here when the steel factory came up. The agreement between Nehru and Willy Brandt, you know. Das looked at my hair, thick, yet slightly fading around the ears, the scars on my cheek, and raised his eyebrows.

I rushed through with my own story. I didn't quite know then the complexities of human life, the long reach of history and its injustices, even in a small town.

Das and I agreed to meet at the raja sahib's place for high tea. In that town, where I had little time to think over things, even the past, there were occasions I welcomed Das's overtures of friendship. The other Germans skulked around, apologetic and quiet, and had a haunted look. They had after all lived through those years. I had arrived in Berlin only towards the end of the war, to look for the man Mama had wanted me to meet.

When the day came, however, I forgot about the high tea, and was late. I had spent the hour after lunch waiting for, and then searching for Samineh, my secretary. All had proved fruitless. The previous evening, several hours after we had met, Tilo had even sent a formal note, delivered by a palace servant, along with some tomatoes from the palace garden. Tilo's summons came with gifts of this kind, to pretend that our affair didn't exist. No one so far had bothered. In the lounge chair, that Tilo said was called a fornicating chair, where we stretched out and made love, those hot afternoons, she often read her poetry out loud, or recited those she knew by heart.

Slipped in among the tomatoes and dotted red by a particularly squelchy specimen, was a folded-up bit of paper. Tilo wrote that she couldn't come by that afternoon or the next. She hoped to see me soon and in the palace, but despite the hint in that message, I forgot the appointment. Samineh might have reminded me. She knew my schedule. I waited, I walked around, I looked at my diary, counted the days since I had left Berlin and then, only a chance glance at the clock reminded me, like a stab on the cheek does, of the high tea, the request and Tilo's invite that I had almost forgotten.

The superintendent's official car was already in the palace driveway as I came up. I was fairly running and breathless, my tie unknotted, my hair lashing my shoulders. Das had said it was a formal occasion, but my shoes were scruffy and sandy, as I rubbed them on the carpet and a footman looked on disapprovingly. I saw a movement up the staircase, a flash of white, but the butler now appeared. He bowed, so did the footman watching me. His name, as I'd soon learn, was Ghana. I was led into a room that seemed a mix between a sitting room and a sun-room. A row of French windows curving at the end, brocade sofas arranged in a half-circle; a high-backed sofa against an empty fireplace. And two pedestal fans at the corner. One of which didn't work. Tilo extended a hand, I offered mine too. Our hands crossed each other, she laughed, and then I bent to kiss her hand. That pleased her, and she moved away, saying it was good I was finally here.

'We think you are much too busy,' she said.

'Not as busy as he is,' I demurred, pointing to Das. Suddenly I wanted her to flirt with Das too, for he was looking at us altogether too steadily. I looked for a comfortable place on the long sofa and placed myself in a corner.

Tilo smiled, her bangles moving gently, 'It was good you could get away. Both of you.' She looked everywhere and chose a spot on the sofa where the light would clearly fall on her. It happened to be next to me. We sat around that sofa with a low wooden table hugging our knees. Tilo's shoe knocked against mine. 'I hope our country is treating you well.'

It unnerved me to see Tilo take such risks, when across the table, at the other end of the sofa, Das sat, at total ease, his lips stretched in his thin smile, his eyes shifting between us and everything else. Tilo looked at me, stray tendrils splayed on her forehead, and her sari, of thin silk, slipped often from her shoulder.

'He is still getting to learn about it, our country,' said Das.

'There's too much to learn,' said Tilo, 'usually one doesn't know where to begin.'

'He's trying to help me,' I said, jerking my head towards Das.

The air surged toward us periodically from the one fan that worked. A pankah, wide as a curtain, and creaking, swung slowly from the ceiling. Every time the pedestal fan turned its head away, its blades moving slowly, the pankah's somnolent movements only brought in more heat. Then the man called Ghana sidled in and crunched himself into the alcove, half-hidden by the pankah, intending to pull it. We heard the measured creak of its ropes, and Tilo's foot slid away from mine. Servants always noticed indiscretions; even I who had grown up half a world away could vouch for this.

The pankah was done up very interestingly in the raw, earthy colors that I had seen in the forest villages. I discerned an impressive hunting scene on its moving pleats, a magnificent tiger clawing an elephant by the neck. But the colours had dulled in other places. And the past had lost itself in the old brocade curtains at the bay-windows, in the many portraits that lined the corridor, and I could swear a rat peeped at me from under the carpet.

For the next hour or so, we remained cocooned thus, in that atmosphere of dungeon-like quietness, broken only by Tilo's small talk, while things we were not aware of, were happening elsewhere: at the club, where at this moment, no one was really overseeing things nor was expected to. Members usually turned up around an hour or so later, for drinks and a round of billiards. Closer at hand, Tilo's laughter at times took on a brittle note quite like the expensive bone china we were served tea in. Tilo talked politics, of Nehru, the leftists, China, and then poetry too.

'I must read your poems,' said Das.

'Maybe you could read them to us,' I said.

She nodded, smiled, her hand briefly and very deliberately brushing my arm, and set off to get a copy.

I stood up, hoping Das had noticed nothing. I looked at the portraits on the walls—those who must have been maharajas in the past, one of them with a foot on an elephant, just shot. Then the glass bookcases with thick tomes of books that all looked alike. The stuffed tiger on the wall, in whose glass eyes I saw myself momentarily, before I turned to find that the butler had come up with a tray, his aging yellow nails and nerves running like strangled brooks into his frayed sleeves. Glancing away, I caught a look of naked desperation on Ghana's face. Directed at no one, his stare carried all the hunger a half-starved face could hold. It rose out of his bony body that creaked as alarmingly as the pankah.

If I had to pick a moment when I began to understand something, I'd pick this one—when I contrasted Tilo's easy laughter with the fatigue on her staff's face, and the decay evident in the butler. 'You can stop now,' I said, waving my hand at him. Das raised his eyebrows and walked the few steps to where I stood, close to the pankah. 'Hans, you're quite the Commie, are you sure you're not an East German?' He laughed at what must have been a stricken look on my face. Ghana bent low and kept on at the pankah. We waited for Tilo and wondered where the maharaja was.

'Raja sahib?' I asked of no one in particular.

The butler shrugged, but there was that preoccupied look he had, the manner of all household staff as they somehow remain in tune to goings-on elsewhere. He moved toward the door, and I heard Ghana utter the word 'club,' before he fell forward and began gently snoring, a sound like a rubber toy being squeezed. Das prodded him with his toe and it was then we heard, through the open door, the swish of someone coming down the stairs.

I saw her then, through the doors that led up to the spiralling staircase, with its white bannister. I would see later that the paint on it had given way in places, and if you looked closely enough, there was a scratch mark or two as well. I watched the way she came down, quite unwilling, her fingers sliding on the bannister, her dress swinging on her calves.

Lipsa's face was unusually flushed. This is what I always remembered, and that I'd always call her Lisa, unable and maybe never wanting to correct myself. She sidled down the stairs, light on her feet, brushing her hair away from her forehead, her eyes alight with curiosity. Later, I'd think about this first glimpse of her and tell myself that it was possible that she was looking forward to meeting us. For she must have known about it for some time. I heard Das's swift hiss of breath and I realized that I had been staring too.

You're already late, I heard Tilo's voice from behind her. She entered with her daughter, nudging her in and then for the next few minutes, Tilo did all the talking. 'My daughter yes, she's almost 18, and I had her when I was 18.'

'She's been reading,' Tilo said after a while, half laughing, half mocking. 'She does it all the time,' and her eyes scoured her daughter's face. It could be concern, or even envy. 'I hope you don't have to get glasses, my dear.'

In that room, Lisa presented an utter contrast to her fair and composed mother. Lisa was nervous, her face patchy red with embarrassment. Her hair, falling out of her untidy braids, bobbed on her neck, wavy and unruly, as she neared, stumbling a little over the edge of the carpet. I smiled, hoping to ease her embarrassment and then started, for Das had his eyes fixed on her, and there was speculation mixed in his oddly tight smile.

'In fact, I am all for her reading, it's too hot outside. The sun, you know. This summer it damages the skin even when you are inside,' said Tilo, her overdone explanation floating over this new silence. She glanced at me, and in her look, I read the anxiety of being compared. It was Lisa's prettiness she was afraid of. Or because I'd never seen her, Tilo, in a setting away from the club or my rooms, this struck me more forcefully.

Lipsa, she had said curtseying to me, the words catching on her full lower lip. Lisa is what I heard, the name I'd always call her by, as she missed her mother's renewed efforts to catch her eye, a warning glance about something, maybe her dishevelled hair. An errant strand had fallen over her forehead, and Lisa did not push it away. Rather, she moved away, as her mother stretched an arm toward her.

'It's all right, Madam,' Das said in his lazy voice as Tilo came to sit by me again, 'the sun has set, or haven't you noticed that. It can't damage or even light up anything now.'

She laughed. It was 1960, and it had been a decade and more since the sun had set on the British Empire in India. Das more than anyone else was all too aware of it. 'I know,' she said seriously as her laughter died away, 'things are different today. In every way for my daughter. That is why I have decided to write something different.' She flipped open the pages of her book, and though a pair of gold pince-nez glasses lay very near her on the table, she read haltingly, very slowly, to us, her new poem. 'Something useful,' she declared, 'for the woman of today.'

We thought no more of raja sahib or why he hadn't turned up yet. It was a change to be here, I thought. Tilo's intense voice, her laughter, in rhythm with the tinkle of the teaspoons and the light catching the orange golden gleam of liquid tea. Lisa sitting quietly to her mother's left and yet not too close. She and her mother both looked up startled when I said I didn't need the fan anymore. And Tilo, solicitous at once, turned to ask Lisa to get me a shawl.

That day she was not the playful mistress, or the imperious clubgoing woman, but the rani sahiba, and she intended to show that her graces were intact. That day, her hands lingered on my shoulders as she draped the fine Kashmiri shawl over me. When Lisa had returned and held the shawl out awkwardly for me, Tilo had taken it from her, impatient. 'Don't be silly. He'd not know how to drape one.'

Das laughed, 'True, our German friend might think it's a blanket.'

Tilo had smiled at us, 'There's an art to it. Come, you might as well learn this.'

I saw Lisa's half-pout, as if she had just stopped herself from retaliating. I got to my feet, awkward, and Tilo proceeded to give me and everyone a demonstration of how a Kashmiri shawl—and this one belonged to the raja sahib—was to be worn. She reached up to toss it over my right shoulder, and then had me lift my left arm as she brought the other end around me. I looked down at her sea-green eyes, smiled stiffly at Lisa who now stood next to her, and looked somewhat amused at my self-consciousness. She turned to ask Das then if he needed a shawl too. And Das stretched his legs, pointed to the pankah, and Ghana began pulling the ropes again in a new burst of energy.

'It's all right, Lisa. Hans isn't used to our weather.'

'But he comes from a colder place. Don't you?' She asked me then. There must have been another warning glance from her mother, for Lisa returned to her place on the sofa.

Tilo's insouciance made her oblivious to most things; what she didn't know didn't matter and when things that did matter came to her knowledge, it was too late, and then she could only overreact. That afternoon, none of us knew how soon things around us would unravel, especially for Tilo and her daughter, but in that moment all that was to happen soon seemed far away. I willed myself to relax. Tilo, soon her old, charming self again, handed me a napkin, Lisa took around the sandwiches, and we moved to discussing hobbies, reading, her writing poetry and photography. When I looked again, Ghana's face was in shadow, his chin rested on his hand, and the fan no longer moved. I could barely make out his silhouette framed on the painted curtain.

It must have been some time later that Ghana's head jerked up, and a knock sounded on the door. Tilo's eyes swept past Das, toward the old butler who thrust himself in apologetically, and then she mumbled, her tone mild, almost as if she hated the interruption. 'So, he's finally here.' Then her gaze moved to Lisa, 'You can go.'

'I do want to stay. Father's here.'

Tilo must have intended to protest but at that moment, raja sahib, the ex-maharaja, Tilo's husband, the man I had been cuckolding, and Lisa's father, walked in. He looked older than I remembered him at the club, but seeing him in his own setting, made me feel self-conscious and somehow trapped.

There were the usual pleasantries. I felt somewhat flustered, or I would have noted the absentness in the raja sahib's demeanour. Tilo's chatter couldn't fill up every void after all. And now, with her husband and daughter in the room, she seemed not to want to try too hard. Her feet brushed against me, time and again. I saw her sari fall away, almost in an unintentional way. A slow tension spread, dropping suggestively like the spoon tinkling against the china. Raja sahib, as everyone still called him, took the chair nearest to the unlit fireplace, waved us down when we stood long at attention, smiling faintly, even absently as Tilo spoke up again, too much and too fast. 'Oh, you can sit. He doesn't bother with all those niceties anymore. It's been so long, hasn't it?' She tossed him a teasing, daring glance. 'Since Gandhi came, and now our raja sahib thinks the Communists have a point or so about equality. He's all about giving everyone every opportunity. Everyone must have a seat at the table.'

Das's face darkened at Tilo's words. He put his cup down with a clatter. I wasn't aware then of how power equations ran. Das, the modern educated man, probably considered all this hypocrisy. This high tea, a near drowsy pankahwallah, the obsequious butler, might have amused me too, but there were the four of us, in that room, caught in a sudden awkwardness.

Her husband's smile didn't falter. Then I gasped as Lisa sank to the floor, pulled out a footstool and rushed with it to her father. My gasp was echoed by Ghana who stood up, intending to do what Lisa just had. Raja sahib's fingers grazed Lisa's cheek. 'Anything else, father?' she asked. He gazed blankly at her before shaking his head. He was handsome in a jaded, all-knowing way. He dressed well, a thin jacket over his barely visible paunch, and thin bags under his eyes. When he smiled, his eyes could crinkle up charmingly.

Now the raja sahib shook his head, waved away the tray of sandwiches the butler held out. 'Our guests first, Biswal,' he murmured.

'These sandwiches are not heavy, sahib,' said the old butler, with the deferential familiarity of someone who had served the family for long. The raja sahib frowned, and nudged the footstool aside, then brought it closer again. That should have given away his state of mind, for he appeared an absentminded host. And when he spoke, he looked at the ceiling.

That was how we learnt that he had spent the afternoon playing billiards at the club. 'I noticed you were not there, Gerder, but I forgot we had this appointment.' Then he rubbed a hand over his eyes, his face. I did think at the time he looked tired, that he and his wife, after Tilo's initial explanation, exchanged neither a word nor a glance. Lisa played with her hands, her hair. She looked at her father, but he really didn't wish to say anything more than what was barely necessary.

Only days later when I looked up my diary, I realized it was the afternoon of that event none of us were witness to. The incident that would soon blow up into a scandal, and nothing would ever be the same again. When it all unfolded, as it would only days after, it seemed to me that the four of us sitting there, were part of a stage scene, that we were actors with no clue as to what was expected of us. When we left, Lisa smiled, her eyes locking into mine, and there were things that even I, Hans Gerder, one of the war's lost, abandoned people, unloved and unmoored, still understood.

That night I could not sleep again, and waited for the nightmare to return. It began with a dream. I had read of the Israelis and their determination for justice. Now they were sending their secret service agents into far corners of the world to track down those Nazi officers who had escaped, even those who had helped them. Poor men, I had thought once, those officers who had professed eternal loyalty to Hitler. They had been doing their duty, overwhelmed by the circumstances they found themselves in, as if this might absolve them of the evil they were committing in the name of some misshapen higher ideal. As if evil existed in different degrees.

I might number among the hunted too if the hunters were truly non-discriminatory. The nightmare returned then, quick and unrelenting. Vignettes of my past. Fast flickering images like seeing a quick-moving documentary in a darkened theatre. I saw myself again the night I was taken away, picked up roughly from a Berlin street bench. There I was, bundled up in a ramshackle car and taken on a journey that took me farther and farther into a deep dungeon of darkness. I woke a long time later, feeling groggy the way I had that morning several years ago. My lips felt gummy, and caked with something I did not recognize. And I felt my face, the way I always did at these moments, the way I had that long-ago morning when I knew instinctively that though I was much the same, I had been made to look different. Operated on, scalped and contoured in places, and made to look like the man I was to stalk, follow and kill. A man I knew from my childhood, someone who had always loomed large over my family. Who would never understand my confusion that a person could not turn away from love, even a cruel love like Mama's.

I woke up with a start, my forehead damp with sweat. The light from the palace shone steadily, and I found that oddly comforting.

2

TRAVAILS OF A BLUE DAIMLER

I wish you dead, man.

Those were my words. Words I had spoken and forgotten. I'd been heard to say them to a man who would be dead in a day or two, give or take a few hours. I had been heard to say those words right to the man's face.

All I knew was that I had not been able to help myself. That I had no idea then who he was. Though he had written to me that very morning. Das would insinuate, in that mild way of his, that I had been heard. 'Just letting you know, old chap,' he'd said in that offhand voice of his, 'that I know what happened but then you were in a bad mood and people heard things.'

Things had begun badly that day. My old Daimler was once again in Idris's garage, nursing a puncture. The Daimler, another of Keith's bequeaths to me, just as he had got it as part of the steel plant's accessories, needed servicing often but I was fond of it. I went for long drives in it, from one forest village to the next, stopping at unexpected waterfalls, or to take photos anywhere I wanted. Of animals, the smaller kind, usually rabbits, and the breathtaking views that often caught my eye. The rifle lay on the back seat, but I wasn't very good with my aim yet. I had to work on this; it was the only way I could face up to the nightmare that grabbed me often with a special fierceness.

This had been Keith's advice too. He couldn't have known about my past, yet that bit of advice, given as an afterthought, had jolted me, making me read his careful, evenly-spaced handwriting several times. 'The forests, getting to know them, is one way you will familiarize yourself with things here. Else you will drown in their sounds, their looming presence. And you don't want to drown, do you?' Those words, was I reading too much into them? Words that made me forget for a moment the trembling that often overcame me, the dizziness that swept over me the very moment my finger was against the trigger. It'd take time, maybe even a long time, was what Colonel Oakshott had once told me in Berlin. You have never really known evil to do evil, he said, and Keith too had left behind that advice in his notes. Both men saying the same thing, almost in the same way. But it had already been several years since my last failed attempt.

The Daimler had let me down too many times already. It wheezed and sighed before coming to a complete halt. Keith had been good with the car. Idris told me it had been sent to the garage less often in Keith's time.

The car. Not just a car, but a Daimler. The blue Daimler had once been in a Berlin garage. A car that had once carried Hitler himself, who often stood in the seat next to the driver. A seat, especially adapted, so it could be lifted, and the man could stand, wave to the gushing, fawning crowds. Perhaps my mother, in that last year as the Reich collapsed, had stood by the road too, waving desperately, hoping to be noticed, hoping not to believe the truth, that the advance of the Russians, the British, the Americans from every side, was a gigantic lie, spread by the papers dropped by the Allied planes that flew deeper, ever deeper into Germany those last months of the war. The Daimler had braked hard when a small Pekingese had strayed into its path and Hitler had lost his balance. He had stumbled, his hands just about grabbing the car dashboard, and the hair falling over his eyes had not managed to hide the murderous glare that flashed in his eyes.

It wasn't the Daimler's fault. The driver had been pulled off his duties. I'd get to know him later when we were both prisoners at the Tempelhof airport. And now years later, I was still coming to understand the Daimler. There was nothing wrong with its brakes, it was just getting old. One of those pieces that had had faults from the very beginning. It was born a sickly child and its wheezing, coughing, stumbling and often complete stalling wore me down many a time. Maybe it didn't want to be understood.

At the end of the War, it had been found in the Reichstag garage. It had been abandoned when the soldiers had simply helped themselves to all the other cars, dismantling them, shipping them around the world. This one was shipped in its un-dismantled state, left just as it was, to this Krupp collaboration at the other end of the world.

I had seen the car often, in the years I had spent virtually a prisoner at the airport, those three-four years of my life. There were times, late at night, I'd been driven in it. With Colonel Oakshott at the wheel, as he took me around the guarded, watched-over city, left bruised and battered. And now, in this city in India, with its new German factory, all the stray children on the roads were familiar with the Daimler. They understood the mute appeal in my eyes every time the Daimler stumbled and stalled on the road, needing a good push on its back. Sometimes this worked, sometimes it didn't. Yet the children waved cheerily every time I drove by.

The morning of the day that was to go horribly wrong, Rao came in, as usual, with my tea. I saw the letter propped against the pot, at the tray's very edge. There was no one I could think of who would write to me. Rao placed the tray next to me, pointed to the letter with his long wizard's finger that bore the marks of several years spent as a cook, first in Burma, and then with Keith, who had passed him onto me.

'For you, hand delivered.'

The lines of writing on the envelope did not look familiar. An ungainly scrawl with letters like ants running in errant lines.

'He came himself,' Rao went on, a trace of smugness on his face. The morning sun that had acquired a pointed intensity very early on, hit me full on the face. As I grimaced, Rao hastened to draw the curtains. The sunlight dropped into tiny golden circles at Rao's feet, showing up his gnarled graying nails and he rasped in his usual way, 'I am sorry, Hans sahib. Just that the man put me off.'

'Who?'

'The one who came with the letter.'

Now I read it, squinting as the scrawl unravelled to tell me that following recent developments about which I had proved totally irresponsible and ignorant, Samineh Ali would no longer work for me. He, the writer of the letter, would come around at four for her last remaining pay and other matters.

I read it again, the indignation I felt at its peremptory tone at odds with the sweetly bitter tea that Rao had brewed for me. The name was even more undecipherable and as I brought the paper up close, Rao's voice came again, from behind.

'Ahmed Ali.'

I thought of Samineh who had been away from work two days already—the day of the high tea, three afternoons ago, was when I had last seen her. Last evening, I had made up my mind to dig her address up from among the many files she had in the cupboard to write her a stern letter of warning. I had been composing that letter in my mind all night as I worked in the dark room, developing my photos of the hills at sunset.

The letter remained unwritten by the time I went to sleep,

looking at the lone light still on in the palace. That light gave me a sense of being in no place, or in any place I wanted: the African desert around which I grew up, the Black Forest where I had been hidden away, the ocean where I had been on the same ship as Adolf Eichmann and we were each other's prey. For I knew that the men who protected him as he made his escape to South America were on my trail too. There were nights like the ones I knew now, when I paced the deck and the passing lights of a ship farther away were reassuring, just like the familiar stars at night. No matter what I thought, or how I felt, I wasn't alone. Except that I could never feel truly un-alone.

The light in the palace not too far away, flickered, went off, and then came on again. This had gone on for a while before things went totally dark. I knew now it was Lisa's room, and that she stayed up late, reading.

'He teaches in the Muslim school,' Rao's voice broke into my thoughts. 'And he is to marry that other Muslim who works for you. Who worked for you, I might add.'

He sounded reproving. 'Rao, don't they have names?' I asked absently. Now he stood, my discarded clothes from the previous night in his arms. The washer-man would come around soon. I refused to look up and saw Rao's toes curl up in a half question-mark. Rao took pleasure in being suggestive.

'They do, but that would make us forget.'

'Forget what...?'

'No, sahib,' he said shaking his head, 'it's too long a history. You come from too far away to understand.'

Samineh had been an efficient worker. I thought of the quiet and unobtrusive way she did her work, in her corner office at the club.

'You should not have employed her. Their kind is always conspiring.' He lowered his voice, almost gritting his teeth. 'First, they break up the country and now they want even more to themselves. East, West Pakistan, Burma everything, so that their numbers are more than ours.'

I looked down at the letter. The anger leapt at me with every word, matching the anger in Rao's voice. The person it was concerned with, was someone whose face I now struggled to dredge up. Samineh, she spoke softly, her voice as unremarkable as the rest of her. Though I had never really looked. Short with fat, stubby fingers, for I remembered her hands from the times I had seen her at the typewriter. Her handwriting, short and round like she herself was. And this man, with the terrible scrawl, this fierce anger, was apparently her fiancé. They seemed ill-matched right away.

'He is coming at four?' Rao stopped. He had the grace to look sheepish, and avoiding my eyes now, he sucked in his cheeks, which made him look even more skeletal. He claimed to have almost starved the time the Japanese ransacked the official palace in Mandalay.

'Why don't you meet him then?' I said, extending the letter his way.

He shrugged, 'I am sorry, sahib, you were sleeping and being who he is, I had to check.'

He saw me frown and shrugged again, his collar bones lifting jerkily with the effort.

'You know how they are,' he pointed to the letter, 'those Muslims can't be trusted. Ten-twelve years ago, they stole our sisters and daughters, our land, and they are planning to do it again. Right from here, from under our very noses.'

He turned away, shaking his head, knowing he had managed to change the subject in some way. 'Ah...! But sahib, you are alone and single.'

I remembered then that the previous day, just as the workday was finishing, someone from Das's office had rung up again, to confirm an appointment. Das wanted to come around at 4 to discuss some urgent matters related to the club and its equipment. The man at the other end had been cagey. It was urgent, he only repeated, and that he couldn't divulge more. I knew then it could never be anything important. Das irritated me then. Didn't he have better things to do?

I cut myself shaving, as I looked at my craggy face in the mirror. There were a few things that always niggled. I was just here to do a job and wished I had been told more about the people here, more than what Keith's obscure, history lesson-like notes revealed. I wished they would be easier to predict, and not so difficult to understand, it made it harder for me to settle in. But did I really want to do that? I was past 30, already old before my time and I had never really been young.

Five years at the most, I was told when I was appointed here. Well, I had four years more to go. All the other Germans felt the same way: a few years only and then we pack our bags and leave. We all knew of course that Germany would be totally different to go back to. Nor was there any place else. I would not be welcome in South West Africa. It was all someone else's country now, someone else's claim. And Germany had cut itself into two separate countries, so that we were like Siamese twins, conjoined, yet divided by a wall, unable to reach each other.

Outside my cottage, there was the makeshift garage that had once been a warehouse. Now it was as empty as my mind. For the last three days, I had been waiting for the return of my Daimler. The thought of the old Daimler, as beaten up, as worn out, as unclaimed as I, was a palliative amid my black thoughts. Idris had assured me the car would be ready in a day, but the Daimler had reached that stage where it seemed to spend more time in his garage than mine.

I looked forward to having it back. My old Daimler. Huge and sturdy, I was proud of it, especially of the bullet hole it still wore, lower down by its side door. A sign that, unlike me, the Daimler had actually experienced war. As for the passenger seat that could be raised, and that I wanted to have nailed in place forever, Idris had tried his best and failed every time. I appreciated his honesty; that nails, and anything overdone in a decorative way, would simply ruin the car. He could not do that. Besides, he asked me, puzzled, 'You're not going to have anyone stand next to you, are you, sahib?'

Rao often advised me to put a garland of green chillies and lemon on the car's fender, to scare away those with evil in their minds, to stop the Daimler from being garaged so often, but I dismissed this as silly. Idris too had said much the same thing when, five days ago I had crunched up to his garage with my car and its one deflated tyre. 'Someone has the eye on you, sahib,' he had said grinning as he looked down at the sorry looking tyre, wearing a flat, utterly squeezed out look. 'A minor puncture, just a twenty-minute job, except that I have some plant cars to fix,' Idris blithely continued. But I knew as always, he would take longer and, in the bill, put in claims for more workhours spent on it. The boys working for him needed to be paid, he said, even though there wasn't enough work for them. And that they didn't really know much beyond the basics of car repair. I was to learn soon about Idris's political ambitions, and how this antagonized many in the town. Ambitions and antagonisms that were historic and had taken on new forms in a new India.

These people just did not understand. All the big things—development, modernization, big steel plants, five-year plans, and the dams—would never work if the old pettiness did not change. Rao, for instance, could never make this connection. He freely helped himself to the supplies—Olson's butter and marmalade, Sunlight powder, and even a bottle of squash or two. Small things, he always said but it wasn't the quantity at all. It's stealing, I would tell him and insist I cut the amount from his salary. But Rao invariably pleaded, wringing his hands, talking of the extreme poverty of his children, and I would then relent, putting the cap back on my pen and warning him, Okay, next time then.

All my errant thoughts came back to the matter of time. That day, there were just too many things about to happen at four.

As it happened Tilo did not turn up that afternoon—she usually left a bit before four, leaving by the back door that led to a small copse of trees. Her cycle was left propped against an old tree, and a broken path led back to the palace. Tilo had already spent several afternoons in my dark room, managing to avoid scandal even as she created it. We sat on the old armchair, where Keith must have once sat, and made love, her teeth biting into my lip, as she pressed herself on me, the book of poetry she read often, resting on the armrest. The curtains lay heavy and thick on the floor. It was the time I ostensibly worked in my studio and everyone slept in the siesta hour. Even the club was emptied of its patrons. To all appearances, she was reading me poetry, and indeed she was, while I developed my photographs of the still-in-progress steel mill. Photos, I'd have to send to the head Krupp office in Germany where they kept track of things.

Her voice lifted and carried through the heavy stolid curtains, dust-ended, and golden tasselled, the conspiringly closed doors, and the windows just open but never offering a view of us. There on Keith's old lounge chair, I could hold Tilo secure between my legs, and feel myself sinking into her high, untuned voice, and the summer heat hung around us like a smoky cloud.

That afternoon, as I waited for her, I also waited for the sound of Idris driving the car back to the garage. The irritable crunch of its wheels, the wheezing groan of its engine. And when the afternoon stretched, and my waiting yielded nothing, I decided to go and meet my old Daimler.

My mood was not helped by the hot walk to Idris's garage. I hoped Idris had not given the Daimler to his assistants to service. The times I had been to his garage, a sprawling fenced-in space that one reached after going down the Main Road that had nothing on either side, the boys working for him hadn't inspired much confidence. His assistants were always converged around one car or the other, and there were always too many of them. I was sure they left their inky hands on the car, and the dirty rags they used in cleaning up never helped much.

Idris was a dark, tough looking man, who liked nothing better than to fit himself into the bottom of a car and come to intimate terms with it. At least people in the plant vouched for him. He's the only one. And you know, you can shout at him. He doesn't seem to mind, even if he never keeps his promises.

Yet Idris had promised me two days ago. 'Your car, delivered at nine in a day. Sharp.' He had made a note of it too, licking one end of a page and pulling a pen from behind his right ear, where a silver ring gleamed.

But my car had not turned up, and neither had Idris. And now in the auto shop, there was no sign of either. I flung open the small wooden gate that grated against the hard ground and walked in, my frustration rising with every step. There was no one within sight. Cars in various states of undress stood around, their innards rudely exposed, metal parts glaring in the heat. Everywhere there was the smell of diesel and petrol. In the stillness, I could hear the merry rattle of rickshaws going past, the insistent call of the crows, and the beat and sound of clanking metal.

Where were Idris's boys? There were always so many of them. They would stare at me every time I turned up at the garage. Boys and men of varying ages in their oily overalls, sauntering about with easy confidence. They looked a hard lot. Keith had said that Idris's garage was the only shop left standing in the area during the riots of a few years ago, and the boys had fought back armed with garlands of burning tyres and welding torches.

Keith had found him interesting and so did I, the times Idris was at his most garrulous. He envisioned an interlinked world, an altogether new country made up of all the countries created since the World War ended. Countries, Idris insisted, created on false pretexts. We were the centre of the country once, Idris would say. 'This part here, right where we stand. It is the exact centre from Bombay in the west to Burma in the east.'

I did think he was facetious but learnt soon enough of his Movement for Centrehood. The maps of an older India affixed to his office walls, showing a region before Partition in 1947; before even Burma in the east was separated in 1935; the files containing all his letters to editors about the matter, all indicated that it was this that was his life's concern, and not the motor workshop. He told me once of his intention to write to all the important people he could think of—the prime minister and the vice president, whom he referred to as the 'wise' president—to apprise them of the urgency of the matter. So far, however, he had had only a small following, the students he lectured at the Urdu school and—as I'd soon learn—there was Ahmed Ali, a teacher in that school who believed in this movement as passionately as did Idris.

Idris sounded like an old, old man when he lost himself in his plans and his movement. He had been in this town since the days it served as a midpoint stop, a resting place for cross-country journeys. People took a break here, stopped for the night if they were travelling across or up-down. It was the gatepost to the deeper, unknown territory that began just a few kilometres north of town.

'We are those,' Idris told me, 'who just stopped here and didn't carry on.' He boasted that his garage had existed since the motorcar first came to India. And because of his garage, he went on, Nehru's government was convinced and went ahead with the steel plant project. Between your country and mine, Hans sahib. It was the first step in changing the face of the country overnight.

'Would anyone expect it, a garage in the middle of nowhere, and now see, I have only been an inspiration for people to follow, even you Hitler sahib.'

I had paled the first time he had called me that. His boys had laughed, and I knew better than to protest too much. It was obvious, Idris, with his terrible sense of history, in this place so far away from where a terrible war had happened, had meant it jocularly. I dared not set him right. My visible anger would only invite more of it.

I looked around for Idris now, waited to hear his voice holler out from under a car, 'Is that you, Hans sahib?'

But the cars stood sullen and silent, some with bonnets agape, others disembowelled with a door or two missing or turned inside out, as in one particularly old looking Morris. I wondered idly who it could belong to when the door to Idris's office burst open, and the man I would soon come to know as Ahmed Ali, emerged.

Everything worked to make sure we would never hit it off. He offered a fresh startling contrast to my own dishevelled, brazenly hot face, unused as I still was to the summer heat. I remember him speaking to me in an unusually brusque way, smoothing down his long yellow kurta with his long fingers. He lifted his face as he came up to me, and his beard lifted too, like a flag. 'Hello, I came to see you today, mister.' People were always addressing each other this way, either this or they were too obsequious with superiors, and brutal with those who just didn't matter. Yet in the letter for all its peremptory tone, he had addressed me formally enough.

'I am looking for Idris,' I told him.

'And I left a note for you today, mister, and your man made me wait,' he went on, 'and wait, till he told me you weren't there.'

I was taller and looked down at him as he came closer, and that was how I remember him. That he had hair on his chin, a goatee like a shaving brush and spoke words that made no sense to me. His kurta stretched to his knees, stiff, yellow and sparkling obscenely, and strapped neat sandals that showed uneven, badly cut toenails. One of this pair, torn and dusty, would be found, only a couple of mornings later, in the forest, a mile or so away from where he was found, on the train tracks. A death that, as the Civic Hospital's doctor certified, had occurred some hours before, in the night. And the doctor was believed, for almost everyone in the town that night had heard the bullet shots.

Yet that afternoon, as he looked at me, a deliberate sneer on his face, I felt unkempt and his next words, made me seem an uncouth cad as well.

'Perhaps you intended to avoid me.'

It was the direct way he said it. I stared at the man, my eyes narrowed against the sun. My shirt was soaked to my back, my feet burnt from the earth's heat searing into me. I felt pinned into place, immobilized by the man's stare and the earth's molten heat.

'I had to inform you that Ms Ali will not be at work ever again. You cannot assure her protection, or guarantee her safety, Mr Gerder, and I will not put up with it.'

He pulled himself up, thrust his chest out and declaimed. 'I will not put up with it.'

I hated his impressive aggression. Still I had no idea what he was getting at. His speech—if one might call it that—seemed rehearsed, and I would have laughed but for that expression on his face. I looked around, remembered something and still did not see my Daimler or even Idris and that was when I said those words that everyone heard. I had felt someone jostling me, jerking me by the shoulder. It was that man, Ahmed Ali, who still hadn't had his fill, who couldn't tolerate the thought of me looking away and so had tried to get my attention back. An action that remained un-witnessed by all those who somehow miraculously reappeared right then and caught the very moment I apparently let loose a volley of choice abuses. That was what Idris's boys said later. That I was furious and had wanted him, Ahmed Ali, dead.

'Just leave me alone, man.'

'You will not go, man, till....'

It was then that I had interrupted him, placing my hands on his collar and thrusting him aside. 'I wish you dead man, you and all that you want,' I said again through clenched teeth, lashing out in quiet fury at the man whose mouth fell open, the smug look slowly vanishing, as my words sank in. Maybe for those moments, he was only reliving the magnificence of his own words. But in that silence, words carried, and there was a pause between his reaction when he laughed nervously, and I stepped back. A pause long enough for the few onlookers to be convinced they had indeed heard what they would report soon, and how one-sided the entire exchange had been.

As Das said, there were at least five people who had heard me say those words clearly. The boys at Idris's garage, a passing rickshaw-puller, and an old beggar woman who lived on the doorstep of the teashop next door. When I could have sworn that on that blistering hot afternoon, there had been no one around, and it was only after I had stood there for a few minutes, about to raise a racket, that Ahmed Ali had emerged from the inside office.

The summer heat had made my head swim, and running into that smooth-talking, odious Ahmed Ali had not helped. Das only nodded as I persisted with my explanation. I had not even been aware of Ali's existence before that day.

Das, however, would not be convinced about the other details. 'You just didn't notice anyone,' he said. 'Your kind never does. There were people around.'

He was so persuasive that I did come to believe that I had missed seeing anyone. Perhaps they had just blended in with the surroundings, I thought unkindly, brown on brown.

In the days that followed, as Das went about solving the murder, with a certain relish, as if it gave him the chance to undo and resolve all the injustices, imagined or otherwise, that he had accumulated since birth, he would manage to provide five witnesses, who authenticated the statement that I had indeed wished Ahmed Ali dead, word for word. That I had said this, not once but twice and had pushed him aside before they had intervened. 'I am not for a moment suspecting you, old chap,' he would say later, 'it's just that one must take everything into consideration. There can be no mitigating circumstances.'

Sometimes I was pretty sure Das carried a pocket dictionary on his self. I wished I had one on me merely to decipher him.

'Die you said, did you?' He looked at me pointedly, 'and remember he did die, and he was found dead.'

Coincidences, I thought to tell him, would make killers of us all. But I was guilty. *Die*. That word. One I had practised so many times, the way I had been taught. *Die*. To say it, as I aimed a clear shot, just once. For on that ship, the SS Giovanni, where we were both passengers, I would get no second chances to kill Eichmann, and I had to push myself on. So, I did believe, under Das's pointed glance, that the word had slipped out in an unguarded, unwary moment. The heat had seared through me, stamped me all over, and had taken me, my words by the throat. I had felt strangled, weighed down by things. Now at Das's exact rewording, the old memory pressed down on me.

You must wish him dead. And you must wish him dead with all your waking hours and then killing him will be easy. Eichmann will be dead. Just as you want.

3

THE HOTTEST AFTERNOON IN YEARS

As evening sluggishly came on, I walked back to my office, for a meeting scheduled with the club's contractors and suppliers. Barely a few hours ago, I'd had that joust with Ahmed Ali and I wasn't looking forward to the meeting. But Singh, the supplies man, and Jhunjhunwalla, the labour contractor, had asked for one. They wanted me to speak to the management committee, evenly made up of Germans and Indians, about a temple in the plant premises.

Singh got himself together as he saw the look on my face. He had been freely sprawled on the sofa, while Jhunjhunwalla sat on the armchair, his chin resting on his long baton. I saw that Singh had been leafing through the photography magazines that had just arrived by post. Their faces were flushed, in pleasure or in guilt, I wasn't sure. I felt like a teacher who had caught them in some obscene act.

'We didn't hear your car,' Singh mumbled as an afterthought. I saw the magazine in his hand. *Life*. Probably he had been looking at the models, staring at their photos in a starved manner. His eyes fixed on the breasts, firm, pointed, unlike the heavy, weighty ones of his wife, whose photo took pride of place on a mantelpiece in his drawing room. What she had once been like, before the children came along. She liked people to look at the photo, admire it whenever they visited her, and I did too. I knew that their oldest daughter was of marriageable age. The younger children were in school. Singh had reached that definite stage in his career where the only thing that urged him on was the prospect of making money; it all went to build up a dowry for his daughter. As supplies superintendent, Singh believed in making money on everything that passed through his hands and needed his sanction.

Singh pointed to the magazine and smiled. It was only last week that he had tentatively broached the idea that had evidently just occurred to him.

'Would be honoured, Hans sahib, if you click my daughter?'

When I looked puzzled, he brought both hands together and crossed his fingers, forming the shape of a camera.

'My daughter, Meenakshi. We must start looking....'

Singh, with great relish, launched into describing traditional Indian weddings, wringing his hands as he described how the bride's father was made almost penniless in gathering together a dowry attractive enough to draw a respectably placed groom. That was why he was hoping I would click his daughter... he broke off, hesitating again, and I responded, filling in the gaps for him, 'Oh I see... to cut costs.'

He turned red before the words rushed out, heedless and tremulous, 'How can you think that, sir? No, no. I have seen your genius. You are great. You can make my daughter look beautiful.... We will get a good husband for her, a well-placed government servant.'

Singh's turban bobbed when he was most insistent or nervous. The man with him, Jhunjhunwalla, the Marwari with the red streaks on his forehead, and who supplied the workmen—the contractual and construction staff— for the plant, looked at me solemnly, rose slowly, his hands folded in a namaste. I waved my hand awkwardly, asking them to sit. I longed to splash cold water all over myself, to ease the memories of the afternoon. For a moment I envied Das and the suaveness that came to him so naturally.

Singh continued to look at me, a gleam in his eye. I thought, a longing gripping me, of the photography magazines, the photos I took and developed, with my Pentax, and the dark room I zealously guarded. Till Tilo invaded it, blithely and casually. One afternoon, at the club by herself, she had come by to my cottage, for a 'guided tour'. This was a low-tiled two-roomed place, located just behind the club, with an alcove for the dark room. It was a converted outhouse really, where the caretaker had earlier lived, but Rao preferred to live in the houses across the rail tracks and cycle back and forth every morning and evening. Which suited me fine. That first day, Tilo had wiped herself with her collar, fanned herself with her book, and then had unbuttoned her blouse. As I just stood there, she said, 'Are you just going to do nothing?'

'They'll never know anything,' she said an hour or so later, raising herself on an elbow to talk. She didn't seem to mind my overlong hair, my sweaty armpits and the frazzled moustache.

'It's afternoon,' she said, 'there's no one besides me and you. And no one would suspect. We are too different, you know.'

'In age too,' I said.

She slapped me as I laughed and pulled her under me.

'You don't understand,' she closed her eyes, and when she had opened them again she had that peremptory look in her eye once more. 'Do that thing you did, again, Hans?'

I bit my lips at the memory and turned away. My eyes caught the calendar. It was a Friday and she hadn't come, nor had she sent a message. That was most unlike her. That first time, she had set her mind on having me and the affair had continued. Tilo was fun, and unpredictable. Now I suddenly missed her. Her conversations, her voice always half-filled with frustration and longing. She seemed to be wasted in that palace, writing her poetry that no one read. All our wasted lives, I thought of the dark room, and longed for the safety and serenity it offered, watching the spectral negatives come to life. I tapped my knee restlessly as I heard the men out again. This was our second, and more formal meeting. I just could not get them to understand. Why did you need a temple to complete things, for heaven's sake? It was a steel plant. A modern temple to India's entry into the world stage, built with technical collaboration with the west, and they still wanted a temple for their ancient gods.

When I made these points, they looked at me unable to comprehend. 'You don't understand, sahib,' said Jhunjhunwalla, pityingly, 'the Birlas have their own temples in their cement plants. It makes people happy.'

'It is a gathering place, Mr Hans,' Singh pitched in, 'people meet at temples. It is a social place, like a club with statues of gods instead of a bar.'

'We could build a church too for you, Mr Hans,' said Jhunjhunwalla again, dryly, watching me with a careful expression on his face, 'there is enough land to please everybody. We just cut down the forests...,' his stick lifted, swished a bit in the air, before he calmed himself, and the baton, down.

I looked at my watch then. I had to get the Daimler back. Suddenly I wanted to sit in it, drive at breakneck speed down the city's streets, and feel the wind tossed up by the forest, uncaring of everything, even my thoughts. We will meet later, I told them.

It was late evening when I returned to Idris's garage, and my car still wasn't there. I looked all around for it, and for Idris too, but there were only Idris's boys watching me with a blank curiosity. I stood there, and then, collecting all the air in my lungs, yelled as loudly and forcefully as I could, wishing that its force would bring not just Idris, but Rao, Singh, the garage boys, the slothful peons, everyone in this slothful, heated-up country to their feet.

Idris, Idris. And this time Idris materialized so fast that I took a step back. He emerged from his office, fixing his fez. I realized he had been at his prayers and was momentarily contrite. But I had had enough of chasing my car.

'Your car. Sahib.'

He looked around for it, as I had done. 'My car, Idris. You are one day too late.'

'Your car, sahib, it is with the rani,' said one of the boys casually and then turned away.

'You idiot,' Idris took off his fez and flung it at the boy. 'Do your work, boy.' The wind picked up the fez and it bickered, rolled, turned over, before two boys caught it. We watched it in some strange joy and stupefaction, and when Idris spoke next I jumped for he was right by me.

'The rani, yes.' Idris fanned himself with his now recovered fez. He flapped it, pointing toward his office, the low steps. The same place I had seen Ahmed Ali emerge from some hours ago. Surely, he didn't think the Daimler was there.

I heard the boys giggle, and now there were more of them around. What did he mean? Was the car with Tilo? She did not know how to drive. Idris spoke in a lowered voice. 'She has left him, sir. I think so.' His voice dropped to a whisper, and the waft of onion and garlic that came from him made me miss some words.

'Something happened at the club. The raja sahib. Something he did, under the table, and she could not take it. With a woman.' His words were all broken, he played with his hands, then his fingers, making odd sinuous gestures. Then looking at me very intently, he did so again. My eyes widened as I understood what he was trying to explain.

Then he straightened, stood akimbo, his chest flung out. 'And we will not take it too. How dare he do this to one of us? No one is king anymore.'

I leaned down, put my hands on his shoulders, from where the sweat and the grime seeped through.

'Where is my car, Idris?' I asked in as cold a voice I could muster. The heat pounded into me with a malevolent force.

'Sir, you do not understand,' Idris said miserably now, his arms dropping to his sides. 'This isn't your country. This is India.'

He swallowed, and began again, 'Sahib....' The pleading tone was back, the sweat ran down his forehead, stream down his neck. 'She was in a bad state. Her husband's bad behaviour. Everyone knows. Everyone.' He stopped and looked up at me. 'Don't you know? You must. After what he did. How could she stay on?'

His voice turned hoarse. It was clear that the moment he said it, something else, the enormity of what he had just described came home to him.

'What does that have to do with my car?'

Idris stuttered in his nervousness.

He opened his mouth, shut it again. His eyeballs swivelled to the very corners. He and I, we were both struggling to make sense of the situation. 'We must talk inside.' His boys were still standing there, hands on each other's shoulders as if witnessing a gladiatorial joust. Then Idris's voice broke through the haze of my anger.

'Hey, you, standing there and laughing. No work to do or what? Showing all your teeth. Idiot, standing and waiting for what? For me to go to Pakistan? I won't. And if you want to work in my garage....'

He didn't finish. He had folded up his shirt sleeves and was rubbing his arms, in some menace as his boys dispersed in haste.

'The car, Hans sahib, please understand.' His voice was stronger now. 'The madam wanted a car. She was going to leave the house. The servant who came to me with her note said she would not live there a moment longer. Never before had someone come up to the house and given them, her, I mean, such humiliating news too. Because of what the raja sahib did.'

He stopped and then as if he remembered something, he glared at me. 'It happened in your club. You cannot allow such things to happen. I would never have allowed it.'

Now he would not be interrupted. The accusation against me, or rather the club, had filled him with new energy.

'Not a minute more did she want to stay on. And she did not want to take the sahib's car and the other cars... see, some of them are here. They weren't working well.'

He pointed to one of those dome-shaped ambassadors, the sun gleaming on its silent headlights like a waiting tortoise.

'So, I sent Salim with your car, sahib. It had to be done. Rani sahiba is right, my friend Ahmed Ali is right too. The raja sahib should not have done this. You should not have allowed it. We are independent now, sahib. Very independent.'

That was the second time I heard his name. Ahmed Ali. Overnight a man I had never seen nor known about had become my nemesis.

Idris was wiping the sweat from his brow, flexing his arms. The picture of the ham-handed, burly Salim, one of Idris's employees, at the wheel of the Daimler flashed into my mind. New waves of fury coursed through me. I looked at the man before me, at his assistants lurking like kitchen insects in the corner, the cars in various stages of dismemberment, and I raised my voice, oblivious of the consequences.

'How dare you? And without asking me? What do you think this is? That you can just take my car and rush off with it, without even asking for permission.'

'She was very disturbed. When she asked me for a car...?'

'And so am I, get it?' I was breathing down on him. My hot breath fanned the thin hair on his head, wafted back to hit me hard. I smelt myself, dusty and old, the smell of old metal.

'Sahib, it will come back soon. I promise. Salim is a careful driver.'

I rubbed my perspiring hand over my pocket. Looked around at the confusion scattered everywhere in the garage, and the boys trying not to eavesdrop.

'He will leave his smell all over it,' I said grimly, 'that dirty swine. He smells like a pig.'

A dark look descended on Idris's face. His face lost its earlier shapelessness and took on a righteously angry look, I saw him swell up with new belligerence.

'Sahib. Sahib. What are you saying? We are all devout people, loyal to our religion. What you are saying is deeply insulting.'

Ahmed Ali's angry letter, Tilo leaving, the Daimler gone, Idris's lame explanations. It was only much later as I looked up my diary that I realized some things. That all that had happened, everything that Idris had mentioned had begun from the afternoon of the high tea. The afternoon of the scandal—the raja sahib caught in a compromising position under the billiards table with my secretary Samineh, which erased, overshadowed everything there had been. Like Lisa's presence, for instance, that had made me so very conscious of everything around: the high tea, the tinkle of glasses, Tilo's low laughter, the slow creaking of the fan, how I had suddenly felt cold. It wasn't a prelude to anything. It suggested an end to something.

4

OF SCANDAL AND LOVE

That evening, without my blue Daimler, I sat on the porch till late, watching the fireflies, and the frogs. As the sky darkened, the faint outlines of cranes appeared, hovering in the distance. I should have got up, knowing this was when the nightmares returned. The endless peregrinations around the ship deck and the man in the cloak, my quarry, rising suddenly from a bench. But tonight I knew, this, and the other nightmares would stay away. I'd not see myself again in the monastery looking down at the road far below, feeling for certain, that the advancing lights of a car meant only doom. Or at sea, just as the ship left port, that at any moment, their boats might come up and I'd be captured again by those devious SS men.

For that night, in my hand, I still had the note Das had sent me through his peon.

Scandal reported. Raja caught in complicit position. Your sec implicated.

Will explain when we meet.

I had to laugh at first. Evidently, Das had a fondness for cryptic communication, and felt he had to take precautions. He had drawn in the raja sahib's distracted look—a man with hair standing up, a table and a woman in a skirt. But for all the obliqueness of his message, I had a better idea of things now. The way raja sahib had looked that afternoon. A certain wildness in his eyes that he, a man of the world, had masked as he brushed his hair away. And then Samineh's long absence. She hadn't returned, instead there had been the appearance of her obnoxious fiancé, and now I knew, of course, that Samineh would never come back to work.

But then were things really that clear? Even if the raja sahib and Samineh had been seen, did it really make things difficult? The women in Berlin, who were believed to be with Nazi officers, were humiliated after the war, as collaborators. But they had had no choice. Just as I, in a different sense, hadn't. I understood them and felt a twinge of pity. There were times one was left with no options. I had come to Berlin hoping to please my star-struck, hero-worshipping mother; and to find the man she had so looked up to: Adolf Eichmann. It was already too late for that, but I reached early enough to witness the fall of the Reich. The Russian army marching into Berlin, the Americans then, the partition of the city, and my own partitioned self as I became a prisoner. First, of the Allied forces, and then those dreaded months, when the SS had me in their grip, a pawn to save one of their kingpins. Eichmann, the man I'd known since childhood. In Berlin, life for me had come to shape a concentrated circle; and I knew how difficult it was to get away from the choices that were thrust on one.

So if Samineh or anyone made their own choices, there was nothing I nor anyone had need to understand. There was nothing wrong with Mama too. She lived in a different time, with a different kind of ambition and hope. She had believed all that she had read and heard. And far away from Berlin, in a city beyond the equator, she had wanted to do something too. Who knew it'd all be so monstrous, so very wrong and evil? I looked at Das's letter and felt strange, recognizing the stealthy warmth in my heart, that I had thought of Mama in ways I never had before.

I heard a cough behind me and jerked around. My hands instinctively reached for the rifle that hung on the wall. Then I saw someone hunched up before me. A hunch not of physical deformity but of habit, of years of deferring, of listening, and being ordered around. I knew then it was the pankahwallah. The man exhausted beyond measure that afternoon. The one whom Das had jolted into wakefulness with an arrogant prod of his toe.

A breeze came up, touched my forehead, and I heard a soft murmur, a movement of his hands. And I said quietly, 'You have to stand up for me to hear you.'

The man rose, and reluctantly rummaged in his pocket. The rest of him looked weighed down by whatever it was he had in his pockets. I heard the jangle of keys and saw him clearly as he emerged in the light. A wire-thin moustache, beady eyes glinting in the dark, and the way he walked, hunched forward. The bones of his feet crackled as he neared, reminding me of those fakirs who leapt nonchalant over burning stones.

'The car keys.'

It was a day of one too many convoluted conversations.

'The car....'

'Yes,' the man panted as he laughed, 'in the garage.'

I looked out, 'Can't see any car there.'

The man nodded, his face seemed to have shrunk, and there was nothing more, I thought, he wished then to sink into the ground.

'Stand up straight, my man.' I had no idea then that I sounded like the Russian commander at Tempelhof, with the stern voice he adopted when he spoke to us.

'There is car,' he said, and then holding up the key ring so it moved like a bell, he went on, 'and here are keys. Choti sahiba said I must give it to you.'

'That was...who is?'

I had never heard anyone referred to that way, and I leaned closer to listen. He took a step away and gestured with his hand, lifting it to indicate someone of his height. I held my breath then. *Lisa? Lipsa?*

He flashed a toothy smile. His hands danced around his face, indicating her hair. He twirled around, the keys ringing in his hand, and laughed, a high thin laugh, before I raised a tired hand.

'I know who you mean.'

But the man was now looking around with curiosity, staring at the walls, at the shelves, taking in his fill of the objects and artefacts Keith had collected. The rifle, the different masks, and the horns.

'Sahib is interested in all this?'

I leaned against the chair, and asked instead, 'The car, you were saying... and this?' I pointed to what he still held in his hands.

'Yes, keys to the....'

He handed them to me. A flash of silver, a clammy cold touch against my fingers.

'Yes, the raja's car. The madam said....'

'The madam, I thought, is gone.'

'The choti madam not gone,' he said stubbornly, and again he raised his hand to show someone of Lisa's height. 'She said I was to give you the keys, so you can drive around.

'Any time,' he added.

What I had in my hands then were the keys to a car in the raja sahib's garage. I played with the keys moving them from one hand to the other. Then I heard him wheedle close again.

'Sahib, you have an interest?'—he fingered the shells, and then stopped at the painting.

'Is that all?'

'Sahib?' He said. I watched him, idly jangling the keys. I was curious now. The keys to the raja's shiny green Austin, the one I had seen in his garage only the other day. I knew I could not ask him the question that had formed in my mind. Why had Lisa, she of the certain height, the twirling gait, that way of curtseying, sent it to me?

'Thank you,' I said with some finality, and the man now jumped and moved away. Walking backwards, facing me all the time, till he walked into the door. He jumped like a stricken moth, and he sidled out, making the narrowest of openings for himself.

I slipped out as stars gathered overhead, and flames from the steel plant sent sparks like meteor showers in the sky. I kept to the very edge of the forest as I made my way to the palace, the light still on in that room. Was Lisa still reading? I had been longing to drive the car, the day I had seen it parked at the very end of the raja sahib's driveway, and now I had the keys to it. My anger toward Tilo, for having helped herself to my car, diminished. She did strange things, in desperate and impulsive ways. I felt a guilty relief that I would not see her for some days. That thought stopped me short. We were taking risks. It was an even greater scandal than what the raja sahib had purportedly done. A quiet, and then an insistent rustling in the Forsythia bushes made me pause. The bushes framed the palace like a wall, and as I looked on, the leaves moved, and I felt a fleeting touch on my arm. Cold, and quickly gone, and then a voice calling me, through a sudden gap in the leaves. Mr Gerder.

Lisa.

I felt her hand on my arm, and she was pulling me through. The gap in the bushes hidden by tall grass that only her mother had known. Lisa's hand felt cold and light on my skin, her breath wispy. 'You scared me,' I tried to laugh, but my voice was a whisper.

'So, you got the keys. I sent them to you.'

She sounded matter of fact as if this was her usual place for meeting guests. I still held her hand, and realizing this, let it go abruptly. 'I was just too surprised,' I apologized, and caught her faint smile. We sat on the dry grass, the leaves brushing our skin, the low shrub against our faces. My hand rested on the edge of her long skirt, and we heard the soft rush of night creatures, the chirp of some insects, a rustling again close by.

Then she said, 'We must sit in the car. There could be snakes.'

'Not here though,' she reassured after a pause.

'You know about this?' I gestured indicating the bushes, the hidden gap in it, and the stone-riddled pathway. She nodded, and I knew then that she knew for sure, what she had always suspected, the thing between Tilo and me.

She said nothing more as she led me through, skirting past the empty stables toward the narrow dirt path that led to the garage. She squeezed through more bushes, holding the thin stalks quiet, careful also not to let her dress catch in the brambles. 'The guard is asleep, and most servants are now off duty,' she said over her shoulder. She had her hair tied neatly back and she wore a pair of divided skirts, and sandals. Then I had a vision of her twirling, curtseying to me, just as Ghana had demonstrated.

'I thought I'd show you to the garage. There's a service door for the cleaners.'

'That's very kind of you.'

She waited, and as we took a few more steps forward, she turned to me, and I almost walked into her. 'Could we go for a drive?'

She had turned her face up to me, a pleading and yet determined look on it. Somewhat like her mother, but not quite. In that faint light of the moon, I saw the light in her eye, the gleam of an earring. I could also see the light on in her room, a ploy on her part, to deceive anyone else. Her head knocked often against my shoulder, and as we walked down that small unused path, sometimes our hands brushed. I felt her soft breath against my arm, and the two of us were enclosed by the night that blanketed everything. The pebbles crunched softly under our feet, and she led me through the narrow door of the garage. Ahead of us I saw the smaller driveway that led out to the back gate.

'I've never gone for a night ride before,' the quiet heightened the words she spoke, 'have you?'

I thought then of Berlin's silent streets at night. A fatigued city, lying on its back, as Colonel Oakshott drove me around in his jeep. And the time in Recife, in Brazil, nearly eight years ago, sharing a ride with the soldiers in their trucks, as they kept watch over a curfewed city.

'You seemed so demure that first time, Ms Lisa.'

She stopped abruptly and tightened her grip on my arm. 'Don't compare me to my mother, Mr Gerder.'

'Why did you give me the keys?' I asked. The night had imposed a closeted informality on us. She shrugged. I saw her try to speak, and instead we stood for a while, our backs against the garage wall. Hadn't this place had more than its fair share of scandals already, I thought, as she reached out a hand and unlatched the old wooden door.

'Take the car down the driveway and out through the old gate. Don't turn on the lights. There will be no one there.'

She reached up and unhooked a bag from the wall. Rummaging inside, she handed me a beret. 'You might wear this. It's my father's. From the war.'

'You seem very prepared, Lisa,' I had to grin.

'A disguise, yes,' she said. 'My father fought the war in Burma,' she added as an afterthought.

'A war hero?' I asked, not telling her my other thoughts. The war I had been part of too, in a different way, in a different part of the world.

'Kind of,' she said, settling herself in beside me. The car lurched and hummed as I eased it slowly through the garage door, keeping an eye out for the guard. Though I saw no one around, she bent and lowered herself as we passed, crunching herself in front of the seat. For some moments I felt her head against my knee. Once we were out on the road, she sat up straight, turned a hand to pull the beret lower over my forehead and went on from where she had left off.

'Nehru never trusted father. Because father was close to Bose, you know the man who led the forces into Burma along with the Japs. But my father wasn't tried. Ma knew people who could speak to Nehru. But....'

She looked away, as she spoke, 'There are more people against him now.'

I listened to her low voice and relished the sound of the engine. She leaned out through the window at times, her arm feeling the wind, and every time she spoke she had a way of turning toward me animatedly, her hands often brushing my arm.

That high tea, I told her trying to make conversation, I would always remember the way she had burst down the stairs and slowed down just outside the dining room. 'Well yes,' she said now, 'I was a bit annoyed when my mother told me about the high tea. Benny Ambrose, the English teacher in my school, had just given me books to read. And then it was nice to see you. I practised the manners I'd learnt.'

I remembered the swish of a gown I had seen, the swiftly closing door, and turned around to see Lisa's impish smile. Instantly the car lurched as something, a rabbit perhaps, dashed across the road. She was thrown across the dashboard, and I reached out a hand, and then stopped myself. When we had covered some more distance, leaving the palace, the club, even the plant some way behind, when I could trust the silence between us, I asked. 'What happened? Where's your mother?'

She was silent. 'I don't know. That man Das came by last evening. There was a long discussion and Ma decided to leave. I know she asked for a car. And then I saw the blue Daimler at the door this morning.'

'You knew it was mine.'

We exchanged a quick glance and she said archly. 'Doesn't everyone know it's yours?'

I had last seen Samineh the day of the high tea. Around the time we were at the raja sahib's palace, the king and the secretary were fornicating, or doing something scandalous, disgraceful, unpalatable, whichever way you looked at it, under the billiards table. Tilo had had no idea, she had been laughing and I felt a twinge in my heart, thinking of her reckless innocence and then her hypocrisy. In her intolerance of her husband's indiscretions, minor when compared to our afternoon trysts, she appeared hypocritical. I had never before been so critical of Tilo, and knew that she would return soon enough. Next to me Lisa arranged her hair, smiled, looking lost in thought.

'That Das, acting like the perfect policeman, said he knew what had happened. He saw it all on my father's face,' said Lisa now. 'That he'd get you to talk to my father too. To admit, to apologize, or something.'

'Do you know anything?' She asked then insistently.

I wasn't sure what she was asking and driving gave me a welcome pretext not to look her way. How could I possibly know what was going on at the club while at high tea? And Das's expression at that time had told me a different story. He had hardly looked at the raja sahib. Tilo had held everyone's attention at first and then Das had appeared riveted by Lisa's appearance. I had been worried that Das had seen through Tilo and me, but now, it appeared he had sensed other things too. The raja sahib's unease, his attempt to conjure a false veneer. That Das had had this foresight or even the perception should have eased my worries, instead, it now made me uneasy.

'I really don't, Lisa,' I said hesitantly. The way things had moved, I would have to rewind time to get a fix on what had happened. 'I learnt quite suddenly that my car's gone, that your mother had borrowed it.'

We stopped where the road curved. On the right it forked out, through some trees that huddled closer forming a copse, leading to denser forests further ahead. This part was deceptive, for at the very end, the land with the trees looming around dipped quite suddenly toward the river Koel. I turned the engine off and waited for the silence to wash over us.

I looked at her, unsure if she was looking to me for assurance. She said nothing, and I reached over and touched her braid. 'Lisa, isn't it too late? You should be at home now.'

I had never spoken to her before and in some situations, such as this one, I felt self-conscious about my English. I had modelled it on Colonel Oakshott's speech, the slow, impeccable way he spoke. The man who had saved me in Berlin and then had embarrassed me and himself one night very thoroughly. I hadn't seen him after that, but there were things he had helped me with, my love for photography, and that measured way of speaking. He said it helped him to think over things, before saying anything out loud. It helped not to reveal too much of oneself.

'Is it a problem?' Lisa had quite a direct way of speaking.

'No?' I asked.

'But what is the problem?' She said impatiently. 'What I just told you? Or the lateness?'

I looked up, the night now encompassed us totally. The trees hovered like silent old sages, and there was the eternal buzz and cheep of the forest creatures.

'You wouldn't understand,' she said, 'I just wanted to get away. Have you never wanted to? Don't you want to get away?' She burst out, tapping on the dashboard.

'No. Not right now.'

She looked at me, puzzled, and I realized she thought I was flirting with her. And I knew she had not really understood. That she was too young, and I'd always been old.

Then I heard the clear, long drawn sonorous call of an elephant. The trees moved in a sinuous graceful line and I knew they were on the move. Somewhere far away, but the earth, the trees, even the sky carried the sound, and trembled to the call. It was picked up by other elephants, for the trumpeting lasted for what must have been several seconds. And it was only in the silence after that we felt the earth shake gently. The car moved, and I patted her on the shoulder, my hand lingering on her left braid. I wanted to tell her not to be afraid. There had been moments like this before. That I had heard them too. Closer. And other sounds too, almost similar.

The drumming neared, and loomed close, ever closer. The trees hummed but did not move. There was a sense that everything was holding its breath, hushed to the strange rhythmic quality of this sound. The Nama drummers of my childhood in Africa were nothing compared to this march of elephants, stamping their presence on the forests.

We had no idea when the sounds, the call, died away, for the leaves shivered and shook against each other a long time, and the branches stayed restless for a while. Long after the elephant herd had passed, the tremors remained. The trees whirred, humming and sighing. The car stilled, and through the moving branches I saw the clouds that had momentarily scattered begin to move, in a more orderly fashion now. I found I was holding her with my arm thrown over her shoulder, and at last when there was silence again she lifted her head and kissed me on the cheek.

I kissed her back lightly, on the cheek, and then again. 'You need to go home, Lisa.'

This couldn't be happening, I thought, as a breeze came in through the window. If I wasn't careful, I would be inviting a new nightmare for myself. It seemed to be a completely insane situation to be caught up in. 'Your father....'

But I waited for her to talk, I waited for the night to return to just the two of us again. 'He's made a mess for us,' she said, 'tell me what should I do?'

'We should be home now, Lisa. It's late.'

And I raised a hand to my lips and pretended to yawn.

'Everything is just getting worse,' she said, almost to herself, as we drove back, 'and I can't even talk about it to anyone.' For the first time, she sounded petulant. 'Talking about such things to anyone would be humiliating and my mother believes talking about bad things would only draw the evil eye. After Das left, I heard her argue with father. And they went all quiet when I came into the room.'

I knew she had wanted to go on a longer drive, she had never wanted it to end. As we saw the palace from afar, I knew that what held that decaying household together was its air of well-worn dignity. A dignity displayed in that genteel silence I had noted, broken only by the polite conversation between her parents, in the sound of wind chimes and cutlery, invisible footsteps, and the smell of musty carpets and brass polish. It was locked inside rooms now used only sparingly as old hierarchies slowly lost their meaning in a new country, and kings became remnants of an earlier age, the servitude due them almost an indulgence. In a keenly maintained driveway, the empty stables, that forgotten driveway at the back. In a flower garden where flowers sprang in wild profusion, but vegetables grew slyly in the back garden, that were then sold, as rumour had it, in the weekly market across the railway tracks.

'Why are your braids so tightly done?' I said as the car hummed to a stop.

'It's the way hair grows fast. The cook did it before she left.'

I tugged her braid gently and then, undid her hair. My hands ran through her hair, and we were enveloped in a fragrance of jasmine. I lifted a strand of hair, wrapping it around my finger, and saw her smile. 'Does your hair feel different now that it's loose?'

There was something in the way her hands brushed my ear. My hands found her chin, and then I kissed her, light on the lip.

'Are you my mother's friend?'

'We are just...friends.' I said, her chin on my shoulder and then her head against my chest. I held her in that silence, sensing her feeling of abandonment, relating to it. I couldn't tell her how I felt. My father riding away, never to return, the cook's unexpressed pity for me, my mother's long wait for letters, only for letters. 'I understand,' I murmured. And then she laughed. 'Did you speak in German?'

'No, that was the Nama language. The one I learnt first.'

'Do you know if my mother will come back?' she asked, almost casually.

'I think she will, Lisa.' I shook my head as she looked intently at me. 'No, because of you.'

I looked at her, knowing I meant that, knowing finally at that moment, that Mama too had meant it when she came to Berlin, that last year of the war, to look for me, even if it was to set me right. I shuffled in my seat, thinking of Mama and feeling guilty. About various things.

She gave a last, quick smile, opened the door and then she was gone.

Lisa ran into the house, up to her room, as if she were returning to a precious secret. I saw her turn right at the corridor, her hair, now loosened, bouncing on her back. She would read into the night and it was the lone lamp in her room I would look at as I smoked my last cigarette of the night.

Ghana came back the next morning for the keys, as he would do for the next couple of mornings. He had to clean the car, he said, and promised to bring them back in the evening. That second morning, he held out a conch shell carved like a boat, inlaid with peacock feather motifs. 'My people made this,' he said.

'I've no need for it.'

Ghana held it out, then placed it experimentally on the shelf next to one of Keith's horns. 'The sahib before liked such things,' he said.

He looked so expectant and that morning, even more bent over. As if the day's chores had already been too much for him. I remembered how he had looked that first afternoon, and reaching into my drawer, found some money, a few notes for him. I had no idea then that all the goods he'd fetch for me, were pilfered from the palace. That Ghana had been lying to me about them from the very beginning. Now he gave me his old toothy smile of thanks and proceeded to volunteer more information.

He told me that things had really gone quiet in the palace. Raja sahib and his daughter lived in separate wings and rarely met. Evenings, raja sahib would leave the house and it would be past supper time by the time he returned. He would sit in the living room like he did every night, till very late and listen to music. Often, he sang to himself, or flipped through old magazines, before giving up and retreating to his study where he fell asleep, again listening to classical music. Choti sahiba, he meant Lisa of course, only emerged from her room for dinner. Father and daughter would sit at the table, watched over by the old servants and no conversation.

Lisa told me that night that she had always been afraid to intrude on her father's privacy. She obviously missed her mother, and took to entering her parents' rooms, when they were both away. In her father's study, she had a sense of the forbidden that enveloped it, a remote faraway feel, as if it belonged to a person she hardly knew.

She helped herself to her mother's books. Erotic poetry, the old love poems of the *Caurapancasika*, the poetry of Byron and

Keats and of late, Eliot. She had brought the books back to her room. She, like me, would never realize, when and how things began to be pilfered from the palace, how they went missing and how unintentionally some of these made their way to me.

The books, the ones her mother was reading, and Tilo read several at once, were arranged in a certain order on the table. The books sat precariously on each other, the one at the top jutting out uncomfortably like a cat about to leap off a high wall. Lisa had crept in on those nights her mother was away, breathed in her mother's sweet fragrance that lingered everywhere, felt the breeze from the table fan, that same fan that stirred her mother's brown gold hair. One evening long ago when her mother was still there, she told me, she had waited nervously for permission to speak. Her mother, absorbed in a book, had not even looked up once. Now Lisa said, I can imagine I am having a conversation with her. Lisa's words echoed my own past. I did not tell her all this then. I thought I would one day, that I'd always be able to. I had already begun to look forward to our nighttime drives.

The call came three nights later, rousing me from sleep. *Listen. They got him.* A voice, muffled and coming from far away. *They got him.*

That voice, faint and from a long distance away, came again. I must have heard it many times. I must have woken up, moved groggily toward the phone, only to hear the same voice, saying the same thing again.

When I woke up at long last, the next morning, I knew the nightmare had returned once again, with more vigour than before. It'd be the night of the debate at the club that would make me late for my usual meeting with Lisa. Things get into your heart quite easily, making you let down your guard. I should have known better.

5

THE UNEXPLAINED DEATH

That evening, only a few hours before his death, Ahmed Ali had been seen by at least fifty people. And any one of them could have killed him, for he incensed everyone with his arguments. Ahmed Ali didn't really care much for what people thought of him or his views. I found that out when I moderated the debate he was part of.

The invitation from the club committee took me by surprise. I was still mulling over the call. For two years, I had had no news from my old associates, and about Eichmann, and had waited for a trunk call, a letter. But would they be bothered enough to tell me anything, to even assure me that I was not hunted any more. I was small fry, a necessary spoke, and it had already been a long time, a decade and more, since I'd been, alternately and against my will, the hunter and then the hunted. Would Mama write or was her brain too damaged by now to remember anything, even the man she once loved?

But what I feared most, I could barely bring myself to name. It was that which took my sleep away. Left me looking out of the window for hours on end; my only succour, that lone light in the palace window. What if I was tracked down now as the second Ricardo Klement, the lookalike, the person made to resemble in every way, even by name, the new identity Adolf Eichmann had taken on hoping to live life out anonymously in a Buenos Aires suburb? The past always catches up with you, everyone told me that, but what about my own past and how had I become a pawn in the world's past for no fault of mine? The years in Berlin when I was first picked up by the men wanting to save Eichmann, when I became their pawn, and then the other side, the Nazi hunters, who knew they could use me to track down Eichmann. The jarring bewilderment I had felt those years in hiding had never really gone. Perhaps it never would.

I had been touched by evil in my years in Berlin and later, but I had taken on that role against my will, even in my ignorance. But who would believe me? The way I had been rescued, the manner in which this job—of being deputed to kill Eichmann as he made his escape—had fallen into my lap still remained a mystery, a series of almost forced coincidences. Colonel Oakshott knew, he was a one-man army, but I had no idea where he was. And the elusive Keith Rawson? Who it seemed had just been waiting for me to turn up, so he could leave? Who had left me notes, but we had never seen each other. I couldn't write to him at Dharamshala asking him to vouch for me. Why was I being told the news now? Did the men who had tracked down Eichmann feel I knew too much?

Why me? I had had no idea that I'd said this aloud, but to Das and Singh, it appeared like mere rhetoric. I had taken too long to reply, and evidently, I had been tempted by their offer. 'Come on, not everyone gets to be President, to chair a debate,' joked Das. But the subject was one I knew little about: India, ten years after independence.

'You are a good speaker,' reassured Singh, his head bobbing earnestly, 'besides, you are not Indian. Definitely not.' And that decided it. As if my not being Indian placed me above the sentiments and emotions that would be generated during the discussion.

It was a mistake to have taken my diary along. Somewhere in the middle of a contestant's meandering speech on history, that began with the zero, moved onto the decimal system and flying machines, to cover all the interesting stuff that had been invented by Hindus, I began my usual doodling. Of the many things that meandered through my mind. Lisa sitting on the big Queen Anne chair in the raja sahib's drawing room. The fear I encountered on AE's face—it was always the initials I used when I wrote about him in the diary—as I came upon him unexpectedly on the deck of the SS Giovanni. The ship we were both travelling on; the hunter and the hunted with roles that were just as reversible.

A fear I have always been at a loss to express. A fear I had seen before on Eichmann's face as I mimicked his escape over the years. From the pantry in the old monastery, to the outhouse, then the boot of the car, the delivery lorry where he was stuffed in with the church furniture. Then the painful overnight journey, spent crunched up and hidden, as we moved over the Pyrenees to Italy, and the terrible sea journey. How far had I travelled in his shadow? Those spiralling lines across Europe and that line that cut across the Atlantic. There is a point I have marked on a map. A point where the southwest coast of Africa and Skeleton Bay was just a night's swim away from the SS Giovanni as it moved across the south Atlantic. But I never dared to jump ship, was never foolish enough to swim in those treacherous mid-Atlantic waters. At night I did once spot that lone whale that followed the ship for part of the journey. The whale that reminded me of one long ago June day, the time of my companionable journeys with father, when he and I had gone to look at the lone beached whale on Skeleton Bay. The whale that died soon after, for all my desperation that it live.

I thought about the call the previous night. It wasn't possible. But it was increasingly certain now. Israeli agents had been tracking down Nazi criminals with increasing success and it was possible they had managed to find Eichmann. But finding him was one thing, getting him out quite another. He could be kidnapped from where he was, in the most secure of havens, but then they would have to smuggle him out of Buenos Aires. All in a matter of a few days, without the smallest suspicion.

The news would obviously travel slowly, and secretly, and so far there had been no mention about Eichmann in the Indian papers. The big newspapers from Calcutta always came here a day late, and in the afternoon, that is if the train was on time. But what the papers never said, my limited knowledge and imagination helped fill up. It was all there in my diary.

Every morning, I noted, if his capture was a certainty, AE would be brought in a special convoy of armoured cars, each one no different from the other, from his special security prison in Jerusalem to the courtroom. No one would know which car he used, and every day he would use a different entrance.

They would appoint decoys—as had been done before—who would enter the courtroom through separate entrances. All this to foil potential abductors from whisking him away. The court itself would be heavily barricaded, with watchtowers and army posts all along the routes that led to it. What chance would a rescue mission have? Could a helicopter evade firing from below, from snipers all around, and land inside the grounds or on the extensive parapet of the courts, letting three-four armed men barge in, hold the judge hostage and take away the prisoner? Had it been tried before? Thinking such thoughts, imagining all this, made me nervous. I took a quick look over my shoulder but around me, were the kind of faces I was growing used to—brown skinned, yellowing teeth, always with too much curiosity. Except for Lisa. As her name flipped through the chaos in my mind, I felt calmness descend, like a coin falling to silence down an empty well.

When it was Ali's turn to speak, his voice had the sneer I remembered. I had not anticipated that he would be a speaker at the debate. That evening, he was dressed no different from the day I first saw him. In a kurta starched so stiff it crackled in the hazy yellow bulb light, and those tight jodhpurs that looked to me too difficult to take off, and even harder to pull on.

I should never have agreed to moderate. How could a man be expected to be fair when Ali railed against the government, against Sardar Patel, and even Gandhi. 'He abstained from responsibility when it was most needed,' sneered Ali. 'He could have avoided Partition, and he chose to give up responsibility. Gandhi knew all the time the rivalry between Nehru and Patel, in fact, he encouraged it.'

He could go no further. There were raised shouts from the audience, but Ahmed Ali would not be intimidated.

'I have a right to speak. Right to freedom of speech is guaranteed in our Constitution.'

'You are a traitor. Go to Pakistan, if you are against our leaders.'

There were more of them standing up now. 'Go to Pakistan, Pakistan.'

He had the mike, so he could effectively answer the hecklers back, but their numbers were growing by the second and a few were now standing on their chairs.

'All I am arguing for is that these leaders did not understand that a united India, from east to west, would have been the fourth largest country in the world. The Congress should have understood this.'

'It was you people who wanted your moth-eaten Pakistan? Broken up and scattered, like a discarded pair of shoes,' this uncouth remark came from a speaker who half-stood, half-sat in his chair. He received loud applause from the audience.

Ahmed Ali persisted, 'You just do not understand. Independence has left us more insecure. Kashmir and Hyderabad...look at the wars we are fighting there. And more important, this is for us, though you may shout me down. Our city, right here, may have been at the very heart of it all. Instead that honour now goes to Nagpur.'

'Nagpur is our holy place. Stop him, Stop him, Mr Hans.'

Some of them, I noted with alarm, now held a shoe or two up, intending to use them as missiles. I closed my diary, hammered on the table with my gavel. 'Quiet, quiet, please. This language will not do. We are deviating from the topic. Mr Ali, I am afraid I must ask you to take your seat.'

He stood his ground. 'Sir, I was only making my point.'

But the audience was determined to shout him out, waving their shoes, whistling and jeering. 'Ali Ali, acting silly. Ali Mian. Ali Mian. Go to Pakistan,' they chanted.

'Quiet please, this is a serious discussion. We were discussing a topic that is important, what makes us Indian? While a person may have other ways of describing himself, these are all personal. Here we are talking of being citizens, and what defines an Indian citizen? I hope I have made myself clear.'

My intervention, something spontaneous and little thought out, was met with rousing yells. And from the front rows, there came vigorous clapping. Ali still made a valiant attempt. 'As Indians, we are all equal, but some of us are now second-class citizens. Our concerns are not addressed.'

The applause gave way to booing, a chanting that rose by the second. 'Ahmed Ali, you are a fool, go to the moon or Pakistan.'

I saw Ali's face then, he bent forward to speak into the microphone, but words had finally failed him. I saw him try, but his face went blank as he looked bewildered at the mike, at me, at the sea of faces chanting those derisory words at him.

'Next speaker,' I said, beating down with my gavel, and another speaker, someone from the city college, rose. I remember little of his speech, for most of his words were drowned by loud clapping even before he had completed a sentence. I remember with relief his last words: 'And so I make my final statement,' he said. 'To truly make our nation forever secure, so that no country will dare cast its eyes at us, a compulsory period of military service. Even the greatest country in the world, America is soon going to introduce it. It will keep us safe from our enemies.'

I looked at him bemused as he came off stage. The three last sentences made no sense yet drew the loudest and the most prolonged applause. When it was all over, we had dinner in the club lawns outside. The breeze had picked up and scattered the yellow wildflowers and dry brown leaves all over the lawn. The bearers had to put away their trays and emerge with brooms periodically, to sweep it all away. The ladies were busy plucking leaves off each other's hair.

I listened vaguely to the voices around me. I was congratulated on my fine, concluding speech, though I didn't remember much about it. Some of what I had learnt in school had come back to me. Being patriotic is fine, but that is not enough. It means making sacrifices so that the interests of the country come before yours.

I had toyed with the idea of bringing up Gandhi again, who, driven by patriotism had given up a comfortable life in South Africa, where he could have become famous in his own right, but he had chosen to come back to fight for his country. But I couldn't bring myself to. Where I came from, for a great part of me belonged to Germany, there had been nothing noble. It had all been monstrously evil, for a time, for some years. Evil done in the most ordinary ways, as in the trains that brought the hapless to their deaths. Evil that ensnared even the most ordinary of people, like the officers and men and soldiers, who simply obeyed. Evil that made a mockery of love, just as it had done with Mama. Evil that stained those who when they came in contact with it, mistook it for duty. I had done the same; having come to Berlin to please Mama, I had taken on for a while the loyalties she could never let go of. What right did I have to talk about a man of peace? I had no claim to anything good that remained in this world, not even love.

I remembered Ali's bewildered look as words failed him. Now I saw him with Idris and others of his own group in a corner, talking with heads bent low, in sullen whispers. No one paid them any attention. That sight disturbed me, the two images following each other in my mind. Ahmed's face at the mike, gripping it for support and then minutes later, the closed circle of men at the far end of the garden, huddled close, gathering strength in their own proximity.

The minibus taking the participants from the college left early, followed a little later by the cars, one after the other. Ahmed Ali left too, shaking hands with the few people he had been closeted with. At one point his eyes caught mine, and all at once, his swagger dropped. He ran a hand through his beard, over his face, and turned away abruptly.

I was left alone, walking amidst the tables, and the scattered chairs. I wish I had handled it better. Everyone in Raurkela seemed to be wishing they had handled it all better. The raja sahib who felt entitled to a careless moment of pleasure. Tilo, whose pride had made her storm out, and everyone knew she had to come back. Singh, Jhunjhunwalla, Idris, and Ahmed Ali, there was nothing better they could do. They were all trapped in their own circumstances. Except for Das. He was, I thought grimly, far too involved in writing, albeit in his own mind, a splendid biography for himself.

It was late when I crept through that gap in the Forsythia bushes again. One minute the smoke left behind by the asphalt burning in the summer heat had made my eyes tear up, the next I was breathing in the sweet-smelling Frangipani that bloomed this time of the year. The light was on in Lisa's room, and I made my way slowly, certainly to the garage, just as I had done the night before.

The Austin was there just like yesterday. Parked obligingly with its front turned to me so I didn't have to reverse awkwardly. I waited for a long time, hoping she would come. I knew it was late, she might have fallen asleep, book in hand. I fiddled with the car's knobs, reached out to rub my hands over its familiar insignia, the gold-plated handles, and then I must have fallen asleep, my head falling forward on the steering wheel.

The night train to Vizag woke me up. I had never heard its horn so loud. It must have been a particularly quiet night. I woke with a start, then it took me a while to get the car started, and by the time I was lurching towards the gate, where the guard dozed on his stool as I passed, the sound of the horn had faded, and the drumming of the train ricocheted through the sleeping city.

The guard sat slumped forward on his stool and stayed that way long after I had closed the gate after myself and driven away. Evidently, he now had a taste for the drink. Lisa had been slipping him wine surreptitiously, and perhaps he had now begun to help himself to it, boldly entering the palace when there was no one to see him.

I drove through the blackened, shuttered city and felt I owned the streets, the houses, the city, even the sky. If I had looked far to my left, I would have seen the light still on in the palace. I drove down the road, past the highway, and then toward the small forked road that led into the forest. I cared not a whit, now that I was on my own. The raja sahib was away as well, the guard's presence indicated that he was expected but no one knew when.

I knew the matter of the billiards table had to be sorted out soon. The raja and Samineh under the table; I somehow could not envisage them together. Shops with shuttered eyes looked at me as I sped past. Men slept in their lungis on vendor carts, and jackals and dogs roamed freely. What did Lisa think she was doing, sending the pankahwallah to me with the keys? Immersed in my thoughts, I did not see the leopard at first in the faint streetlight. But there it was, sleek and wonderful, its gold spots rippling in the thin light. It stood on the small traffic island maintained by the plant. It stretched and yawned, and as its eyes met mine and the car headlights spilled over across the darkness, the creature took off in a dash across the road, into the forests around.

Almost in reflex, my feet stepped on the brakes, and the car lurched and tottered, a slow-moving clumsy creature when pitted against the leopard's grace. I straightened and gingerly felt my nose, the nose I had been given, when the time came for Eichmann to be secreted away out of Europe. A nose that despite these passing years, never felt like my own. A nose that had been made to look like his, or rather Richard Klement's, the name Eichmann had assumed, and the name I had in the one passport I had to keep hidden away forever. A nose that had been accidentally broken the time I had been found in a ditch in Durban, so that in some ways, it was at last my own.

When I drove back, the town was asleep like before. On the main steel plant road, the lights had dimmed, some flickered in their dying throes. The sky still bore traces of the orange sludge, like fireflies flying too high. I rolled down the windows and, changing my mind, turned back into the dirt track road that led to the forest. The night rose around me in degrees. I had the sensation of being nowhere. I could well have been the only man on earth. The world was just a hand-span big. A breeze came in through the gaps in the leaves. The trunks of trees seemed to take on animated features, and I felt I was being watched. The world was not mine alone then, for into my reverie, came the sounds of a plane overhead. Planes that had no idea of the life simmering below. Planes that would never descend on this part of the earth, any time soon.

The aircraft's low buzzing filled the forest. The top ends of the trees shifted in indignation. If they could, they would shut their ears to this. The young birds moved restlessly before being hushed back to sleep.

I slumped in my seat wishing I could go to sleep right where I was. But of course, that would be foolhardy of me. There were the elephant herds that moved across the forests in the dead of the night. Or the tigers. It might not be so thrilling to come across them in the dark and all alone. The raja sahib for all his bravery in shooting one down had half the village helping him. There were people who said he had not done it at all. That the tiger skin had been procured with special help from the sanctuary officials at Simlipal. It came from an old tiger who had fainted on coming across those giant herds of wild elephants that roved through the corridor of jungles that stretched from Assam, through Bengal and into Orissa. From here, they would go further west, and south, meeting other elephants on the way. On certain nights, and I can vouch for this, especially full moon nights, the gathering was bigger, and you could hear them stomping through the forests, trumpeting wildly in pleasure.

So many lies, the supplies man Singh had said with relish, the raja sahib had had to say to hold up that one lie. That he had indeed killed the animal. I had chuckled, listening to Singh. It was not easy pursuing royal pursuits in an independent country. Just like Israel, determined to write a new history, picking up all its persecutors one by one. How long back into history would it go? My grandfather, who had worked in Krupp's giant steelworks, and moved to South Africa, believing in Bismarck, and the great vision of German industry, would have made a likely target for similar blame. Mama too. It was a good thing perhaps she was incarcerated where she was. And my father, ever curious to learn more about the strangers in whose midst he found himself, where would he be in this strange new world the war had created?

A long while later, I awoke with a start, feeling the cold night wind through a gap in the window. I reached out a hand, and felt the softness of a shawl, Lisa's. She had forgotten it the other night. I lifted it, brought it to my face and it was then I heard the gunshot, ringing out loud and clear.

I jerked upright and through the mist that had formed circles on the glass, I saw the men watching me. They appeared to have just stepped out of the darkness and looked unlike anyone I had ever seen before in these parts. Their heads were half-wrapped in shawls, and their bloodshot eyes peered at me through the glass. It must have been only a second or so, and there must have been just the two of them as we stared at each other. They were carrying scythes, for I could see their pointed edges from over their shawls. They could have belonged to any of the communities that Keith had written about, who moved in the forests at will, bringing back twigs or grass that they had gathered, and were armed as they had to be, against the forest's animals. I stared, unable to look away, and then heard voices. A shout from somewhere. It could have been an animal, but it could have been my imagination too. The forest bore down on us, silencing us in every way.

I waited, the men did too. It must have been a few seconds this time before I lowered my window. It was then we heard the second shot. A crack in the stillness but further away this time. Everyone, and everything, the watching men, the trees, the tall grass that brushed the car, stood frozen upright. As nothing moved, nothing turned, we heard footsteps. Someone running ahead. For the sound of tramping carried, though after a while I could not be sure about the direction it came from, or where the person was running to. The two men who were almost one with the trees, stepped back and melted away. I was no longer sure what happened first or in what sequence. My lowering of the window, the men disappearing, the running footsteps. Or was it the footsteps that made the men disappear, and I had then lowered the window for a better look?

The forest narrowed where the valley of the river Koel plunged to one side. On the other side, the forests moved toward the hills. Behind a dense copse, where no one ventured, ran the train line. And the city began again.

I got out and ran in the direction of the unknown footsteps. Later I realized this had been a foolish thing to do though tigers did not normally hunt at this time of night. I could hear the faint sounds of a train as it hissed somewhere and the first creak of wheels. Also voices in the distance, but how could people be carrying on a conversation in the middle of a forest? I took more steps forward and could hear, as I stumbled, the man panting ahead. Then as I stood against an old tall tree, its bark smelling bittersweet, I heard another shot. Closer this time, and from within the dense grass, the low leaves around me, I heard and felt a thousand rustlings, the animals murmuring and calling in distress, and over all this, a hooting. It was an owl, but it sounded like anything else one could have imagined. Later I'd question this too. How long and how far had I run? And had I heard an owl or was it something else? A tiger? And as these different sounds filled up the forest, I knew the footsteps had died away. Whoever it was had stopped or I had lost him. It was in this sudden pause that I heard a different sound, the sharp thunk of metal striking wood. I stepped behind a tree and looked back cautiously.

The silver of the nozzle caught the light drizzling through the trees. The gun lay on its side in a hollow under the tree, and the faint wisp of smoke died out as I watched. Then the footsteps rushed away. And then they were lost in the sound of train wheels that now picked up slowly. I knew then that the night train had not passed but had stopped for what must have been an inordinately long time.

I advanced and then gingerly picked up the gun.

When I heard the footsteps again, this time far ahead of me, I must have fired almost spontaneously. For there was the shot

I heard again. I had no idea I had fired using the gun that had fortuitously come my way, my breathing loud in the stillness of the forest. I fought back sudden nausea as I looked down at the gun; a revolver, no bigger than my hand. It was still warm, and I believed then that I must have pressed the trigger, almost instinctively. The silence now stretched, as the train too lost itself in the distance. Now the only breathing I heard was my own. I slipped the gun into the car's dashboard, stuffing Lisa's shawl over it. I turned on the ignition, revved up the engine, so loudly that it woke up the entire forest, the threshing in the branches increased and as I drove on, alone on the road, I noticed that the harsh cawing of crows disturbed in their sleep, had yet to go away.

I drove to the palace fast. Everything was just as I had left it, when I had passed through. This time, I did find Lisa. In the garage, leaning back against the wall, half-asleep, her stole slipping down one shoulder. My heart rate picked up, harder than before. She had been waiting for me.

'What happened?' She asked, a tremor in her voice, her hands clammy on my skin, and then a moment later, she had steadied herself. 'I heard the shots.'

'The shots?'

'Didn't you? Where were you?'

'I was just driving,' I sounded disjointed to myself. 'Yes, I did. I did.' I held my face in my hands, trying to keep the old nightmare away. On the SS Giovanni, the time we had gone around the deck, once and then twice. Eichmann, the man I was chasing, with the gun in my pocket. I just had to reach out and fire. Now in the forest, I had fired once too, or had I? I still felt the heat on my fingertips but now I wasn't sure. Perhaps whoever had fired, had thrown away the revolver. 'But why?' Lisa's words broke into my thoughts.

'There were some shots,' she went on. 'Three or four. My father....'

She shook my hands and pulled them away from my face. 'Hans,' she whispered urgently, 'my father. He isn't home. Someone may have....'

I held her by the shoulder, she drew closer. We drew comfort in that. The car hummed quietly, I had not switched off the ignition. The pebbles and leaves on the roof above skittered in a thin breeze, but only for a moment as the buzz of heat made everything else fall silent.

'No, I am sure...' I didn't know what to tell her, or even if I could. She was too close, my own pasts from a decade gone by, and what had happened less than an hour ago, mingled in ways I wanted to figure out and couldn't. My hand shook, as I heard the panting again. My nightmare returned briefly. Eichmann, my quarry on the ship that night, had been afraid. He had stepped back, on to the lounges on deck, knowing something was amiss. And I had seen the other shadows rise.

'I did wait for you, Lisa,' I said, and it took all my effort to keep my voice steady.

'You were late,' she said, 'I was in father's study.'

We sat in the car, the walls around us, and we faced a thick bush and above it, the overhanging branches of a mango tree. At times I saw her turn away, lifting her head as if listening for something. She was worried. The raja sahib was evidently out later than usual. But now she rummaged through her bag and pulled something out. An ivory horn. 'I wanted to show you this. The time of my father's hunt. It brings good luck, but it could enrage the elephants too.'

I stared at it, and the moon shining through a gap in the roof turned the horn whiter. I realized it was now very late.

'Lisa you can't be out at this time....'

'No,' she attempted a laugh, and I knew she was high strung and nervous. 'I was just afraid after all that's happened. I found it in his study as I waited for him, I hoped it would protect.... He scares me.'

She gripped the horn so tight her knuckles turned white.

'Who? Your father?'

'No, that man Das.' My hand folded over hers on the horn. Once again, I felt the tension in her dissipate. Her shoulders moved slightly. 'I don't know what he wants.'

I held her shoulders. For an instant I guessed that she felt as I did. That day of my childhood when that man had come with all his promises, and soon after, things had broken down forever between my parents. The world had been almost destroyed in my time, I thought holding Lisa, not knowing it was the last time I'd hold her. And even before the war, the world had been destroyed for smaller people, like me, my parents. And the years of impersonating another had, I felt, hollowed me out.

I found myself telling her a shadowed, dressed up version of my life—moving from Southwest Africa, to Berlin; Brazil for a time, then back to Durban in South Africa. Now I saw the way her eyes had widened, the way they had scoured my face. I remembered how the light from windows lit up Berlin's dark streets, a cat skulking along the lamppost, a man and a woman in a bus riding past, and Oakshott's nudge on my shoulder, almost accidental, as he drove me through.

Things Lisa now said reminded me of things I had forgotten. 'I didn't know things about my parents, now I do, now they are not together. He loves music, she loves poetry.'

Lisa told me how her mother cried to herself as she read.

Mama, I too would then see her, alone at her table, the candlelight on her face, reading her letters.

We are never truly able to share, to relate to another, what we feel most strongly about. I thought of Mama, listening to Lisa's soft voice in the quiet night, and I knew that it is only in secret that we sometimes find ourselves. We must be caught out with our past.

We must have fallen asleep in the car. The spasm I felt in my neck and the frozen sensation in my arm jerked me awake. Lisa appeared even more embarrassed. She straightened her hair, wiped her face and surreptitiously tried to catch herself in the mirror. I wanted to tell her that it was okay (it really was), that she looked beautiful (but that would be flirting and perhaps a lie). I wanted to tell her that none of this mattered. That it had been lovely. And then I cut those thoughts off. 'You must go to sleep, Lisa.' And my voice must have held a harshness in it as I rolled up the window almost angrily.

When I had said nothing for some time, she nodded, turned to the door, and it was then I had to ask her. 'Will you be at the window some time when your lights are on?'

She wiped her face quickly. 'It's all right. Mother will be back tomorrow.'

'Yes.' I whispered to myself, not knowing what to think about that sudden bit of news. But Tilo had to come back, sooner or later. We were whispering; it helped us concentrate on keeping our voices low. 'I am glad your mother's back soon.'

She stood in the darkness looking at her own lit window. I got out of the other side. The stillness of the night was punctuated by the crickets playing in the bushes, the flapping in the leaves as a restless bird turned over in its sleep, the sounds in the far distance, a truck along the highway, the call of the jackals. The steel plant lay trapped like a butterfly, its wings pinned by golden heads of light. Occasionally, a flare rose from one of the silent spires, as if a giant lay stretched out on the ground, smoking lazily. I walked back with her toward the copse of mango trees.

'It'll be good for you to have your mother back.'

'She will see you in the afternoons again.'

I looked at her, touched her hair, and smiled. 'We will have to be on our best behaviour from now on, won't we? Everyone is being watched, and everyone is a witness too.'

'How?' I had confused her for no reason and relented.

'Aren't you one for your mom?'

I was teasing, and in that half moonlight, under the tree, I kissed her.

Her lips were sweet and moist. I don't know what I felt when I kissed her. I did intend to comfort her, but there was a hollowness in my heart that I couldn't understand, not just yet. Tilo was so overwhelming a presence always. She was there even when she wasn't there. It was not just how she appeared in our conversations but in most other things, like in the way, Ghana, the palace servant, talked about her. It was always the rani sahiba who decided things, he told me once when he had come a bit early. 'Now there's no one to ask really. We do what we do.'

'Lisa, we mustn't meet again. Once your mom's back.'

'Are you no longer my friend?'

I wasn't sure how to answer that. I was not even a friend to myself but saying that aloud sounded too easy, too pat. 'I have never been anyone's friend, Lisa.'

We waited in the darkness. She might have figured out my lack of response as a dismissal and didn't want to learn more. I struck a match, and caught her face in its light, the shadows on her neck, her eyebrows, and the way she pulled at her dupatta.

She said almost conversationally. 'I know what really happened between my parents. My father found someone, and my mother, I know, likes you.'

'That happens. But it's not something...,' I shrugged looking for the right word, 'big enough.'

She looked away, scratching the tree nearest her. We heard the raja sahib's jeep then, growling up the driveway, slow, and deliberate. The raja sahib was back, and I felt her really relax then. We heard the dull metal clank as the butler lifted the heavy bars nailing in the front door and heard him shuffle slowly out to the porch to wait. The orange lamps on the driveway stood looking dolefully at the thin circle of light that had formed around their feet, a few frogs hopped around on the raised platform that housed Tilo's cactus plants and croaked in vain. It was a night taut like a spider's web that could snap any moment.

The raja sahib was back, but he had parked near the gate and we heard him furiously lash out at the drowsy guard.

'Every day he seems more drunk. I should kick him out. Stand up and salute. Salute me.'

The raja sahib said this again and again. Lisa's hand tightened on my arm, as we saw the butler stumble and then rush forward, though it took him all his will to speed up. 'Sahib, please you go on, I will see to this. Go on, sahib.' The old butler spoke to his employer paternally, almost indulgently.

We exchanged one last look as she ran, making for the back door, and then I left too.

That night, I fell into the same dream again, and awoke much later, sweating profusely though the window was open, and the forest breeze came in. I had relived an old nightmare. The time when reality had had me totally confused. The incidents of the night before had conflated with all that I remembered and struggled to recover from. But the images were even more vivid this time. Images that would never go away. The time I had been picked up from a street bench, or rather kidnapped in the middle of the night, pushed roughly into a ramshackle car, on a journey that took me farther and farther into an all-enveloping darkness. I had woken a long time later only to realize that I was no longer the same. I had been made to look different. Made to look like the man I was to kill. A man who would be my fellow passenger on a ship bound for Argentina.

Shivering now and fully awake, I saw the faraway light on in the raja sahib's house and felt relief slowly flooding me. But then I had no idea that in the space between that night and the morning that would break only two hours or so later, things would change drastically. For by then there had been the death, or rather, as the police would insist, the murder. Ahmed Ali's body was found only a few hours later lying on the railway tracks. The night train to Madras had already passed and then there had been the herd of rampaging elephants that had moved past, close to the tracks. And the shots had been heard by many people in the refugee settlement, and in the town as well. Everyone had heard them, though as would be soon apparent, there was no consensus on how many shots had been fired.

As Das would report later, it was just too convenient. There were several reasons why people would have him killed—'you remember the anger he drew at the club?'—and there was the matter of those gunshots. The raja sahib's own guard, and the butler, had heard them, and they knew the raja sahib had returned late. 'He says he was at the club and then at the lodge, but you were not there, were you Hans?'

But all this was for later. That morning I stood by the window thinking of the men I had seen in the night, the ones who had melted away into the forest. Those men could be the Adivasis who had lost their land and were rumoured to forever roam the forests. From Keith's notes, I remembered reading about the Roullias, the black magic practitioners, who had given their name to the city, but now lived deep in the forests. Their numbers were dwindling, as fast as their land was being taken away—by the plant authorities, by the government, by the new settlers. Had I been one of the lucky few to have seen them?

6

SHOWDOWN

My letters had a strange way of being intercepted. Close at hand. First it had been Rao and then it was Das who got to the next one. But about this, I had only myself to blame.

Rao must have placed the envelope on the front table in the lobby some days ago. Then he had taken a few days off. I had indeed seen the letter the previous nights when I had come in late. I recognized the clear blue insignia of the postmark that gave away its origin but had done nothing. The newness of present-day events had upended my habits and crowded out my past.

That morning I first came to life blurrily, my sleep broken by the welcome and familiar sound of keys falling on the table outside. Rao always did that after the cleaning boy had done his job on the car. The metal clanked dully against my ears and I must have asked in my sleep, 'Has that idiot washed the Daimler properly?'

The Daimler, never the car. A Daimler can never be another car.

When I next awoke, the fan whirred heavy over me, churning the hot air that curdled and spread over the entire room, and the cleaning boy was frantically knocking on the window.

'Someone for you, sahib.'

It was Das waiting for me in the only other room in the cottage, a makeshift living room done up with a settee, a round table and a cabinet holding all the curios Keith had collected and to which Ghana of late had added some objects. In my annoyance, I remembered we had barely met a few hours ago, and now here he was again, unchanged in appearance. He loomed over things, as he fanned himself with a very familiar looking envelope. It was possible he now took up more space than before, for he had only grown in his own importance, but the rooms in my cottage weren't very big to begin with. Two people could crowd things up.

He looked very dapper, in well-creased, slim pants, and he had an altogether strange smile. Too brilliant, overly bright. Far too happy, I'd realize later. As if he had it all figured out. 'Something's happened, old chap. I need you to come along too.'

He wanted to meet the raja sahib, he explained. 'And it's best you come along.' I thought of the sunroom, of Lisa, and simply nodded in agreement. As I turned away, indicating I needed to change, he called me again, his voice very light. I felt myself go still as I looked at the letter he held up. A calendar flipped in my mind, I saw its pages move in a wayward breeze, numbers in black and white swirling past. It could have been the same postmarked letter I had received seven, or eight years ago. That was the last time I received news about Mama, of her being committed to a home.

This letter that Das held up, was quite like the last one, in the same kind of envelope. It could not be about her death, of that I was certain. Sad news always came in a few lines, a bare slip of paper. This had to be some administrative matter.

'It's from some institute,' Das was looking closely at the letter, holding it against the light. I cursed Samineh under my breath for not being there anymore. She would have placed the letter in my personal file.

'It is,' I was carefully offhand, 'just a magazine subscription.'

He smiled and handed it over. We left soon after, and I, now fully awake, lightly asked him what the matter was, and if I was really needed. His jaw tightened, and he looked away as he said crisply. 'This whole matter involves you too and it's gotten more serious.'

I waited for him to finish. 'I am surprised, old chap, that you're the manager of the club, and you don't make inquiries. Your secretary leaving, her fiancé coming up to you... and the rani sahiba leaving. In a huff. Something happened but now it's more serious.'

He looked around, dropped his voice.

'Look, we must get to the bottom of this, root the whole poison out.'

It was only much later that I figured out that when Das spoke in such abstractions, it meant he did not have a clue. He was gazing at what was not even a puzzle, just some events that had followed each other almost by coincidence, and he was trying to piece them together. Understanding dawns later, years and decades after, and by then the past has changed irrevocably.

'Mishra, call him what you will, the raja sahib or whatever, he still feels he is entitled to his feudal privileges. He took...' Das groped for words, 'some liberties, and all that, with the girl. Under the billiards table.'

'The girl, oh you mean Samineh?'

'Yes, and now he's gone and killed the man.'

He enjoyed the shock that splayed itself all over my face. 'Yes, old man, there's been a death, last night. And we are looking at it as a possible murder. And that is what we must get to the bottom of.'

It must have been related to the shots I had heard. It must have been when I was in the car.

He must have seen my face change colour, the confusion I felt. 'What's wrong?'

I stopped deliberately, willing my hands not to tremble, bending down to make a show of arranging my hair against the car window. Das's driver stood waiting, holding the door open. I took my time, lifting my collar, pushing my hair back.

'The shots,' I said, looking back at him, 'someone might have been out hunting.'

He looked taken aback before he laughed abruptly, 'At that hour? But come along,' he said, impatient now, 'I do have to make inquiries. Why was the raja sahib out at night? His jeep was seen on the jungle road, late at night.'

'Is that so? I never heard it?'

I had let myself be bullied, and now as I stepped into Das's official car, and he moved in to sit beside me, I felt a clammy hand around my heart. What would Lisa think if she saw us together?

'But why did you want me to come along?'

'No, I was...' he looked at my face before he answered, 'I was hoping you'd help me understand things. I try to do things on my own. Now the guard at the palace can't remember clearly which car he saw. It seems he was drunk. The raja sahib still won't dismiss him. What does that make you think?'

I made my face go very blank. 'Should it make me think anything?'

'The raja sahib is duty-bound to answer some questions,' he told me in a lowered tone, as the car revved up. 'He must have been out late that night. When I called up the palace the butler told me that sahib was sleeping late. He had gone to the lodge.'

Das leaned back against the car's soft cushions and then said a tad too loudly, for the driver's benefit. 'There have been some important developments, and we need to go meet the raja sahib.'

The main gate was shut, which was strange considering that it was morning. We had to get out of the car and walk down the driveway, for the gate remained firmly stuck on its rails despite the best efforts of the old guard and the driver. The guard was most unwilling; muttering under his breath that the sahib had expressly wished not to have visitors, or anyone enter the palace, but he was careful not to let his words reach Das. Weeds had entwined themselves around the rusting bars, dandelions snaked around the old padlocks. The heat outside was now stronger than ever, beating heavily down on my head.

Lisa stood at the window, as we neared the portico. I had a fleeting glimpse of her, before the window took on the habitual blank transparency of all windows. A curtain still moved. Das walked beside me and now resumed his monologue, his voice tickling my ear, his breath hot and hard on my cheek. My confusion had given way to irritation. Inwardly I cursed myself for not getting my hat along and for being here in the first place. Das had been in too much of a hurry and I had to get him away from the envelope and letter within. The man made too many unnecessary observations, saw too much into things. Why didn't the heat addle his brain as it did for everyone?

'It shouldn't take us so long to get here in the future,' he was now saying, 'if there's a road through the forest. They cut down a part of the forest when they built that south-eastern railway line. And raja sahib wanted his share as well, for the line was built over some of his land.' Das waved a hand in disgust, almost wishing the palace away too. 'We, the government, had to compensate the people who lived there. It was their land really. There were, as you well know....'

He turned to me suddenly and fell quiet in that menacing way he had.

'You seem preoccupied.'

I jumped out of my reverie, I had been looking up at the window. Das paused and took out a speckled green handkerchief from his pocket and wiped his lips dry. I realized that he was nervous too. He was preparing himself for what lay ahead.

The raja sahib was surprised to see us. His eyes were bleary with sleep, and when he spoke, his words were stiff. He had us ushered in and then stood at the stairs and called for his daughter. *Lisa, Lisa.* I heard it the way I called her. Her name resounded in the high-domed lobby, rose up the stairs, and for some moments, I was full with her name in my ears, and everywhere around me.

'Lipsa, tell the servants to have tea ready.'

In an earlier time, perhaps, the raja sahib would never have done this. But then, he must have been frazzled, almost at the end of his tether. But now holding his pride in check, he leant against the stair rails and called again for his daughter to come down. It was quiet except for the sound of the wind chimes. Then as we waited, she appeared, hesitant and demure, her face devoid of any expression, nodding to her father. We sat in the same sunroom as before. The raja sahib seemed to have forgotten our earlier meeting, as he showed us in, saying it was comfortable in that room.

I could see her through the half-open door, as she supervised the servant setting the tea tray at the table. He was slow and fumbled often, and Lisa, impatient, leaned towards a glass cabinet and brought out a new tea set. She brought the tea in as well, overriding the servant's objections, and the frantic signals of Biswal the butler.

She kept her eyes firmly on the tray, almost afraid of the delicate chinaware that sat on it. Was I the only one who saw her nervousness? Did she feel that at any moment she could trip embarrassingly on the carpet? An expensive carpet her grandfather had got from Kashmir, one of the things Tilo had revealed to us that last time.

'My daughter, Lipsa.'

'We have met,' and Das rose to his feet. Still trying to follow the situation and Das's recent revelations, I was a bit slow. 'We have met before,' I wanted to say but the words never came. I rose, then promptly fell back onto the sofa before I gathered myself again. She bit her lip then, suppressing a sudden giggle. I smiled too; it became something of a conspiracy between us.

The morning light had left shadows on her cheeks. There was also no Tilo to dominate the proceedings. She looked angelic. And preoccupied. And I saw myself reflected in the dusty gilded mirror on the shelf opposite and realized I needed a haircut. My hair, stringy gold and long, like the pictures of Jesus Christ in all the missionary schools.

'Lipsa, my dear, these two gentlemen are Mr Hans Gerder at the steel plant and Ranjay Das, the superintendent. You would remember him from an earlier time.'

She placed the tea tray on the small table next to us. 'Thank you, my dear,' said her father again. She smiled, and it seemed forced. She turned back and ran up the stairs to her room. She did not meet my eyes the second time and I knew then instantly, feeling the heat rise in me that it was because I had come with Das. Which to her meant I was on his side, and so had turned against her family. I looked down at my hands, at the truth staring at me. I wanted to explain but did not know how. I had not wanted her to leave. Those drives already seemed far away. I no longer wanted to follow the conversation. Das took an elegant sip from the cup, wiped his lip with the napkin, cleared his throat, and began.

'You were seen. At the club, in the billiards room.'

'It isn't what you think, Das,' began the raja sahib. There was a deliberate heartiness in his tone, but he ran a hand over his face, evidently fatigued, and the bristles made a scratchy noise under his fingers.

'You were, you made the entry.'

I put my cup down and stared. What was Das up to? I thought he had mentioned a body being found. I shook my head. It had been a long night, perhaps I had not heard him right.

'I played billiards, that's right.'

'The lady says you insisted on a, on an...' Das coughed delicately, wiped his face and said again, 'exchange of affections.'

Raja sahib looked puzzled and distant, 'Well, I really.... But I've never disputed a woman's view so openly. Someone was there, some people. I introduced myself.' I wasn't sure if the raja sahib was having Das on. They were clearly on two different trajectories. I wanted to tell at least one of them to stop.

'More like...you introduced too much of yourself. And why did it have to be done under a billiards table?'

'I was not doing anything. I have said this before.' Now the raja sahib's voice was louder. He calmed down and said instead. 'You seem to go on about it. There is no proof, is there, is there? Any photo? Or....'

Das looked at me, and all round, placed his cup down and delivered the kill. 'Well, it does seem there's a dead man now.'

'Under the....'

The raja sahib couldn't finish, instead his wild gaze flashed my way. I spilled some tea. Then almost as if I had conjured her up, Lisa appeared. Evidently, the raised voices had alarmed her. His face turned white and I turned my gaze and thoughts away.

Her father paused, looked at her as if lost, though he nodded all the while. Then we heard him repeat the words again, and then again, 'I do realize. I do realize, indeed.' He said it between pauses and in that silence, we heard the low rumble of thunder. It never took long for the tropical heat to crack up, and now the clouds had gathered heavy on one side of the sky, though the sun, unrelenting as always, still shone along the porch. I knew then that Lisa had been listening in all the while.

'Madam,' Das said clearing his throat, and then bowed to Lisa, 'madam, who is not here now, has let me know that there is danger to your daughter if she's left alone.' He made a show of pulling out something, patting the pocket of his shirt, and then gingerly feeling his trouser pockets. Lisa came in, stood next to her father, her eyebrows raised in mockery as we looked at Das.

He presented a ridiculous figure for all his officiousness. I tried hard to hold onto my smile.

But that was a mistake. Das caught my eye, his jaw clenched, as he said tightly.

'I assure you the matter is most serious.' His eyes had a coldness in them, and I felt sheepish, and anxious too. Das had one too many weapons up his sleeve. My eyes stayed fixed on Das, who now fumbled more deliberately in his pocket and pulled out a letter. 'Madam gave me this letter, that I produce as evidence. It is from someone,' he lifted the letter for a closer look, to add to the theatrics of it all, and read, 'called, I think, Bernard Ambrose. A letter that was apparently sent to your daughter.'

I heard her gasp. It was clear Lisa had recognized the letter and she was now shaking her head insistently. 'It is from the English teacher, he teaches in the high school.'

Das flapped the letter as he held it high. He seemed to like doing this with all letters. 'It says,' he read on, 'that he would like some acquaintance with your daughter. To teach her the classics. At home.'

I saw the raja sahib's eyes widen.

'Father... I had left it on my table, it is of no importance.'

Raja sahib's face was set in grim lines. 'Yes, how did your mother find it? More, why is she using it against me?'

Lisa looked distraught, her explanation hurried. I wished I had not come. The letter, she stumbled as she explained, had been on the table for a long time. Her mother must have picked it up when she left the house. She must have read it over the last few days which she had spent in her ancestral house in Brajrajnagar. A letter that was now a trump card for her mother to show that Lisa was better off with her, not her father. He just could not keep an eye on her.

The storm broke in the middle of Lisa's explanation. A streak of purple lightning flashed against the window, and the thunder rolled out moments later. Das's driver ran up the porch seeking shelter. I saw him through the window, shaking off the sweat and raindrops as he stood under the awning. The raja sahib who had listened to Lisa expressionless, stretched elegantly before the fan. He had recovered his poise and now didn't appear put out one way or another.

'It's only a letter, from someone she barely knows. This isn't relevant at all. Tell me, Das, are you going to make this a morality test, like the club incident? And involve my daughter too?'

The thunder crashed overhead again, and there was the sound of a door slamming shut. The chimes shook somewhere in the house, like an alarm. Outside, we heard loud heated voices of servants berating each other for being caught out in such unexpectedness, and then just as suddenly there was laughter. The storms were unpredictable and never lasted long. We saw the purple flashes of lightning that looked different from every window. The thunder that followed, sometimes sounded near, sometimes not.

Upstairs the wind slapped a window shut in a room, and we heard the urgent creaking of a half-latched door, the clothes hanging out to dry in an upstairs balcony now flapping in alarm like frightened hens. I hoped the storm would quell the chaos inside me as well. I waited for what would come soon; the gentle peace that would descend, the smell of wet earth and newly washed jasmine that would hang in the air, as if, like the cars in Idris's garage, everything had been given a fresh wash. We looked at each other, knowing it'd be hard to make ourselves heard in the din, and then came the distinct sound of a car driving up. I looked up with delight. I recognized the sound of the Daimler. Then I saw Tilo run up the stairs to the portico, glancing back once at the police superintendent's official car, and smiling in her casual way at the stupefied and delighted butler and a couple of other servants who had materialized out of nowhere.

We rose as the Raja sahib did too. Then he did a most surprising thing. He stepped closer, and I felt his touch on my arm. 'Gentlemen, on no count are you to mention Ahmed Ali's death to her. Not yet.'

There was a firmness in his tone, his eyes moved to mine, and I saw his look of swift appeal. I nodded and smiled more fulsomely at Tilo as she came up. Lisa melted away, she moved behind the curtains, an intensely serious look on her face. She had misunderstood the pleased expression on my face. The Daimler, as I looked behind Tilo, was its familiar serene blue self as it stood against the Forsythia bushes that edged the driveway.

Tilo walked right up to her husband, stopping to bestow a smile on us. Like the raja sahib, her regal demeanour would never slip. But she was flushed, and her voice quivered as she made to speak. It was the raja who beat her to it though. 'Well, my dear, it seems your friends got here before you did.'

We did not react, and Tilo looked up, her chin tilted back, and she faced her husband as she declaimed.

'I returned.'

'I can see that,' the raja sahib, looking bored and blustery again, 'Though it is going a bit too far. The letter is perfectly innocuous.'

'We are talking about your conduct as well,' she said.

I felt embarrassed to be witness to this. The raja sahib shrugged, 'The matter must be settled. I was helping her look for a pen...a pin. A safety-pin.' Now he looked furtively at me, desperate for an escape. Tilo turned to me as well, smiling most apologetically. 'Mr Gerder, please accept my apologies. I am sorry your car was dragged into service.' Her tone had changed from accusatory to mollifying.

Das shuffled and coughed. 'That is fine,' I said hurriedly, then bowed, remembering raja sahib's desperate request to us just before she entered. 'We must let you rest now.' I looked significantly at Das who leaned back on his heels, placed his hands in his pockets and said, 'We were here on business, to press for an apology, but things seem more serious. Yet we must leave, must we not, Hans? Can I say goodbye to your very charming daughter?'

With all that he had just said, what he asked for last seemed to be the least shocking. The raja sahib, looking somewhat ashen, called for his daughter again, in loud, somewhat abstracted tones.

Lipsa. Lipsa.

I felt a prick of concern sensing Lisa's vulnerability. I remembered being called down by my mother the time Eichmann had visited our corner of the world: Luderitz in Southwest Africa. But Lisa emerged soon enough, and Das turned his smile toward her. His eyes scoured her face. In another time, on another occasion, that glance might have appeared abrasive, but now, with the things that had just ensued, it merely seemed somewhat odd. As if he wanted to be remembered, and this moment too.

'It is always a pleasure to meet you, Miss Lipsa.'

Her mother now rushed toward her and hugged her tight.

'Lipsa, how are you, my dear?'

I had never seen Tilo this way. Neither, I was sure, had Lisa. As Tilo surged past me, I smelt the raw perfume and the sweat. I felt the agitation rising and falling in her. The chandelier swung overhead, and it seemed to me that it moved in an ever more frantic manner, but it was Tilo, her reflection caught in it, a whirl of black amidst other still standing figures. The raja sahib was rolling his eyes. And then pointing outside to where the weather had cleared, he led us away stopping on the way to murmur to Tilo.

'My dear, do show some restraint. You were gone just five days.'

He left us at the door. As we stood at the porch, looking at the clearing sky, Das looked at me, his lips twisted in that smile I knew. 'Why do you think he did that? Asked us not to mention Ali—that's guilt no?'

'I don't think so. It's because....' I scratched the porch steps with the end of my shoe, 'I think he knew Tilo would consider him guilty as well. That's two of you making a case against him. Just what were you doing, Das?' I was careful to keep the anger out of my voice.

'There's no proper case. I am building one, Hans. There must be the necessary steps one has to take, some questions that follow each other....' He paused, brushed his hair back, and continued, 'All in proper order.'

We heard the raja sahib's voice from inside, clear and low. He had walked back to Tilo, and he was now shaking her by the shoulders none too gently. Her back was against the banister, her bangles slid down in a musical cacophony and Lisa sat on the stairs, looking totally bewildered.

'He had only given me a book,' Lisa said almost in a wail.

'It's all right, Lipsa,' her father said, looking from one to the other, 'your mother will do her best to turn you against me, but remember not a word is true? Do you hear? Not a word is true.'

We heard him too, as he indeed meant for us to. The next moment, I forgot everything again as I saw my Blue Daimler parked in the driveway. Das noticed too. When we shook hands, the sweat of his hand gummed into mine. I had forgotten about the envelope but Das evidently had not. As he walked to his car, he left behind one casually tossed question, 'By the way, old chap, that envelope of yours?'

He must have seen my quizzical look, as he stood there, his elbow on the open car door, 'The overlapping postmark...did you notice that?'

In the blinding light of the afternoon sun, his teeth were white and menacing against his swarthy face. The fatigue rose like a cloud in my mind, but Das was unrelenting, 'It has a home ministry stamp on it, over the German postmark. Now, are your letters being screened?'

7

BERLIN IN 1945

Seven years, I counted again. Seven years ago I had received a similar looking envelope, after which I hadn't thought much about Mama. As with that first time, this letter too was from the reverend Maria George. A whiplash of a woman, with lips set in a narrow line like a stingy river. Perhaps I knew this from the way she had used her words in that first letter. Terse, and pointed as if she had no time to waste. *Your mother wishes to have no further communication with you*, that first letter from her had said. *She will not stand for those who abandoned the cause, who gave up too soon*. Poor Mama, she might have lost her head, but never lost her hopes. Perhaps her insanity saw her through the hell of those last years of the war. How could anyone, even the blameless, the ordinary, live on, when you've lived so close to evil?

Seven years ago, in Durban, sitting on a garden bench, I had read that scalding first letter, my mother's words in a stranger's handwriting. The contents, I can recite them from memory. So terrible in its implications, that I had shredded it to bits, tossed it away—the casualness in the way I did it, I remember even now. I watched the bin swallow it up, and walked away, straightening my creased old tie.

That memory had underscored my reluctance to open this other envelope. It had just been there on the tray, ever since Rao had left it, and had drawn Das's attention. Now I opened the letter, steeling myself to read it, recognizing in myself a despair as to whether I'd ever be free of the past.

Herr Gerder

We have been forwarding your mother's letters and are deeply disturbed that you have not bothered to reply. We are planning to dispose of her old collections of magazines and newspapers. She is receiving treatment and the doctors have ruled her unfit to appear before the tribunal.

I stopped at those first lines. What were these letters that the reverend Maria George was referring to? I had not received any. They did not know where I was, where I had travelled to, after her first letter in Durban. My eyes scanned the letterhead, and I saw the date Maria George had most recently written to me. 1 November 1959. More than six months ago.

Frau Gerder is in no position to read and understand the magazines. We also have not encouraged her to read these magazines and their seditious contents. They upset her even more, make her even more delirious. But since most of these remain unopened, they are taking up too much storage space, space that could well be used for other necessary articles of daily use. The proceeds from the sale of these magazines and Frau Gerder's books will be used for the benefit of the other women in the institute.

Dear Reverend Sister, I thought, you must have given up on me already. The gap between letters, despite the ones I never received, seven years was suddenly a bit too much. The missing letters were my missing years. And that is a frightening thought, for time, especially when you are young, is too precious to be lost.

Mama, she came to mind sitting at her desk, murmuring to herself, always, glancing over her shoulder. This is how I remember her, from the time I was nine or ten. Was it my imagination or did she look fearful then? Of being overseen or spied on? Did she move to cover the paper she was writing on? With her hands, so hardened and strong, that I flinched every time she touched me.

The years passed like the ever-ticking second hand on my old watch. Sometimes I forget the exact sequence of events. Almost 16 years ago, in 1944, I had left our home in Africa for Germany. Mama, with her callused hands and faraway face, whom I left one day in Windhoek, began writing to me soon after. Her letters were cajoling and full of recrimination in turn. She wrote as if holding her breath, stopping only if she had run out of paper. Till the time she must have sent Ujwima to get fresh supplies. Looking back as I held the nun Maria George's letter in my hand, I knew it was my father's long absence that had made me go away. The man whom I feared, was also the man I missed. He had never returned since he had ridden away one morning. I could not stand that intense silence anymore. A sense of waiting, of not doing enough.

It wasn't surprising to think that Mama had been successful in tracking me down in Berlin, in those days of that terrible war. No one knew then that the war would end soon. It seemed to have gone on for ever, and the cruelty, the madness had only increased. Suspicion and fear lay heavy everywhere, like a sullen, unwavering cloud.

As a card-carrying member of the party, Mama had her contacts. I received her letters at the Tempelhof airport, always some weeks too late. I was late myself, too late in registering myself for the cause, when the war was almost over, and I was close to losing my own will. There had been days when I had seen the officers fighting amongst themselves, screaming themselves hoarse, and the senseless executions, carried out on someone's passing whim. I skulked in near anonymity, often helping the older women pull things—old, valued, and most times, utterly useless—out of the rubble, or playing with the kids amidst their destroyed houses. In those last months, the delay between her writing her letters and me reading them, in my soldier's cell by the light of the lone lamp that strayed through the window, was exact, never varying from the usual seven weeks. The letters always reached me too neatly folded, crisp, to all appearances unread. I believed that she could find me then if she wanted. But she had chosen not to. Perhaps he, the man she'd forsaken everything for, wouldn't let her.

For till the very end, Eichmann or AE, the way I referred to him in my diary too, was planning the movement of trains, the meticulous transportation of all passengers, recording them, so that after the war, the humiliations of retreat and the ignominious defeat, all of them, all his crimes, would become known.

The last letter I had from Mama was one morning in June 1945. Later that afternoon, as we had known all along, the Soviet troops marched in.

They found the letter in my pocket when I had barely had time to read it through. Perhaps I might have tossed it aside and shrugged off any knowledge of it, but you could not trust anyone. There were some of us, who had trooped into the Soviet commandant's office and betrayed Gerard Mannhaus, the supervisor to the soldiers. His body looked ridiculous, bloated in the wrong places, as they hanged him on that pole near the gate. His tongue lolled out, his eyes still bulged, the way they had when the soldiers marched him off only some hours ago, as he sat pompously in his office, his eyes over the last day's figures.

We did not have long to wait either. He was still dangling when we were herded into the storage hall with the old dismembered pieces of aircraft standing around like museum pieces. They frisked us roughly, looking over our identity cards, running their rough, scabby Russian hands through our pockets, one pocketing the five Deutschmark note I had, and then there was the letter. I read it out loud standing on a makeshift stage, repeating lines when prodded, their laughter harsh, guttural in my ears.

They patted me on the bottom, pinched my cheeks.

An airport is a strange place to spend one's detention. But I did, while most of the others were taken away in vans, to the sound of the Russians jeering and saluting. The thud of their boots as they cocked their mock salutes, the laughter in their raised voices, resounded in the terminal, and made us cringe and feel very afraid. At the airport, now much shrivelled in importance, fewer planes landed, largely American planes that refuelled and went their own ways. I heard the low rumble, saw their vanishing red lights and remained unfree, in my state of limbo, waiting for my case to be decided. We knew waiting was better, there could only be one of two options: Siberia or a terrible death. The Russians had to avenge too many things. Soldiers came and went, weeks passed and then months, I remained while my fellow soldiers and co-workers continued to disappear overnight or very suddenly. Other men came in looking already dead. They were taken away for questioning and some never came back. And later we learnt that they had been sent away to Siberia or to work in the mines of Ukraine.

When my turn came, there was always that last incriminating letter from Mama.

It was a letter so overcharged, and so unlike Mama that it had to have been doctored. In her usual letters, she would begin in a cold way, and we could well have been discussing the day's weather before she began a long harangue on my failures. Mama realized soon enough she was not getting anywhere with her letters. That I would never understand how I was wasting my time loitering around Berlin when the Fatherland needed every hand at its disposal. Why was I not meeting the *Obersturmbannführer*? She had written many letters to him, and I had simply to call up the office and speak to him. Mama would never understand that Eichmann might not want to meet me or anyone. His office was not where Mama said it was and that he himself was most times on the move, assessing things for himself, making the best transportation plans possible. There was a certain desperation, targets to be met in those last days. He worked late into the night, diligent and meticulous always with his plans.

The last lines of that letter left no one in any doubt. How it had been changed, how someone had had a good laugh at her and at my expense too. Even the censor officials needed some amusement, even if they had to conjure it up for themselves. It was evident in how they changed words: Baby for son; rejoice for fail and of course, messing up the most crucial information of all.

You are my baby ~~son~~ *but I am distressed to note that you seem to overwhelmingly* ~~fail~~ *rejoice in your* ~~duties~~ *failings.*

I have tried to be of help to you, have tried to provide you every possible support. I have even provided you the commander's ~~commandant~~*'s address.* (It was this word that was flagrantly and very foolishly written over.) *I intend not to write to you any more or to ever extend any offer of help. I regret giving birth to you. But in case you have a change of heart, here are the details once again.*

Obersturmbannführer
AE,
Reichs Central Office

Her own suspicions were already clouding her sanity. The abbreviations gave it away, too many shortened, brief sentences as if Mama expected to be taken away any minute.

That night, as they poured buckets of hot and cold water over me, this was what I was asked, repeatedly and insistently. The tones always changing texture. My questioners could sound casual and offhand at times, even dulcet, and gruff at other times, brooking no nonsense. But the threat lay suspended in the air like frost that chills one to the bone and refuses to dissipate.

Who is this man... the *Obersturmbannführer*? They squinted at the initials, that had been struck off, written over several times. RF or it looks like an A, or is it RE, some Nazi official? Big one?

I do not know, I always said. I did not know, and I did not want to know. They came closer, ever closer, the lights never going off in that room in which they questioned me. But they still asked me, time and time again, and I could only moan and groan, suspended in a morass of agonies that rendered one numb and killed all memory, even the ability to conjure images, especially those long lost.

I was tossed aside once they had their fill for that day. They never wanted to kill me, for some reason. I guess I was younger than the rest, or, as I think now, that I simply didn't fit in. I just looked different, and even spoke German differently. But for those days, this didn't deter their cruelty. The torture inflicted on me happened like routine once a week or every time a new corporal came up.

For all this, they could not decide what to do with me. But I remained, even as my fellow inmates changed, as the contingents around me left and were transferred. And luck finally shone when the Soviet troops left, and the American Sixth regiment arrived. Colonel Oakshott, bald, reddish in hue, rigid and stern before his superiors, and who wasted his time, we thought, taking photos of everything around, especially the city in near ruin everywhere, and of us too. But he was, I soon understood, a bit like me, a nowhere man. An Englishman in an American regiment. A steely man who could not admit that differences of habit, of taste, and outlook, made him lost, and an outcast.

There were stories about him too. Of how he liked taking natural photos, the way he spoke of muscles and the beauty of the male body, and the embarrassed silence, the nudging of elbows, that followed when he entered the mess.

He showed a curiosity about me that was flattering. And an affection that made me suspicious. I remembered the way Oakshott would lift my chin with a finger, trace the bones of my face.

Can't place you, he said. It wasn't his photographer's sense but something else. He saw something about my face, its malleable contours that made for skilful impersonation. When I was caught, and my face altered, I wondered which side he was on, where his loyalties lay. And if his shifting, shadowy loyalties held the key to my escape.

German, I'd insist before the Colonel. But I never could hold myself straight when I said that. My chin dropped, my eyes shifted. Germanness took hold of me slowly, and then came easily, like an overcoat one could take off and put on depending on the weather.

In the dark room that he converted a part of his kitchen into, he showed me how to develop photos he had taken from his camera, an Agfa. As I worked in the dark room, I could hear the questioning that went on in the rooms around me, and the conversations the Colonel had on the phone. Sometimes in the darkness too, I'd know that he watched me. One long night, when we had developed several photographs of the city and its people, I found him smiling in fatigue, and then he came around the table, and kissed me full on the lips. He smelt of cigarettes and beer, and I smelt hungry most of the time. But we both drew apart shakily. I could only stare at him and wonder if the stories about him had been true. 'My...boy,' the words came out of him in a long-shuddering sigh. 'Sometimes one weakens. You must try and forget this. And forgive me.'

That night he went on his drives through the city. And came back late. He no longer asked me to accompany him. I remained in the dark room. For days after, Colonel Oakshott would go out for his rides into the city, always in the late-night hours, and one night he did not return.

There had been times before, when as the skies darkened, and the lights dimmed over Berlin, and the lone fighter aircraft drifted over the night sky, he would call me out for a drink. The silence was swallowed up in the darkness, it was like nothing I remembered. Sometimes when he was in the mood or was upset with the superiors in the Allied high command, he would between guffaws deign to teach me a bit of Hindustani. Only later would he tell me that they were the choicest abuses he had ever heard. In a mellower mood, he taught me the meaning of some Urdu ghazals. The true language of love he called it. I came to like the metallic haunting voices of Amirbai Karnataki and Gauhar Jan. Music I later heard from the raja sahib's study that afternoon—as the door closed behind him. That was why I could never really think badly of him.

Rumours also floated about that the Colonel had been killed by the same people who later got me. The same people who transformed me. The Gestapo, or people who made up the Odessa after the war, many of whom were still on the run. People among them who had experimented on skin, on changing shape. All for an escape, a possible getaway of their own, when the time came. The Gestapo who would rather I become a pawn, just so one of their own, someone higher up in the hierarchy, could escape to safety. Did this fit in or was it contrary to my mother's hopes for me?

But I have always believed that the Colonel disappeared. Anyway, they gave up the search for him too fast. The Berlin Blockade was to last for over a year, and by the time it ended, I found myself suddenly a free man, at loose ends. For I had grown used by then to living an imprisoned life.

It happened in a matter of weeks or just a month. I spent my initial days of freedom longing for the regimentation of a cloistered life. I did not have an appetite, I shrank from crowds, slept on park benches, and time and again must have passed the house that was soon to become Mama's prison. A banker's house to a recruiting centre and finally an asylum. Under the fountain where I slept, the same graffiti would appear every night. It read like a madman's rantings, a warning that the devil had an eye on everyone. It was rubbed away every morning but reappeared almost by itself by nightfall. And then came the night I woke to find someone shining a torch on my face.

I barely had time to scribble something on the bench, perhaps an inchoate, garbled message, before I was whisked away. The office I was taken to, men speaking in accents of my former comrades, voices that I had only recently been familiar with. The instructions, the money offered, and an assurance that I could begin life all over again. On one condition. The man I'd impersonate had to be safe at all costs. I was to be the perfect foil, to throw pursuers off his track. I'd be making a great sacrifice and in the end, I would be compensated in a land far away.

Those years I suffered the torment of travelling in cramped buses, stuffed into cars, and then the nerve wracking sea crossing, down the gentle Mediterranean, past the northwestern coast of Africa, and down the rough South Atlantic, before I finally found myself in Durban, a city that became my home for a period of five years, where I found safety and anonymity of a sort in the city library.

Once she reached Berlin, Mama wrote for a while and then never again. All through my childhood, Mama had always threatened this, to leave us, no good father and son, and pack off to Berlin. For her, life was always there. She would describe its clubs, its operas and the Saturday picnics in the forest. Her wintry gaze froze as it lay over the heat of Southwest Africa. A heat that fossilized everything. Her mind was always on a bigger cause.

The nun's recent communique to me had carried more disturbing news about her. It wasn't just about the magazines, but the veiled message that soon followed. The tribunal was instituting a case for treachery against Frau Gerder. The charges: collaborating with the Nazis, helping in the escape of noted war criminals. The evidence had been found in some of Frau Gerder's letters to the Nazi Hero Mission. Frau Gerder however, was in no position, owing to her ill-health, to appear before the tribunal.

My mother, a war criminal, I thought, putting the letter away in my pocket. And there seemed no way I could get away from my past.

Letters from her, or about her, would always pin me down. That first letter about her, the one the nun had written to me seven years ago, had been forwarded to my Durban home, a room in a lodge. It'd be some months before the advertisement would catch my eye and it was in desperation that I applied. It had been left pinned to my locker in the library. It struck me later that someone had deliberately done it. But that would mean I was still under watch. And I did not want to countenance that thought. The advertisement for anyone willing to be posted in a new Krupp plant in central India. The position: administrative manager, fluency in German and an ability to pick up languages.

I remember that I had that appointment letter for a long time. As if I had to look at it to believe in it. It was still in many ways, strange, this place I had ended up in, in central India where the heat never seemed to relent. Suddenly I longed for the cool winter. The winter here lasted a bare two weeks and was gone as fleetingly as the swallows that I saw every summer.

Lisa was at the window again. The evening sun was fading and as the night spread, I missed the drives with her.

Later, the phone rang, broke off, and then rang again.

I knew it was an international call when it broke off the third time. I still waited.

A voice came over the line, the fourth time. *We have him. Homeward now.* It took long seconds before I recognized the heavy thudding around me. It was the blood rushing heedless through my veins, my heart beating so hard I had to hold tight to the window. My eyes were swimming with the import of the news. I thought I had outrun them but they knew where I was all along. Everything blurred momentarily. The light turned into another golden globe gliding silently down a long river of light.

8

THE BILLIARDS TABLE

The billiards table, as my files showed, was the standard 4.5x9 feet in proportion. Made of rosewood and polished aluminium, it was a prize find, and had been a gift from America to Germany. It had been shipped to the new plant by the German government. Das asked for these exact specifications, as the scandal got murkier and murkier.

It was no accidental death. It was a murder. Das simply wanted a motive to join one dot to the other and frame the raja sahib.

Men came from the police superintendent's office to measure the table, comparing them with the measurements recorded in the file in Keith's hurried handwriting. Das looked at the new measurements carefully. He came down himself when the discrepancies seemed too large. Taking the tape measure in his mouth and a scale, he worked out the exact measurements all over again.

'It's short of 9 feet. Around 8 feet, almost a foot short,' he said rising to his feet, and rubbing his back, in some self-satisfaction. 'So despite what the cover note says about the Americans, even they took short cuts.'

'Do you think it got chipped in places, during the transportation?' asked Singh. He had no business to be there, but he happened to be in the club at just that moment. Singh now got into a long discussion about how crates shortened in size as they came from Calcutta, and their contents too never matched up.

Das looked at me, rubbed his chin and looked back at the table again, then he tapped all around its silver inlaid edges, peered into its corners and even sat on his haunches to tap the underside. The rest of us watched him, waiting for the billiards table to yield its secrets.

There was a short, animated discussion that followed between Das and his deputies on American mechanical expertise, the bombs and the spaceships they were developing. Again, it was Das who had the last word before he moved on to the matter he had really come about.

'The Soviets,' he said, folding up the measuring tape, and putting it in his pocket, 'they are smarter, you will see. They will pip the Americans to the post.'

The laughter came late, a few seconds after the look of incomprehension had passed. It took time for Das's fondness for the idiom to sink in. I would have to ask him later for the measuring tape, it was club property.

'How do you think a man who is 6 feet and some odd inches tall, could fit under this table?'

In the silence, everyone trained their eyes on the table in front. Outside, the metal clanking of the steel plant started up again, and through the windows the heat rose from the red-hot gravel, and a dusty breeze wafted in, bringing behind it dry yellowing leaves. It was left to me to break that awkward silence. 'Um... depends on what position you are speaking of?'

The laughter began jerkily, the men looking at each other nervously, each one waiting to be prompted, but like a wave, the laughter burst forth and went on for long minutes till the bearer came with his tray of pakoras.

'The legs are too stout, you can see that,' went on Das, the oil from the pakoras shiny on his fingers, 'and the sides are low enough to ensure some er...er...privacy.'

'We need to know what kind of shoes he was wearing.'

This time the silence was thick, no one dared look at each other. I looked at the dim lights overhead and switched on a few more bulbs; now the baize shone violent and ugly. The few black spots on it showed up stark, and with its stout bent legs, the table had the appearance of a sleepy prehistoric creature, the inlaid stones in its pockets resembling sleepy eyes.

'Or boots, sometimes he would come in straight from his hunting...,' someone said.

'Yes, he found his prey under the table, it seems,' I could not help responding and this time the laughter was instant and loud, and earned me many back slaps. 'Hans, you wicked old thing,' said Das, wringing me by the shoulder, 'I would never have expected this from you.'

I sat next to him in the cosy foursome we made up at dinner. As Singh and the man who gave the plant most of its workmen, Jhunjhunwalla, got up for their refills, Das let slip in an undertone, having grabbed my attention with a kick on the ankle. 'The raja sahib will do anything to save his skin. Now he is off to the capital to plead with the chief minister.'

'But why? When no charges have been brought against him?'

'It is important that we build a case against him,' Das was almost talking to himself. 'No one seems to remember. But it's all very funny. He came late to the high tea, but no one heard him. Even the car....'

He scratched his chin thoughtfully and I ventured to add, 'But was the man really killed by a gunshot?'

'It is a bit complicated. His body was found across the train tracks. And then his cycle found somewhere else.'

'Perhaps he had been running?'

'From something. That's the part of the road which has been

cordoned off,' mused Das in reply, 'and then he, or the body, was run over by the train.' He raised a finger in a teacher-like way, 'Which, I believe, had stopped. It was late. But the raja sahib could have got it to stop.' He shrugged, 'Old privileges, you know.'

Das picked at his teeth with a fish bone. I smelt the fish on him strongly as he tapped the bone against his plate.

'And you do know who he, our dead man, was engaged to?' Das toyed with his scuppered bone, as if he was picking apart a corpse. A waiter offered him a toothpick and he now used that to push the bone all over his plate.

'It looks very bad for our friend, very bad indeed. It's true, it could have been an accident, the death. But there were shots heard.' He stabbed the bone with his toothpick and left it standing there.

'Yes, I heard them too,' I murmured, then stopped. What had I heard? Three shots or more, and perhaps one had been my own. I had felt the heat on my fingers. The gun had already been fired. Then I remembered the gun I had left behind in the raja sahib's Austin and looked guiltily away.

Das still did not seem to hear me. 'True, everyone did hear the shots. They keep coming up to the police station to report this. We have a table listing this. Day, shots heard.'

I interrupted, 'Just how many shots were there? I can't seem to remember.'

But Das appeared not to have heard me. 'And what's more, the raja sahib was seen driving out in his jeep, not the Austin. Which meant he had intentions to hunt,' there was a very satisfied look on Das's face, he had it all worked out already. Then he said, 'Don't you think, old chap, it looks altogether too convenient. He wanted to get Samineh's fiancé, Ahmed Ali, out of the way. We just have to prove it.'

Did he intend to make the raja sahib confess? For I didn't see how he'd connect the dots or if there was anything in this at all, except a series of unfortunate coincidences, and a tragic accidental death. But I'd have no idea what precisely Das had meant, for it was at that moment, the lights went off.

I sat in the dark next to Das thinking hard. I had clearly heard the first shot the night I was out alone, when the elephants had stampeded across the forest. No, that had been later, I frowned. But the train had stopped when I had heard the shot. I had also heard the man running, and I knew it couldn't be the raja sahib. Not that it would be incongruous or even undignified, but the footsteps had been lighter, the panting heavier, more frantic. Then there were the other people who had appeared around my car and quietly disappeared. Had that been an illusion? A creature watching me in the dark. I knew I had been fooled.

After the seconds of blackness had eased and our eyes could discern the shadows again, the nervous laughter was more easily heard, as well as the sound of cutlery. A few more minutes later, the waiters emerged with the foul-smelling, hissing paraffin lanterns. Das's face was now half yellow, half black, and I heard his voice, the words swirling out like the black wisps of lantern smoke that left black laughter lines on every lantern face.

I knew he had been looking at me, then he rubbed his hands and said, 'The matter is making you curious is it not, old chap, I always think you know more than you let on.' Our other two dinner companions returned then, their plates loaded, giggling as they sidled into their chairs. 'The lamb curry got into the custard,' said Singh and broke into giggles.

'It's all a coincidence...,' I said.

'And you see no connection at all?'

'Even about the table, you don't seem to be surprised?' Das's voice broke in suddenly.

'About the discrepancy in measurements?' I shrugged, 'I will have to look over the files again, but the table came before my time.'

I was silent and then he spoke up again. 'You think I am making too much of a fuss about it. Do you know something,

Gerder, as a German...?'

I felt the skin tingle at the back of my neck. It was odd hearing that on such a muggy night, the likes of which I had never seen before either at Lüderitz or Berlin or...or...strange that the thought of the city where I had spent a year could still make me nervous, and Das still watched me too carefully. Recife, I remembered...the port city in Brazil where I abandoned the cause and had hidden away for a year, till I knew I had to escape. I was lucky I could stow away on that ship to Durban.

'As a German, you ought to know that the table has pockets. And that's the English way of playing....'

Das laughed at my startled expression. Suddenly there was an animated look on his face. 'You might say I fill myself with all kinds of strange information. Billiards or French carrom, old chap, is played on tables with no pockets.... But did the table really come from America then?

9

LÜDERITZ 1939–40

Before she became obsessed with the great cause, my mother read Goethe and Mann. I never saw her talk, really talk. The way people converse; sitting back and letting the words out or just to say something aimless in another's hearing. There were the orders she barked out, the remarks short, abrupt, and rationed to my father and the absent-minded monosyllabic responses to me. I learnt soon to keep questions to myself. To make up for her silence, Mama wrote. The letters I received on her behalf every time she was away for a week or two to Johannesburg or Cape Town. Secret missions, she told me. And my father would shrug, and say she was away, fund-raising.

And if I asked more questions, he, or even she, would add, 'For the Fatherland.'

There was the one time she raised her voice. A month or so before that man came in his Maybach, my parents had a big quarrel because my father refused to have anything to do with it.

'That man is preparing for war,' he said, and he pointed to a picture on her table. Of a man with a brush moustache, a fierce, angry look in his eye. 'As if Germany has not suffered enough in the first war. As if we haven't caused enough suffering already. Haven't you seen the evidence here?'

'It was a war to keep us down,' my mother retorted, 'the Americans, and the British, they would do anything to keep us Germans down. Now that we are as powerful, as strong and with colonies of our own, they can't stand it. Wilson, that George character, everyone is determined to get us down. And they encourage our people, the Nama, the Herero to band up against us.'

'They are not our...,' but my father stopped, gathered his breath and went on, 'it would not serve anything. Our presence only alienates us more among those we live.' He had been reading the paper, and he lifted his mild eyes, the colour of which sometimes shifted with his mood. Now they were brown, inscrutable, giving nothing away. And his voice too was mild and low, often straying in my direction where I looked out of the window to watch Ujwima weeding out the flowerbeds.

'There will be no peace in our time as well. The League of Nations is a showy body with little power.'

Mama rose swiftly from the table. For all her thinness, she was an awkward woman, and the cutlery jangled as her hip caught against the edge.

'I am proud of what I am doing,' her voice was harsh and grating, at odds with that faraway look on her thin face. Her chin looked more pointed then. The villagers would stare at her as she went by, nervous, falsely imperious on her bicycle. These were the times when she rode out to collect the post, or when she was forced out by the doctor. 'Get some air, some air,' had been his diagnosis. But it seemed Mama could not stand the heat, the sullen air all around. Whenever a visit was due from the doctor, when he flew in on a special aircraft from Windhoek, the front and the sitting rooms were aired, occasions stamped like a rite in my memory. Mama, a cloth over her face, barked out her instructions that Ujwima and the other houseboys found hard to keep up with.

I liked the way the sunlight strayed into the room then. Beams of light and the dancing dust embedded in them. 'Keep away from my books, my books.' She might well have been haranguing the sunshine, but it was the houseboys she was warning not to stray too close to her shelves. But my mother wasn't done yet. She would warn them about the table too, where she wrote all those important letters and sorted them out. 'The table, the table,' she would say, swatting the air, pointing in some desperation.

She had a habit of repeating things twice, for she knew they did not understand her. 'They stand looking at me dumb and sullen, like slaughter animals,' she would tell my father and he laughed at that, wiping his mouth, looking up to only say, 'how apt and how sadly true.'

In the files on her shelves were her letters too, carefully slotted. These came for her every fortnight or so and were brought to her by the special aircraft from Windhoek. Sometimes I received them when she was away. The post office was a small red brick building with a tin roof under the shade of an acacia tree. A lost-looking building, unhappy with itself, for it did not fit in among the bushes, the people in their coloured dresses and the huts with their helmet roofs.

Neatly numbered and bound in black and blue, Mama's files aroused my curiosity, but they were off-bounds for me. As I grew taller, I could easily reach for them, after climbing up on her heavy wooden chair. She made sure though that nothing was ever done about the noise in the shelves. They creaked and moaned every time they were opened. And she would wipe the old glass panes herself, testing them for clarity by moving across the study, next to the grandfather clock and trying to read their labels. Sometimes she would make me do it too. Force me to stand on the gardener's ladder and read the names aloud when I had not even learnt the alphabet properly.

At her table, I'd watch her in secret, as she devoured the contents of the letters that came for her. The hurried slitting open of the envelope, the frantic speed with which she read it the first time, the second look always more leisurely, with that thoughtful look in her eyes. She would return to that letter time and time again until the next one came. Her eyes would dart toward where she had kept it, in some numbered, precisely dated file. She would keep the letter open as she penned her reply. A letter drafted and redrafted several times and then copied out painstakingly, several copies that she sealed and addressed herself. She carried them with her when she took the train to Johannesburg.

From there she wrote to me, and others, letters written in so fervent and rigid a manner that I could imagine her as she wrote them. Letters, she delighted in writing, as she raised money for the Fatherland. 'It is a noble calling,' my mother wrote several times. 'The Fuhrer knows that there is no race like ours. The world has long denied us our due and it is time we Germans stood as one.'

When she wasn't singing the Fuhrer's praises, she was denouncing my father in equally vehement terms. 'Your father is a traitor, an idiot, a sentimental fool. A disgrace as a German. He is totally unsuitable for the job. If I were not married to him, a decision I solely blame on my parents, I would have exposed him to the Fuhrer at the earliest.'

'He mixes around with those we call the Untermensch,' she said once, when she returned from a trip to Johannesburg. There was a new sparkle in her eyes, followed only by a new set of household rules. Mama forbade my friends from the village to even enter the house. She sprayed the house with perfume after the helpers were done with the day's work. She scoured the floor carefully every time Ujwima, the gardener's boy and my oldest friend, departed though he used the back door. Of course, when my father was not around, Ujwima was even denied permission to enter. She would see them staring at her, through the netted windows, and pull down the curtains one by one, shouting at me to do the same, when all I wanted was to play outside with Ujwima.

'Don't you go playing with them,' she would say. The time she was home, and not at her table, she watched over me with an obsessive protectiveness. I would see her eyes on me precisely the minute I stepped outside, which is when I got into the habit of hiding myself in strange places. In the cellar, in the old ruins of the king's palace and now in the dark room.

But when she was away, I'd always discount her warnings. I enjoyed the days of freedom then, as did father. I heard her, shrill of voice, as she gave instructions to the maid, and watched the calendar with a longing I tried hard to hide. The stronger the longing, the greater were the chances of the train to Johannesburg being somehow delayed or held up because of some rebellion on the border. Her plans and mine would fall apart. The packed bag would be opened, her clothes and papers replaced in the cupboard in the same manner for them to be repacked again later.

Books arrived for her in the post too, and she would closet herself in her room for hours, even for an entire day. She would emerge, her eyes red-rimmed, whether from crying or fatigue, we would never know. She would alternate between being sullen and berating my father on several counts.

For all her antipathy towards him, she shared father's love for books. Their tastes ran in different directions though. My father, in a job he did not want, in Lüderitz, South West Africa, in a factory churning out cars for the Fatherland, saved himself for a while with his curiosity. Curious about the people he was with, he was eager to learn everything about them, and was desperate to right, all on his own, all of history's wrongs in this region. He was also keen in a secretive way to prove all those impressive eugenics theories wrong.

'Their culture,' he said referring to the Nama, the people who had lived in this region long before the rest of us came along, 'is just different, not inferior in any way.'

'Might is not right,' he added, 'it is just brutal.'

'Going native,' my mother would describe it, a snigger in her voice. He ordered books too, and they took longer to arrive. Sometimes they did not, for the rocks and the fog around Skeleton Coast could be treacherous and it was rumoured that too many ships had ended up there, broken and devoured by the deceptive, half-hidden, rocks. Finally, he decided to help himself, and began the greatest project of his life, a book on the Nama, their history, their language, and customs. And because Mama would not let them in, he went to them. Riding out to their villages, seeking out the tribal elders, travelling with them across the vast dunes to their settlements on the other side, making his notes the nights he was home.

The times he did attend office, it was all half-hearted on his part. He hated it when I interrupted him. When he found me in the office swimming pool, he had me locked for hours in a closet, shivering and wet, before finally relenting. We rode home that day on a speckled young horse, with me seated in front, wrapped in a colourful Nama shawl. Yet he always suspected Mama put me up to such things, to spy on him. Mama couldn't discount disloyalty, either on his part or mine. Only I knew of the secret afternoons he spent with the Nama women. I learnt this the time I followed him and we both paid a heavy price. He lost his job, his self-respect and I, my father who had tried to reach out to the world, in the only way he knew.

As I grew older, it was in those few days of freedom, with Mama away, that my father began taking me to the settlements even farther away. 'My objects of study,' he told me, as we rode out. I liked the way my head flopped against his chest for I had not learnt to ride yet. That, and his voice over my head sometimes making a few strands of hair stand up, and the thudding of the horse's hooves over the rough gravel. Once we saw the rounded mud huts, we would cover our heads with the coloured turban, and I felt like a bandit as we rode up.

The children who gathered as we rode up sometimes became my friends. Though I think they merely tolerated me. They stared just as they do now, looking on with unblinking, uncurious eyes. My father left me with them before he, suitably turbaned, closeted himself in one of their rounded huts. The children mocked my efforts to keep up with them. The way they walked into the desert, cold by the evening, or how they calmly sucked the nectar of a cactus. I was wary of getting the red desert sand into my shoes and kept away from the cacti for fear of the red scratch marks they left behind. Mama would inspect me carefully every time she returned and there was always a way she came to know.

Something in our eyes. She would tell me enigmatically. And while she did not accost my father openly, the servants would change. Ujwima survived somehow while the others rotated. They became faces familiar to me, for those Mama had long forgotten, would return after a while. But then she had never looked at them in the face, even when she addressed them. For a few trips that Mama made, the cook moved in. I was certain of this for she seemed to be there whenever I would go into the kitchen hungry. At that age I always was. The kitchen, a big room that looked like a war room, with the heavy metal utensils dangling overhead like shields, pans that looked like war helmets and ladles like medieval swords. The storage bins arranged next to each other like generals. It was where sometimes I found her asleep. The cook plied me with the food my mother denied me, bananas and cassava, for fear they would make me soft. But I hated the blanched meats Mama fed me, and the boiled potatoes, insisting this would make me hardy and strong. I was not allowed second helpings of desserts and chocolate pudding.

But the cook, Najime, was especially indulgent. I hung around the kitchen watching her with starved, greedy eyes as she made supper, breakfast and even lunch. My father hung around too, laughing and joking with her, an eye constantly on me. It was only later that I caught them in the cellar, my father patting her bum, his lips on hers. It was she who was first alerted to my presence. I can still hear my father falling on the vat, as he tried to back away hurriedly. I ran away and hid inside the tree trunk. Later, it took two men, the gardener and his assistant, to lift my father with a back sprain out of the cellar, moaning and crying, leaning on the gardener for help. He later told my mother that he had been looking for something to eat, and the cook had been totally useless. Of course, she was sacked, and another appointed in her place. I'd soon learn that this just helped keep my father's relationship a secret. Now he'd ride out to the village to see her.

After he recovered, the first time he was able to, father took me hunting. He sought me out from the garden, as I built a treehouse with Ujwima. Father helped me fix straw on it before asking me if I was ready. The smile on his face was broader than I had ever seen. My father said he had hated being injured and cooped up in the house and knew I must feel the same way. A day out in the plains would be a good idea, he thought. And he said no to my mother's suggestion of a packed lunch. 'That would send the hyenas after us, Marian,' he laughed.

I knew the hunting trip was the price my father willingly paid for my silence, for promising not to give him away to Mama when we returned. I never gave his game away to Mama, though the promise I extracted from him helped him. Every time now, I accompanied him to the Nama villages. He left me to roam with the children, as they herded their cattle, and he did his 'studies'.

It might have been a sense of futility that made him finally leave my mother. She waited for letters from the man in Berlin, the one who did come to visit us once on a secret mission. The one I knew later as Adolf Eichmann. But once the war began, the man in Berlin had no time for Mama. As for father, he never really believed in theories that created special beings and alienated others. Or that he finally chose between the women he loved: my mother whose insults he had put up with all through their early years of marriage, or the other woman, the dismissed and disgraced cook, Najime, silly in very many ways, but who loved him unquestioningly.

AE came to visit Mama on the afternoon I lay in bed recovering from a scorpion bite. That stopped me from accompanying father on his visit to the Nama village. The scorpion had crept out of the bush as I played with Ujwima. A sharp, piercing pain that left a lasting bow-shaped scar on my upper arm. A bite delivered as I lay full length on the ground, playing a soldier. Mama watched over me anxiously, and even called the witch doctor in. I heard her ask him, desperate to make herself understood, 'how long, how long?' I can hear her shrill voice still, echoing in the house and corridor, while the shaman kept his eyes firmly shut, shook his head morosely and rubbed a green gooey paste over my bite.

That day, as father left, I stayed at home. The pain in my arm was excruciating and I denied it for all it was worth hoping my father would relent and let me accompany him. Instead he tossed me his old pistol, and as I reached up with my bitten poisoned upper arm to catch it, I collapsed in agony. My father laughed. A schoolboy kind of laugh, then he shook his head, as he picked up his fallen pistol. I remember watching father leave on his horse, with his assistants, Obje and Mukama, riding alongside.

It was an hour or so later that the rumbling Maybach drove up. As it came up, I stood at the staircase window looking down. It was the newest in fashion but appeared much the worse for wear, with sand encrusted on its tyres and front; but the man who emerged from it seemed untarnished by all this. I saw the carpet being unrolled, the way Bonjo, the houseboy, saluted. It was ridiculous as I remember it now. His palm straight up over his nose and forehead, his bandy legs trembling, as he tried hard to bring them together. Ujwima and I would take turns kicking at his legs or aiming the ball right through his splayed-out legs.

But I did not laugh then for my eyes were riveted on the man who waited to step out but was thwarted by a three-step ladder that suddenly appeared. My mother stood at the doorway, her hand over her head, biting her lip. The step ladder embarrassed her. It was too high of course and impeded his descent. She clapped her hands and once again Bonjo and Kavila rushed forward to move it away. The man inside wore shiny black shoes, the buckle caught the sun and glinted. It was his shoe that smiled first. No wonder then that in his time as a prisoner, twenty or more years later, when forced to wear scruffy torn shoes or the Soviet-style bandages over wooden clogs, he flew into a wild rage.

When the man finally stepped out, it looked like he had emerged out of a mirror. His fairness was startling. My mother smiled nervously as she stood in the dress that made her look younger than she was: the floral printed one with a sash at the front. The cook had helped starch and iron it and it had hung on a curtain close to the oven for a week.

As he kissed her on the cheek, I saw my mother's eyes close and wondered if she would faint. The moment lasted longer than a moment should. I had never seen nor would ever see again the same rapture on her face. I remember how my mother laughed then. Her tinkly glassy laughter broke the silence that stretched over the driveway, car, bushes, and Bonjo and Kavila who looked on, smiling, uncomprehending.

I remember the car and its exact details even today. The dark green of its colour, its silver headlights, the insignia that glinted each time the sun strayed. The number and the sign next to it, some of Mama's letters had had that sign.

When Najime touched me on the arm, and I heard her say, Hansie, I flinched. I would have moved back but there was no place.

The ledge and the dusty, heavily breathing curtains held me. She made to touch me on the cheek. Her callused fingers always cut a jagged course on my skin, and I ran down the stairs, afraid to see her pity for me. A brass flowerpot tumbled over, the door opened, Mama ran out, and came to a shocked stop seeing me there.

She always thought I had been spying on them, eavesdropping on what they said. I had had no idea then of its importance. But she dragged me in, into the room where the man, her visitor, sat at ease on the chair that was Mama's, behind a haze of smoke and papers that fluttered everywhere. Her books arranged so neatly on the shelves now lay upended, or half-open on the table. Mama had never tolerated such disorder before.

He wasn't smoking as I realized soon enough; it was the fireplace that was alight. Its flames blue with the paper burning in it. I froze when he beckoned me with his finger. He had the most intense blue eyes I had ever seen. He rose to shake hands with me, and I was surprised that he really wasn't very tall, or that I wasn't too small for him. But his sharp assessing gaze tore into me, and I felt my mother's nails dig into my shoulder.

'My son,' and her voice quivered too, 'he can keep secrets.'

The man smiled thinly. 'No secrets here. It's a great cause. We are just careful.' His hand fell away, his feet clapped sharply on the floor, and his eyes took on a faraway look. One I had seen on my mother's face too. Then in one swift graceful motion, he extended his right arm, his face took on a trance-like expression, and he spoke louder, with a fervour that filled the room. *Heil Hitler.* My mother did too, her shoes clapping hard on the wooden floor, and her other hand pressed hard on my shoulder. I knew I had to follow suit. *Heil Hitler*, I said, my new gravelly timbre trembling a bit.

At the end, the man smiled. He said, he will learn soon enough, to which my mother blushed, her hand on my shoulder now gentle. She had been more nervous than she let on.

I remember the way my knees shook and knocked against each

other as I left the room. The man and my mother remained for a long while in the study and I heard them rummaging through papers and the sound of the typewriter keys being hit furiously. I remember too, my mother's hands on my shoulder again, as we stood on the steps to bid him goodbye.

That night my parents left for the party at the Old Nest Hotel. The impressive yellow and white painted building with a red gabled roof that mirrored the sunshine and surf. I hated its cavernous insides, the way it swallowed me up when I walked in. Its forbidding doors like a grown-up's closed-up, all-knowing face; its high ceilings, and then the ballroom, with its pillars and columns, their fluted capitals like the intestines of a giant whale, the kind I had once seen washed up on the coast of Skeleton Bay.

It was already dark when my parents left in the old Austin that had once been my grandfather's. Mama looked like someone else, and my father stiff in his bow tie and creased trousers. They were like two people I had never known before. The house became mine for a few hours while they were gone. I crept into my mother's study again, rummaged through her books and her notes. The fireplace still gave off the smell of burnt paper. Later, I would remember what I had only carelessly glanced at. Among those loose papers that had fallen away and lay scattered around the fireplace were some with elaborate diagrams on how to create extensive encampments so that rebels could be kept away, and peace maintained. There were stories and clippings on the life of the man whom everyone now called the Fuhrer. His success story, his genius, his love and concern for all Germans regardless of where they were on the globe.

I fingered my father's riding gloves and stood in his muddy, rubber boots. I roamed the corridors and rooms of that empty house, touching every part, feeling once again every nook and corner where I had hidden myself away. I touched every door, switched on every light, stood in the circle of light each one made. I paused at every window, trying to find out which ledge provided the best shelter, but it was no use. There was always something that interrupted my game. Perhaps it was the dust that hung in the old curtains, or the sound of a lizard scurrying past. One window was located too close to where the night-watchmen had now gathered, around the gate, and I heard them talking, telling each other stories. Or else what sounded too near was the stray, raucous laughter that came from the servant's quarters, the raw, spicy smell of their food being cooked.

My parents came back stiff and unsteady on their feet. Their voices raised and ugly as they continued the quarrel that must have begun once they left the hotel. The driver stopped at the gate to explain to the other night-watchmen. I watched them titter from where I hid. On the widest window ledge that overlooked the portico, all the way to the driveway and the gate. Stick-thin figures in the yellow darkness that moved like puppets.

A glass broke, my mother shrieked, the door to my father's study banged shut. By morning, it had all been wiped out, a quiet lay over everything. My father had left, Ujwima told me later. My mother packed her books and rearranged her shelves. The room was wiped clean of the most recent past.

The house mocked me now, every window, every door wore a forbidding look like a secret that would never be let out. I saw Ujwima sweeping the driveway. The Maybach that had come up the previous afternoon had no presence left now, the driveway soon looked deserted, the portico barren. The man had made my mother laugh, my parents quarrel, and my father had now left the house. Nothing would ever be the same again. It was only much later that I learnt that the man I had been introduced to was Adolf Eichmann.

10

THE OTHER SIDE OF TOWN

The raja sahib's green Austin waited at the level crossing for well over ten minutes. That afternoon, the train that ran across the country, cutting it neatly at the abdomen, was late. The train to Bombay ran thrice a week. A long train, and an important one, it made itself heard over a long distance, its horn forcefully cutting through the silence of the afternoon.

The Austin was easily recognizable; everyone knew to whom it belonged. The men on cycles, the bus to Cuttack and the odd bullock carts kept a distance from it. Passengers leaned out of the bus, fanning themselves with papers and palm leaf fans. The lazy bullocks flicked away stray flies. All eyes were on the signalman and on the car, that stayed with windows shut, away from the gaze of the world.

Minutes passed, not a leaf stirred, the lever did not lift, the signalman remained at his window, his neck craned, trying hard not to look important. In that somnolent silence then, the car door slammed, the uniformed old driver, Abdullah, lurched out, blinked his eyes in the sun. The heat and everyone's stares zoomed in on him.

'How long?'

It was Lisa who had finally asked that. 'How long? Do find out.' The driver, then got out, shouted out the question to the signalman, now leaning on his window, the green flag drooping unhappily, its one end caught on an old rusting nail. The signalman in turn shouted across the barrier, the hot rails and the sleeping buffaloes. 'How should I know? Some work on the tracks.'

Das and his men had cordoned off the tracks in their search for clues. Some three or maybe four days had passed since Ali's body had been found, and the police had just begun looking for clues. Rumours had carried of some new developments relating to the case. I felt relief for Das did not trouble me, though I let the accounts languish instead of putting them in order, as I had promised myself. I had had no idea how the billiards table had been changed or rather how its specifications had been altered. Now I told myself that it really didn't matter; in the forest Das would probably find clues bigger than a billiards table.

The very sight of those yellowing, smelly papers always turned me off. Endless reams had been wasted on menu details, carpenter salaries, light fixtures and most boring of all, details of drainpipe fittings. There was nothing more about a billiards table. As Keith's own inattention to the matter showed, a few inches or a foot here and there, really made no difference.

Das made the roads his own, I saw his car with the red beacon everywhere, determined to chase clues down. But his real quarry, the raja sahib, had long since left for the capital.

The driver stood at the barrier for a long time. Everyone waited, Abdullah's hands moved across the wooden railing, he kicked at the rails, at the stones, and moved back to the car. The car window at the back slowly rolled down, in expectation of an answer, and it was at that moment, the train horn sounded again, nearer and nearer.

Tilo didn't know what infuriated her more. The long wait, the futility of the driver's vigil or the way the vehicles surged forward once the rail barrier had been raised. The bus sounded its horn unrestrainedly, people looked out of windows and sneezed or spat like a last goodbye, bullock cart drivers woke up with haste and whipped their wards into shape. Only the raja sahib's car, an Austin of somewhat vintage descent (as I well knew) took its time. Vehicles rushed around and then past it, while the driver turned the ignition on once, twice and succeeded the third time.

The raja sahib's car, headed for the Anglo-Indian colony on the other side of the tracks, had been kept waiting for the first time that day. It was afternoon, and most people were inside their homes, most shops had closed for a siesta. Yet Tilo had underestimated people's curiosity. Waves of dust rose from every side of the muddied road as everything surged through, including, at last, the raja sahib's green Austin, with its frilled white curtains and rolled-up windows. The gravel surged up, into the high porches, the latched gates, through the louvred windows and brought everyone out of their homes, many still sleepy-eyed and in various stages of dishevelment. Lisa watched through her rolled up window. Among the people waiting at the crossing was one Benny Ambrose, who had recognized the car and was now trying to desperately wedge his cycle in with other waiting cycles, hoping to avoid being seen. He felt embarrassed. This led to another fracas. As Benny looked at himself in the cycle mirror and his hand rose to flick away errant strands of hair, for he liked to keep up with appearances, he lost his balance, and fell over, knocking over a cyclist, and a vendor's cart packed with plastic toys. A scuffle broke out, it held up the last of the traffic before two constables managed to restore some order. And reports reached Das how the raja sahib's car with his wife and daughter in it had caused some disturbance in the streets.

The passage of the raja sahib's vintage car became an occasion witnessed, to Tilo's chagrin, by over fifty bus passengers, bullock cart drivers, and the lazy tobacco-chewing signalman. Tilo, like those of a certain class, had never waited. The old ways had changed too suddenly. What angered her now was not that she had been seen but that it had not been made into more of an occasion. And being Tilo, her indignation vented itself on other things. She insisted that things had to improve, it could not go on like this. Trains should run on time. She would bring it up before the government, the next time she was in Bhubaneshwar. She said this once Lisa and she had reached Mrs Hutchins's house. Mrs Hutchins taught in the local high school and would now tutor Lisa before she left for college in Calcutta or Delhi. To Tilo it was clear that, following the scandal, Lisa could not continue her studies in the same town, where there would be too much gossip. As Tilo rang forth about trains and their now habitual unpunctuality, Mrs Hutchins's alarm rose in degrees, till she pleaded, wringing her hands, asking her not to name her husband in the letter. For it was well-known in some circles that her husband, Mr Hutchins, drove the train to Madras that passed through the city every second night, and that he had the habit of stopping the train arbitrarily, just on a whim, many a time.

For Lisa, apart from her mother's indignation that expressed itself with an opinion on everything, there was the mortification of noticing Mrs Hutchins's daughter Pat, and her mocking looks directed towards the oblivious Tilo. Pat, whom I had seen at the club at times, for she had been Samineh's friend, was not one to hide her feelings. And Lisa was made aware, all of a sudden, of a protectiveness about her mother. It was inevitable the two girls, near about each other's age, would never be friends.

Tilo told me more the afternoon she called me home. She still hadn't gotten over what had happened and just wanted to talk. I wanted to get a look at the raja sahib's Austin. The gun that I had hidden away in its dashboard; I understood the urgency to retrieve it as soon as I could. In his zeal to investigate Ahmed Ali's unexplained death, I knew sooner or later, Das would hone in on the gun.

Tilo had left the doors open, the windows too, and now looking out, asked of no one in particular, 'How did things get so scandalous...?' She meant to talk about her husband but couldn't. Her face looked drawn, and suddenly she seemed much older.

'We could always run away,' I said, quickly, half-desperately for I didn't want to pursue this line of conversation. It had made people go off into tangentially different directions, as with Das, and I didn't want to complicate things more for Tilo. Already, my afternoons with her were something I wanted to forget now. There were other things I wanted to remember and this despair on her face was making it hard. But only a moment later, I regretted my words. She leaned over and brushed a hand against mine; then turned quickly to check if we were seen. 'It's too late now,' she said, 'don't you want to return to Germany?'

I went cold, and heard the tremor in my voice as I answered, 'I haven't thought of it.'

Slowly the cold hand eased itself off my chest, and I thought of Lisa. She had to be somewhere near. I lied to Tilo instead: 'I'd miss you then, even if I can't see you anymore.'

She gave a loud sob and managed to turn it into a laugh. When a light-hearted conversation takes a turn for the serious and the sentimental, it is because one party feels a certain helplessness. We both felt it and couldn't say anything else. We knew about the servants; the bigger the house, the more ubiquitous and observant they were. Tilo's life was crumbling around her and still she held herself together. It was always the smaller things that did you in: the inevitable return when she had left in a huff; the unexplained wait at the crossing. Now I saw her creased sari, the sweat gathering on her neck. Something the Tilo of old would never have allowed herself.

She lifted her elegant shoulders and buried her head in her hands. We sat in the room I was already familiar with, but it was warm and muggy. The pankahwallah was missing. Perhaps Ghana was off duty or his nightly sojourns had tired him out. Somewhere not very far away, it had begun raining, for I saw the grey clouds lining the sky, but here all we felt was the stifling heat that left behind a thick sweaty imprint.

'Tilo, you are needlessly upset,' I finally managed to say. She sat in the armchair where her husband had sat the afternoon of the high tea, and so much had changed since then.

'All this ruin, and devastation,' she told me, once she had gathered herself up, 'directed against the state of things. Nothing seems to be going right. The British had a sense of discipline, a purpose, and now things are going to seed. Trains are not on time, people don't observe rules and are rude, and there's....'

She never finished for she was weeping now, her shoulders heaving. She sobbed so loudly that I was alarmed. I looked for the bell and then refrained. It was a fading household, like everything else, and what would the butler do if I summoned him?

I ran out of the room, looked up the stairs, and knew I had to see Lisa. I was halfway up the stairs when I remembered that she was with Mrs Hutchins. I should not then have opened the door that led to the rooms of the first floor, I should have run back the way I had come, but I didn't, and that was how I met the English teacher for the first time. That door, with its carved wooden frame, stood in a corridor all on its own. Its brass handle turned without protest and I found myself looking at the man who had just stepped in from an open window. It was an old house, but people—and cars too—did have unusual ways of entering and exiting it.

'We have met,' he said.

I scratched my head. I smelled burning leaves somewhere, and the slap of the ivy creeper against the window.

'I am the English teacher, Benny.'

I knew then it was he who had slipped that incriminatory note to Lisa in her borrowed copy of *Pride and Prejudice*. An innocent note that became a trump card of sorts for Tilo, the day she had returned.

Benny Ambrose held out a hand but withdrew it abruptly as he brushed the stray leaves off himself, ran his hand through his hair, then stamped softly once, and then again. The straggly weeds and leaves that had been clinging to him fell onto the floor between us.

'I also beat you at billiards...I am Pat's friend, and was with her at the club the other day.' He said this with a sort of schoolboy pride, his chest puffed out and part of a cottony vest appeared through his pale blue shirt.

Samineh had been there too, that same evening at the club. I had seen her only as I turned toward the light at the other end of the table. She was at the cupboard riffling through the files, the secret of which only she could decipher. I hated having to lose in front of her, and there was Benny Ambrose again, patronizingly explaining the rules, pointing out the pockets, the way the score was kept....

'But a billiards table has no pockets,' I had insisted that time, and he had watched me puzzled, then laughed pleasantly. Had I mixed things up then? What I remembered of the table from all those years ago in Berlin, my attendant duties, every inch of that table so imprinted on my mind that I'd never forget it all. Would I mix up other tables for it too?

'Hans, Hans,' and I heard Tilo's voice from downstairs as it broke through our silence, and Benny Ambrose's kind friendliness soon changed to alarm.

'Just a second,' I called out.

He had vanished the next moment. I heard the thump of his feet on the garage roof and the rustle of the creeper. He looked up one last time, 'It was nice meeting you again.' I stared at his retreating back, as it vanished behind the thick leaves of the mango tree.

I had caught Pat and Samineh under the billiards table once. Did it really have pockets even then? There had been a great heaving and shaking as Pat had emerged, holding up a cue ball. She insisted it had fallen through the pockets. I had totally forgotten that detail.

Tilo caught up with me as I turned to walk down the corridor and we looked at each other across the steps.

Hans. She grabbed me by the hand first, then her arms reached out for my collar and the hair that brushed my neck. It was strange that the house, till then empty and unoccupied, now had servants everywhere. They seemed to materialize from behind the furniture, the potted plants, the curtains, seemingly busy in their everyday chores. The corridor was suddenly very crowded, and Tilo's hands on my shoulders, my hands on hers, appeared too blatant a gesture.

'Why did you go up there?'

'To look for...,' but I did not tell her, could not utter the name.

'To look for the servants,' I said tersely, 'you were upset.'

'I was...I am,' she was still agitated. I smelt her, the sandalwood fragrance now wearing away, the hot damp sweat that showed up as tiny beads on her forehead, on her frilly blouse. There must have been a moment when I held her close, to comfort her. But I felt her hands tighten on me, and then I was holding her, my hands on her hair, and my words in her ears, 'Tilo, it's all right.'

For a second or two, I could swear, a look of cunning appeared on her face. It made her look unfamiliar, totally unfathomable to me. Her face moved, and her eyes moved down the corridor to the rooms at the far end. When she looked back at me again, the beguiling smile was back on her face.

'Let's run away. Didn't you suggest...?'

I stared at her aghast. I could not give up my life all over again, as I had done before to please my mother. But then, just as quickly, in a very Tilo-like way, she changed the subject. She went on to talk of the letter she had to write to the government.

I let Tilo ramble on, and as I stood there on the stairs, before an open window, I caught sight, just as suddenly, of the raja sahib's Austin in the driveway. I had to get the gun out somehow, and before someone caught on. Even the slow-witted driver, Abdullah, could take it on himself to rummage through the dashboard. And I would also offer Samineh's old job to Pat and ask her to lie as well. That Samineh had never been under the billiards table with the raja sahib. It was time I used my weapons too. I'd make Lisa realize that her associating me with Das had been a total mistake.

•

Barely a day after I put up the notice for the job—a formality—outside my office, Pat turned up and volunteered for it.

I asked if she knew anything about filing.

She nodded enthusiastically and everything else I asked: keeping records, writing notices, and bringing memberships up to date. She could type a bit and had completed high school. She did intend to get a typist's certification soon, she assured me.

The man temporarily updating the register stared, as did the boys working in the garden. It was as if their eyes had been zapped into big round holes by a machine, for they could not look away. It was Pat's hello that had drawn their attention and now it was her big bouncy breasts that held it. Suddenly my office was much too small for her.

Patricia Hutchins was rounded and ruddy, with a halo of wondrous blond curls that fell to her shoulders. She also had a way of saying hello, in a rousing, joyous way that would have everyone jerking up to look her way. She would sometimes help in the club, or in the fledgling library, where she would enter the new books and update the records. But she was bored most of the time, and in the past, I had often found Samineh and Pat giggling away, a couple of times under the billiards table. I thought once that she was a particularly bad influence on Samineh.

I remembered the way the table shook as they emerged from under it, after I had looked for Samineh all over to help me look for a particularly important file. She scrambled out, her dupatta trailing and her long plaits swinging, reminding me of a spaniel, and Pat followed later, sheepish like a shaggy Pomeranian, though built on bigger lines. But now, with the chaos I was confronted with, the absent Samineh and the missing and misplaced files, I knew I must call for Pat again, despite her tendency to shirk work, something I found truly annoying.

The billiards table had wobbled and nearly crashed before the two of them held it up, still giggling. The table was still shaking and heaving before I called some helpers in. I didn't notice the pockets even then. Even when the table had been fixed firmly in place, and I had checked it for myself.

11

INNSBRUCK, IN AUSTRIA, 1950

At the special underground room in their headquarters at Tempelhof, the men of the Odessa played billiards, making plans each time the cue hit the ball. Bent low, they whispered secrets to each other, secrets left obscured by the sad rolling of the balls on the table. And I waited with the powder canister in my hand. They noticed me during one idle period as I arranged the table with Fredrich, who would be killed not long after, just for a moment's indiscretion.

They blew his head off in what had once been the ballroom with its impressive rounded columns and secret alcoves, while the Allied planes flew low and near. The droning of the planes overhead and the raucous laughter below drowned out the shots and I could do nothing, not even look away, let alone warn Fredrich, not to stoop too low, not to strain his eyes in such desperation. He made for too obvious a spy. For they were desperate too, the men of the Odessa, and would stop at nothing to get their own way. And that was why the hideout so close, right in the Tempelhof airport, was innocuous, yet downright dangerous. The ground floor had all the records, materials and files and that was where the inspectors of both sides, former enemies, continued to meet, poring over old papers, microscopically examining photos and identification cards to ensure that the Nazis did not get away. Only a floor below, in the secret underground chamber, the men of the Odessa relaxed, played their game of billiards and made their plans.

My nose and the back of my hands were white with powder, but my palms always glistened with a warm, terrible-smelling sweat. One evening well into summer, I met Eichmann again, the first time in many years. He had no recollection of me—how could he?—I had been only twelve at the time of our first meeting. But I knew who he was all right, though he looked sharper, crueller and had lost his hair. My heart beating fearfully, I was careful to keep my ignorant face on. My eyes always trained on the table, learning the sounds the different balls made, the different shots, the rules of the game. Never looking up, for like Fredrich, we were all marked men.

In the oddest of circumstances, I was to become Eichmann's saviour, for some years at least, someone who would aid him in his escape route. I suppose I would never have left that house on Rue Strasse if I had not bent over, my hands trembling, Eichmann's cue stick not far from mine, and someone had not remarked on a certain resemblance. From the corner of my eye, as I arranged the balls once again in the centre, I saw them nudging each other, their heads nodding, and finally the voice of Commander Strauss.

'You there. Been here long?'

They looked at me, some of them Hitler's famed generals and trusted lieutenants. Now, all of them were men on the run. Yet they had lost none of their former pomposity and menace.

Someone else answered for me, in a whisper. And I was asked no more questions.

But a couple of months later the Americans marched in, after the Soviets left. For a few blissful months I felt free. But I couldn't help feeling I was a marked man. Then Oakshott, the man who had tried to help me, who had partly for this, become the butt of ridicule, disappeared.

Some days later, and I have no clear recollection of this time, I was found on that city bench, and despite all the graffitied warnings that I should have heeded, I was bundled into a van. I came to in a ramshackle building on the outskirts of Berlin, the windows of which looked out into the dense forests and picnic spots that Mama must have frequented as a young girl. The darkness and the blinding flash of lights going on and off is what I remember of the time I spent there. Voices faint and distant that came and went in a thick cloud of consciousness, and the smell of chlorine and disinfectant. A photographer who set up his paraphernalia in that house by the forest and who photographed me many times over, one full face and several profile pictures.

In the hospital, I had woken up to the light streaming in through the high windows but in fact it was the powerful lights that were trained on me. The white coated figures, the nurses—one of them pretty with brown curls framing her face and wide green eyes—all stared down at me. And a gloved hand reached across, hovered over my face, turning fuzzy in the light before it struck me on the nose. Someone else rapped on my nose, pulled it, and then I felt the tap of knuckles against it. Then I heard a man's voice, someone who leaned forward to ask, 'Do you feel all right? You had a bad fall and were brought here unconscious.'

It was morning outside, for as the lights were turned away, the hard sunlight fell through the overhead ventilators and hit me squarely in the eye.

'You have been here a week....'

'Ten days or so,' said someone.

I returned in due course to the billiards room, familiarized myself again with the smell of powder and the hard-wooden balls but by then I was a different person, in every way. A month later, when I finally left that place, I was given a new name too, and a passport, something I had never had before. And in that photo, I looked different, the way I did after I had been operated on. A thinner lip, and the nose just a little flattened. I was advised last of all to keep that cap on. All the time? When I asked that, my answer was a pointed gun, a blow to my cheek. *In our cause, we ask no questions.*

At Innsbruck I saw my own reflection for the first time after a long while, and thought it was someone else. But it was morning and besides a lingering toothache, I was sleepy. The car ride had been uncomfortable, and jerky. All the while as we passed check posts and sentry barriers, I had to crouch in the makeshift hiding place built into the car's leather seat. There was a place near the border where watchful soldiers subjected the car to a thorough search, they thumped the seat so that the hard leather-bound wood slapped against me time and again. Soon after, I was moved to a truck packed with vegetables for the monastery at Innsbruck with the two guards who had been with me since my last evening at the club where we had even played a last game of billiards together.

A pain shot through my back, the truck jolted, swerved too quickly, and I came to only when the vehicle jerked to a stop. I was led blindfolded up the stairs, I counted fifty-nine in all and knew I was in an attic somewhere.

There in Innsbruck, I soon received instructions from the men of the Odessa to visit the Golden Roof. Instructions delivered in an ordinary tourist brochure that left me in no doubt. Any visitor to Innsbruck had to pay a visit to the city's old quarter and see Maximilian I's Golden Roof for himself.

From the Golden Roof, I stared down at the sea of faces and the Alps not far away. The clouds had lifted, and the white mountains had a sheen that hurt the eye. I tried to put on my glasses but was stopped by the two guards who followed me everywhere.

'No glasses, stay as you are.'

I wore the brown striped coat, gloves and the wide brimmed hat as I had been further instructed. It was all in the note left beside my washbasin at the inn we reached late the previous night. The two guards now pushed me unobserved into the crowd of people who were visiting the Roof that day. 'We need to know if the operation is working.' The guard had an odd sneer on his face, his eyes raking my own before he nodded to the other in some satisfaction. 'It'll work. A face just like this.'

There was relief on both their faces. And I felt relief too. I was tiring of their intense gazes on me, I knew I looked different and I was getting tired of feeling different. A guide moved us into a circle and delivered a long uninterrupted monologue about Maximilian I. The guide was a turbaned Indian, and spoke English the way I knew the British did from my time with Colonel Oakshott. But now I could make out little of what he said. It was a new world I was being pushed into. A world I was still hoping to find a place in.

I was pushed up another flight of stairs, following the droning guide, my two guards behind me, who trained their eyes on me even as they tried to remain unobtrusive. I remained part of the eager, enthusiastic crowd, who were mainly students and couples in love. It was 1950, and Europe after the war was beginning to breathe and love again. In the crowd, I made out who the policemen were, and secret agents too, trying, as best as they could, not to look like themselves. But as a man who had spent time with soldiers on either side, I was not fooled.

We moved up toward the balcony, and below in the square there were the agents again. I sensed my guards move away a bit then, and I breathed a little more freely. As a few tourists passed me, I pressed myself against the glass panes and for the first time clearly saw myself as I now was. It had to be me, the new me, for my first reaction was to brush away the hand that came up to meet my own before I realized I was touching glass. I stared at myself for only a moment before I was pushed away again by the advancing crowd that hung on the guide's every word. All I remembered was the nose that looked too thin for my face. The lips were different too, in an odd curling way. In the pale winter sunlight that filtered in through the windows on the other side of the room, I saw myself, etched in a halo of lovely colour.

The shot rang out just then. And then another. A moment's stunned silence gave way to panic and once again I was pushed back down the stairs. I felt a hand on my back and then a different hand, as people pushed, jostled, and shoved each other in their frenzy to get away. It was like a huge frightened snake, chased out of its hole. I tripped once but did not fall. I was held up by the retreating back of another tourist, someone with a wide back, who wore a tweed coat. He turned around, glared at me but panic overtook us soon enough.

In relief we burst out through the door and found ourselves in the warm sunlight that doused the square. There we could acknowledge our relief with nervous laughter but soon the voice of authority asserted itself. The body of the murdered man, dressed like any other tourist, complete with a brown striped jacket just like mine, woollen mittens and leather boots, was cordoned off. The few policemen were whistling all of us away and some were assessing the windows on the other side. Anyone could have waited there and picked his victim, who lay not very far away, his arms outstretched, his hands still gripping his camera that a guard snatched away even as I looked on. Near his head, where the blood now oozed out slowly, was his hat, a wide brimmed, felt hat—not very different from the one I was wearing, had indeed been asked to wear.

12

IN THE HEART OF INDIA, A TOWN CALLED RAURKELA

I came to know about the protests some mornings later. I hadn't been around long enough to recognize the signs. But the boots I had placed out in the portico the previous night remained unpolished, and no one had come by to collect the garbage left out by the gate. 'Lazy fellows,' I muttered. Probably the maintenance boys had had one of their festivals; it must have ended in a drunken orgy and all of them would turn up late, sheepish and sullen. It irritated me. The somnolence, the meek acceptance, that could, as I would learn soon, give way to a sullen resistance at times.

Someone in the club gave me the news. That the junior staff had gone on strike to protest my decision to give the assistant job to Pat Hutchins. She was not really one of the locals. She was an Anglo, and besides, she was a woman. There were, the staff felt, other, better-qualified men who could have done the job. Rao—and I was never sure whose side he was on—appeared from nowhere to give me more complete information. 'They feel they could do a better job. And you won't find them under billiards tables too.'

'But it's a very junior position,' I was more bewildered than irritated by Rao's sneering all-knowingness, 'and it's a temporary job.'

'That Muslim...,' Rao was dismissive, 'she will never come back, sir. Never.'

The other man with Rao, whose name I have forgotten now, elaborated. 'No, sir, it is the government that is making it a small thing. Using people, making them leave their jobs and giving jobs to whites or half-whites. Now they are going to protest in a big way. They are even planning to go to Bhubaneshwar because the prime minister will be coming.'

By afternoon, there were posters up on the walls. I saw the on-strike workers sitting by the road, holding their protest signs a notch higher as I passed, to ensure I did not miss anything.

Down to the raja sahib.

Jobs for locals only. No half-blood, or outsiders

Manager. Resign now!

I was left more bemused now, unsure of whom they meant and how they had managed to conflate two entirely different things. But of course, if you asked someone like Rao, the connections would be clear. If the raja sahib hadn't done what he did... would this have happened?

I did believe the strike and the disaffection over Pat's appointment, would be over in a matter of days. How long could they sustain this? You couldn't sit around with a placard all day, shouting slogans at the jerk of your leader's baton. Professionalism had been ingrained at the giant steel plants of Krupp. And even under the Nazis. To work with a cool, cold-blooded precision that bordered on the inhumane. For a time, the world had admired the Germans. Now all of it was in ruins. My grandfather's house in Dresden, the steel plants, everything that once stood for grandeur, for magnificence. Yet, here in the outposts of the old British Empire, in this steel plant, where Krupp's name was whispered in awed tones, such devotion to work was easily discarded. Even I was guilty of dereliction. There must have been something in that summer heat.

The raja sahib and Das, wearing his police superintendent's uniform were waiting for me in the office. They both looked agitated and tossed me absent-minded smiles as I walked in. They were here only to resume where we had left off some days before. To me, they looked like boxers padded up to fight.

'We must stop meeting this way,' said the raja sahib, weary but still elegant, 'shouldn't we, Hans?'

Das was having none of this flippancy, 'Denying the whole thing will not help, it will only worsen matters.'

'Nothing happened, I tell you.'

The raja sahib spoke in bored tones, but I saw the whitening of his knuckles, and the sweat drops on his forehead. I entered the discussion casually.

'Hello Das, any more news of the murder?'

I meant it jocularly, to ease the tension, but Das's face darkened even more, and the raja sahib's face was shocked as his gaze swivelled from me to Das, but he had his answer rehearsed.

'She had lost her safety pin, I told you this then, and I am telling you again. I was teaching her billiards....'

'What kind of billiards?' A cunning look had come over Das's face.

'Pool, the simplest kind of course.'

'Mr Gerder says she was on duty. And according to his records, the table was quite small, quite difficult for you to get under....'

I shrugged then, 'Actually people did get under it, but with considerable difficulty. I've caught the girls under it.'

Raja sahib looked at me in half gratitude. 'Yes, this time, there was one, who was looking for the safety pin and I helped her out. It happened while I explained the game to her, of course.'

'You could have asked one of the servants,' said Das.

The raja sahib looked reproving, then said in lofty tones, 'We don't have to ask the servants for everything, Das.'

'In fact,' I interrupted again, hurriedly, 'when I was in the office once, it was Pat who was under the table.'

'Who's Pat now?' The men asked the question almost simultaneously. The raja sahib with a new interest and Das with irritation.

Pat. I jerked my head to indicate the outer office. The two men looked at each other. I knew what they thought.

Rao emerged from the shadows then, holding a tray of lemon juice and all of us automatically shut up.

Das said, somewhat frustrated, 'The measurements don't quite match up. Evidently, there's some discrepancy.'

'It was the palace one,' sighed the raja sahib, 'as the one ordered by...,' he nodded at Rao who stood deferentially before him, holding the tray. The raja sahib was being served first and this annoyed Das no end. Rao sidled away quietly, scratching his ear, trying to tell me he had heard nothing.

'You mean the former manager, Keith Rawson?' I suggested.

'Yes, that one for some reason never arrived. So I allowed him the use of the palace table. I'd forgotten...yes.'

It was true then, as Singh had said once, that entire things could vanish in the space of a night, or during a journey. A thing destined for a certain place never arrived. The billiards table might still be somewhere, unassembled and crated up in Calcutta, or it had perhaps been sent somewhere else.

'Ah!' We looked at each other

'That explains...,' said Das with some relish.

'What does it explain?'

'That you know it so well,' said Das to the raja sahib.

'I do, so to explain things to others,' said the raja sahib thoughtfully, 'as a matter of fact, I did.'

Das rubbed his hands as if he were clinching an argument, 'And to whom...?'

It was then I decided to intervene, for things weren't really getting anywhere, and I was sure Rao was lingering outside, eavesdropping unashamedly.

'And now gentlemen,' in as firm a tone as I could manage, 'there was some other matter you had to discuss?'

Das cleared his throat, rose to his feet. 'Yes, we have been digressing. I was trying to convince Mr Mishra that now the time for outright denial is long gone. For the news of the scandal has already spread. Everyone saw the madam drive away.' He turned to the raja sahib who now sat back, his eyes closed, his chin resting on his palm, 'You cannot close your eyes to the truth.'

The raja sahib slumped forward, his hand had moved to his forehead as if he could not believe Das's persistence.

'I tell you, it was just the matter of a safety-pin.'

'It is not. It is much bigger and has gone too far. Your car was seen, and now there is the strike. They will not call it off unless....'

I did not interrupt again, but it surprised me that once again Das had not mentioned the dead man. But now the raja sahib too had got to his feet.

'Unless what...?'

'You admit.'

'Admit to what...? This is getting ridiculous.'

'Yes, you admit it, and the lady can return to her job.'

I saw a grim look appear on the raja sahib's face. 'The lady may not wish to return anyway. But what else might you ask me to admit to, Das? This is a witch-hunt.'

The tension was getting to me now. I yawned, extravagantly and with genuine seriousness.

'I think we are all over-reacting? Marriages break up all the time.'

They stared at me, there was a mix of frustration and amazement on Das's face, and one of genuine interest on the raja sahib's. 'Have you ever been married, Gerder?' He asked, 'You look very...,' he spread his hands out, and then finished, 'experienced.'

'You men just don't understand,' Das was very agitated now, running his hands through his hair. He was progressively disintegrating; he had all his arguments ready and just wanted to follow them cleanly through. He hadn't quite bargained for these unforeseen complications.

'Please understand the gravity of the situation, gentlemen. These people will not take things lying down. The incident matters, and that's why everyone is upset. We are independent now. And we will not be exploited or used, just like that.'

'There was no exploitation, damn it all,' raja sahib was now pacing in some irritation. He turned back an elegant cuff and looked at his watch, 'Stop making it out to be an issue like that. And don't you dare make this out to be something it isn't.'

'Are you threatening me, Mr Mishra?'

'Are you threatening me, Das?'

The other man lunged towards him and this time I was forced to get up, to intervene before it became a free-for-all. 'Gentlemen, please.'

The tension buzzed, echoing the throb in my head. The heat, the screeching of the birds as they congregated in the tree outside, the men standing still, their breath harsh and audible, and the papers on my table moving in the low breeze. Everything around appeared to be marshalling forces, placing damp, sweaty hands on me.

'They...they,' raja sahib said pointing to Das, 'need to be taught a lesson. They are getting fancy airs.'

'And you,' Das said pointing back, 'must know that the old way cannot prevail any more. We too are independent and have our self-respect. You cannot continue to use or molest our women and expect us not to retaliate.'

'There was no question of molestation,' the raja sahib snapped, 'and don't teach me about self-respect.'

'Gentlemen please can we let the matter rest here.' I held my head in my hands, despairing. I heard the sludge fall from the high cranes lighting up the sky a Cezanne orange and the heat stamped itself on my back. I was homesick suddenly. Thinking of the knobby hills and the brown spaces of my childhood outside Lüderitz. Wondering what on earth had pushed me here. Then the phone rang, once, twice, and it stopped before starting up again.

'What kind of a call is that?'

All three of us stared at the black instrument, resplendent on its doily on a squat table. My breath came faster, I held onto the table to still my nerves. But I managed to get the words out. 'It's from outside. Getting a call from outside the country.'

They looked at me, afraid to even exhale. What had happened now?

I learnt later that night, much later, when the call came through that they had managed to get Adolf Eichmann safely out of Buenos Aires.

13

A MONASTERY IN FRANCE, 1950

That evening at Innsbruck, I took the bus back to the inn, with my ever-solicitous guards a few seats behind. It was late when the call came, and the guard shook me awake. I walked groggily down to the reception, and in the light of the mirror behind the desk I saw myself again. It was little wonder that my voice sounded different when I spoke to the Lieutenant over the phone.

It wasn't me, I thought, though my voice was the same and the man in the mirror made the same motions I did. Looking outside it was still night, but I was wearing my day clothes as I had been instructed to.

The Lieutenant laughed at my bland answer. 'Next time you may not be so lucky. But the operation works, it works. No one can tell you apart from him.'

I had known better than to ask questions and sure enough, he grew more eloquent.

'You got away, and that is good. Remember you are serving a good cause, you understand, a good cause. You are a good soldier, Gerder. And now listen carefully. For they know what we are up to. The methods we will adopt to help one of our own escape. And remember,' he paused, before laughing gutturally, 'you will have made it possible.'

I didn't know what that meant, though I spent hours thinking over it. As the sky lightened a few hours later, my guards finally fell asleep. I found them leaning on each other's shoulders, shivering. I escaped, returning only once to place a blanket over them. Gently, even fearfully though there was every chance I'd be caught if they woke up. I walked out into that cold morning, shivering and wrapped in a blanket I had filched from the inn. I paused to look back at the inn where I had stayed briefly and the place where I nearly lost my life. It could have been me caught by the sniper's bullet. Still puzzling over questions, I walked out through the small gate I had seen from my window. It was obviously a service lane, and soon it meandered into the snow. Not very far away I could see the few faint lights still on in a nearby village.

I turned right, I did not want to be seen but realized that it led straight to the mountains. I must have walked in a daze for several hours. For it was afternoon, the time the mountains give off a blinding white light when I saw the figure walking ahead of me. A shadowy figure that, against that landscape of white, looked black and shaggy, and I followed it in some relief. The unchanging Alpine landscape had begun to make me jittery, as did the gnawing emptiness in my stomach. Now the sun, instead of leading me south westwards, towards Switzerland, seemed to be everywhere, beating heavily on my head, my eyes blinking away the undiminished shine of the mountains.

The road led past small rounded hills, and then there were pockets of sparse grass. Sometimes I could hear the tinkle of bells, the sound of herds on the move. I sat on a boulder to catch my breath and when I looked up again, the figure ahead had vanished. Instead, the sun had sunk and there was a greyness everywhere. I had lost count of the hours. As I panicked, I heard the gunshots, the sound of a train not very far away and I despaired for I knew then I had only been walking around in circles.

It was true I let myself be caught. For I sat on that boulder thinking of nothing and watching the evening sun disappear, leaving everything in inky black. The men who came up to me spoke Italian, but I was too exhausted and hungry to respond. My clear thinking did not desert me however. I said I had been sleepwalking and got lost. They asked me about someone, describing him in broken German, and I told them about the man I had followed. Hallucinations, one of them said, before offering me a bowl of soup.

He has escaped. It wasn't me they were talking about, but someone else. The soldiers I was with now were from a military base and the man had been a prisoner—a Nazi, among the worst of them all. When they shone a flashlight on my face, one of them exclaimed, before the others shut him up. It could be him, said the first. No, don't be silly. We don't want to make a mistake. It was then I had my first suspicions about the surgery performed on me.

They stripped me and subjected me to a thorough search, but the tattooed initials that mark out every man in the SS were not on me. I felt a sense of shame and relief. The surgeons had been clever but had missed a crucial thing. I was not marked by that giveaway sign.

In the two nights I spent at the base, I met disoriented and mad men. The screams reverberated in the small base, echoed in my ears and beat inside my head, leaving me with a constant, throbbing headache. These were the men who had been kicked aside, unwanted, lost, and disillusioned after that great war. Their base was a place full of high open windows, high vaulted ceilings; a monastery that had been burnt down and converted into this base. There were two doctors, both Indians, and they were forever at each other's throats, each cursing the other's religion and hoping for a time when they could live separate from each other forever. Little did they know what would happen soon after the war. More violence, more divisions. Half a world away from where I was, there would be paeans sung to independence amidst bloodthirsty war cries.

From their arguments, and conversations, I learnt more about India, a different side, than what Colonel Oakshott's stories had taught me. Here there were no rampaging tigers and murderous tribesmen, but neighbours who betrayed and turned against each other, who thought nothing of raping and killing women they had once played with as children. Until the night I was picked up again, by men who drove up in an ambulance and wore the Red Cross uniform. Yet at first glance, I knew they were not who they claimed to be. I was now part of the other side, those who would be on the right side of history. It silenced me forever about my past. It made me agree to whatever they would want me to do.

They produced papers and took me away, this time to another monastery. 'You could help us get our man.' One of them, a blond officer with thin lips and clear blue eyes, smiled encouragingly as he told me this. And though I was relieved to have been rescued, his words made me feel I had only come full circle.

It was another long journey. I knew this for when I awoke I could smell morning in the air. The scent of cherries, apples, and freshly mown hay lay ripe everywhere. I could not tell for sure where I was. I could not see the sun from the cell where I was detained for most of the day, and I could never navigate my way out in the ocean of stars that could be seen at night.

I lived among the monks, painstakingly copying out old translations of the Bible until the day I found the coded message in there. They must have seen me at it, the monks in the library. Sometimes I would feel watched, a presence behind me, as I copied out note for note, symbol for symbol even while I longed to explore the outdoors. One day, my heart beating fast, my fingers clammy all over again, I stared at the monk directly in front of me. Later I would wonder why I had not recognized the Colonel before. But we were never alone and in that half-dark, always enclosed space, I was afraid of speaking out of turn.

Perhaps it was in the very alien nature of my surroundings, the hidden, fugitive life I had led the last few months. I had indeed begun to read meaning into perfectly innocuous circumstances. But the high barrel-vaulted library, the endless corridors, the cell like room, and the barred windows held only the straitened truth. There were monks who escorted me to my cell from the dinner hall. I never saw their faces, hooded as they were all the time, and the torches cast an eerie yellow light on the floor and the roof. But I became afraid now of stepping out, for each time I did so, there was a faint white clothed figure watching me, unmoving, statue-like.

At the time of the head bishop's visit, there was a flurry of activity. I was interrogated at length, photographed time and again. And they showed me the photo of the man whom I thought I had left behind forever.

I was questioned by a balding man wearing black glasses and walking hurriedly, but with a stoop. I always imagined it was the Colonel, but I couldn't really be sure. He never let on, and I never had the chance to ask. But I was now more curious, secretly so, of my surroundings. The more I thought of it, I wondered why it had not struck me before. The Colonel's army stints in India, and the base where I had been taken for two days after my escape; the two doctors there, who spoke Hindi and Urdu, one a Hindu and the other a Muslim, and who constantly bickered, yet looked out for each other when they sensed danger. In the monastery, I tried to look through the darkness outside the cell window and would see the ghostly lights of the few candles flickering behind curtains, and these were snuffed out well before dinner. At night, as I paced in my cell, the monastery vanished in the darkness, its white walls like ghost columns rising out of the mountains.

'That man...the one you are impersonating. Where is he?'

They asked me again and again. The windows were shut, the curtains pulled closed. They were doing everything they could to snuff out their voices. Their voices were lowered, and some spoke through clenched teeth, their eyes watching me carefully, striking me hard on the hand if I raised my voice the barest notch.

'Where is he?' One of them looked down at the paper and repeated, 'Where is Eichmann?'

'We must get him this time,' said his companion, leaning over the table, pressing down hard on my fingers.

This was all because of Mama, and her madness, I thought, but my replies were never really what they wanted. 'I don't really know who that is,' I said. 'I don't know anything,' I repeated.

'You do,' they came nearer, still nearer. 'We know where your loyalties lie.' It was like the questioning of the Soviet forces five years ago.

'No. No.' My voice was the barest whisper. My nose was bleeding, and there was the metallic taste of blood on my lips. Even the insect crawling along on the opposite wall made a louder noise. Someone sighed in disgust.

Then the head bishop, whose ruby ring burnt brilliantly in the candlelight, leaned forward, and looked at his watch. Evidently, his visit was over for the day. But now he spoke directly at me, 'Clearly, the chicken farmer has left no trace of his whereabouts. Or else, his avatar has lost all memory. We can go ahead then.'

There was a general burst of laughter, but it was smothered right away by the frantic shouts that came from outside. 'Be careful,' said a voice to someone who made to open the window, but it was too late. There was a volley of shots and I saw the monk totter and fall, a thin stream of blood spurted from his neck, staining his pristine white robes.

'Under the table quick, quick!'

As I made to duck, I was pushed to the floor, my face on the carpet, and I found myself bound and gagged again. Then they were lifting me up, four of them, and I found myself, unstable and unbalanced, carried away, down some steps, past an uneven rubble-strewn floor, and then I heard the thud of a door being kicked open. Perhaps a secret door. As we ran through a dark tunnel, the hum of silence closed in on us and sound of bullets grew fainter and fainter.

It was a long run. I heard my four escorts panting breathlessly as they ran. Somewhere there was the smell of dampness, the gurgle of water nearby and what must have been rodents of some kind, brushed past me. I heard too the flutter of wings, felt the brush of wildflowers against me. 'We must stop here,' someone said. And I breathed in the pure night air, felt my own breath abate and settle down, and heard the distant sound of a ship horn. We were somewhere near a port.

'Now listen,' as the man spoke these words, my blindfold was opened. It was night, a clear starlit sky, and through the shrinking copse of trees, I saw a lone barge glide down a river. We crouched in the darkness, my head in the grass as my escorts tried to evade the torchlights flashing on either side of the forest. And then clearly, I heard the voice in French say, 'Anyone there?'

My escorts held their breath while I waited too, puzzled.

The barge moved silently past, like a medieval creature, its torch-like eyes razor sharp in the darkness. Once the lights faded, the golden tinge giving way to a blackness, we crept forward again. I crawled through the tall grass, my hands scraping against small stones and mud. I found myself dumped into a small boat hidden in the small grass. My back hit the bars and I yelped in pain, but the sounds were smothered by the furious paddling, the sound of water rising and slapping me on the face.

I must have slept again but was woken rudely when someone gave me a very un-monk-like kick in the ribs, aggravating the pain in my already sore back. My blindfold was yanked off again and I blinked to adjust my eyes to the steadily brightening day. I had already lost count of the days, of morning and nightfall. On either side the forests still loomed, the wind slithered down the trees and along the towpath by the river, straggly groups of people stood around minding their own business. No one really glanced at us.

'Come on, you can give a hand too.'

They were not whispering anymore. And they looked different, for their robes and cowls were off, and with trousers rolled up to their knees and vests, they looked like ordinary farmers off to a village market. To make the subterfuge complete there were sacks of carrots and potatoes in the boat which slowed us down a lot. With my head bowed, I tried to understand my surroundings, but they sat on either side of me, whispering instructions, asking me to nod if I had understood everything they said.

'You must get him this time. There can be no doubts about this.'

Someone laughed grimly, 'Or you can bet that your so-called friends will get you this time. They know you know their game. You're the impersonator, the one who got away, who is with the wrong side—us, the Nazi hunters. Make no mistake, the men of the Odessa will aim for you, for you are their evidence.'

'Eichmann will travel by the SS Giovanni, you understand. There will be men to guard him always, you can be sure of that. And they will know you, after all the effort invested in you and the operation—my god, it is very convincing. If the Colonel....'

There was a meaningful cough and a sharp voice broke through reprimanding him. 'Don't be stupid, J. You are....'

'I meant that they know you and you are easy prey. After all, with the operation, you can almost pass off as him, almost....'

I remembered again the attic, the constant sunlight in there, or was it the bright light that shone on me all the time in the hospital? There was that hollow drumming in my ears, the vision of the cats dancing on the skylights, and the haziness I often found myself in. The man reflected in the windowpane. That was who I had become. The same man but different. What else had those doctors done? Did I think differently? With my head bent against the bars, my arms straining at the oars, I thought of my mother and to my relief felt the old anger surge in me once more. But this was nothing compared to the terror I felt, the breathlessness that gripped me every time my eyes strayed towards the water. Every time I tried to look up, to reassure myself with the sepia-tinted leaves of the trees, the calm river, the sound it made against the boat, the grey morning invaded everything. But my head was pushed low every time and the instructions continued, the four of them leaning forward and whispering them into my ear.

I had twenty-one days in which to do it. To kill the man whom they never named again. But I knew. Adolf Eichmann or Ricardo Klemet, the name he had assumed. The name on my passport too. The man who had come to our house, who had destroyed us, who had been my mother's inspiration. The man whose death was now my mission. The only way I could correct my own past. Without the help of any photograph, and no means to identify my victim. I had only to look in the mirror.

But that was precisely what I was most afraid to do.

I avoided looking at my reflection in mirrors, in windows, or even in the water. That night on board the ship, when it was mandated that I kill the man, I saw a shadow instead, a black hulking figure looking over the deck, and did not realize it was me. That is why I skulk in the shadows, walk in the darkness, and my windows stay open all the time.

For a day we sailed down the Canal du Midi. It should have been an idyllic ride, for the summer sun was gentle and drizzled down on us through the plane trees. Dead flowers floated out to us and there were the occasional farmer boats that trawled by, with a casual nod at us. The end of the war did not mean the end of suspicions. There was the smell of oranges and grapes in the air. Of faraway shouts and friendly whistles. Of the sun's warmth tangible but unseen everywhere, the smell of fresh hay, farmhouses where bread was being baked, pigs fed in a trough and barn horses at work in wheat fields not far away. The sound of the oars lulled me to sleep and I would wake now and then to the clip of horses riding by on the towpath or the sound of a ferry not far away. I smelt horse manure, falling leaves, dust, coal burning in old stoves. I smelt a summer that was not mine.

I must have been drowsy often as I rowed, coming awake every time my head banged against the bars, or a ferry horn sounded particularly near. But they were still talking when I felt a sharp prod on the ribs and someone interrupted the monologue to whisper sharply, *look up, look up.*

It was dusk, when we appeared to be entering a dark tunnel, but the overhanging rocks turned out to be mid-sized ships anchored off the canal as we entered the port of Sete. My arms ached, my back hurt and I was unable to follow the order at first. When we had set off, the sun had been low, and the day had not yet broken, and the sun was low again now, its warmth fading. I blinked away the day that had somehow absented itself from my life, and the fatigue too. I felt the buzz in my ears that came from hearing unwanted words for too long.

We rowed past the ravine of ships quietly; there was the odd sailor on deck, standing aimlessly or smoking, perhaps they were people like me, nowhere men with nowhere thoughts, just caught in a port town for a brief while.

'We wait here,' said a voice to my left.

We sat in the boat, motionless, watching the lighthouse swing its beam in an arc from one end of the sea to the other. The ships slept, their insides creaking with the lives inside them, the water moved, I sat with my eyes closed, afraid to look, afraid that the water would once more reveal its secrets.

It was the splash that jolted me upright. Looking up, biting my tongue hard to stop the inadvertent scream of pain that came shooting up from my back, I saw the stars, the real ones and the ones colouring my vision, as I fought off the nausea. Near me, I saw in the seconds before I fainted, were the bobbing heads of the men who had till then been my escorts, my zealous guards. I have no idea if they were killed or if it was a ruse, to throw our chasers off track. As instructed by them, I flattened myself on the boat and waited. I was left alone, in a boat, with a crescent moon and dark, hulking ships for company. The water seemed grey, frothy, terribly menacing, and when at long last, after several hours, I raised my head, weak and dizzy in the new light now shining right at me, I swear I saw the ship advance slowly, the torch shining steadily and then the creak of the gangway being lowered.

14

STRANGE ENTRANCES AND EXITS

The phone stayed silent, another call never came through. Later that night, holding the nun Maria George's months-late letter in hand, I felt an urgency. Was Mama still alive? And was her mind alert enough to take in the recent news? Destiny had finally, once and for all, caught up with the man who had crowded my childhood, kept my mother away from me and my father, and all I felt was pity, an urge to protect her from the news. I wanted to reach her, but first, I had to reach the West German consulate in Calcutta. I walked to the club then, intending to use its phone to place a call. I didn't come across anyone, and the club looked unkempt and forlorn like a neglected child. The creepers hung over the railings and stray leaves brushed against my face as I walked past the walls. Around me, there was the buzz of insects, the musty touch of cobwebs that trailed the curtains. I smelt the dust, the dirt in my own office. No one had come to clean it; the strike had become a welcome pretext to shrug off work. The darkness flowed over me, a sludgy river of black that welled up from under my feet.

It took me three matchsticks to light a candle. I would have to make sure to throw the matchsticks away later. You never knew what could make people suspicious. It took me three calls again to get through to the telegraph office and then I placed my telex through to the consulate at Calcutta. *I was a German citizen and I had to get to Berlin, to meet my sick mother.* But the man at the other end was either sleepy or a complete dolt for I had to spell out every word, and then elaborate.

In the end, he asked me again. 'Your name, sir.'

'Gerder...and it's the third time you've asked me that,' I snapped, finally. The man had the temerity to giggle and this time, I spelt it for him as slowly as I could.

'And what's your name?' I asked.

'Das, Sir.'

'Full name please.'

'R C Das. Anything else, sir.' He seemed to be indulging me.

I put the receiver down, pleased that I had had the last word. At times, the night could enforce a sudden intimacy on the unwary and the unwilling. It was later as I walked back home via the short cut that I realized I might have been made a fool of. The man had the same initials as the police superintendent.

I had not seen Lisa since her mother's return. We were all planets in our own orbits and never really reached one another. The raja sahib had gone away again and not returned, and Ghana, who came by almost every morning, told me it had already been two weeks since he had been gone. And the green Austin was still in its garage, with the gun hidden away, wrapped in Lisa's shawl. I had to look for a way to retrieve it, for with Tilo back, Ghana no longer came around with the keys. There was other stuff he brought though. Masks, and ivory ornaments, and he was happy with the money I absently handed over.

The labour contractor Jhunjhunwalla came to see me a day or two later. I was in my office at the club when Rao, who believed in giving people a quick identification check, announced that the Marwari had come, 'on some money-making matter as usual'.

'Now, but the payment's due only...,' I cast my eyes around for the calendar. The money for the workers always went to Jhunjhunwalla, who took his own cut before doling it out to them. One could safely assume that his cut was a hefty one judging from the rings he wore, all embedded with precious stones of one kind or another. Rao smiled his wise man's smile and whispered, holding his finger to his lips, 'It's not about that. Some big matter about politics.'

The Marwari folded his hands with an unctuous smile as he walked in. He always took the seat in the corner, the one that gave him a full view of the proceedings. He had two other assistants who sat behind him, fading into the background.

'Very very good morning to you sir.' His greeting was a bit forceful as if he was trying to convince himself. The room was still dark, the old heavy furniture had a menacing look about it that dispelled only when I drew back the curtains. Almost immediately, he changed position, taking a seat away from the window that still left him in half-darkness. Instantly, the two men with him moved too.

'Do not think I came to discuss matters with you, sahib.' He laughed, flashing his many rings at me. They were there to ward off the evil eye, he had once explained. Every year the dangers changed, people were even more envious than before, so he always had to get a new one, and now some fingers sported two rings, and his knuckles bulged out horribly. He played with his fingers as he sat himself down, and his rings struck against each other, like a child's xylophone at work.

'Time enough to discuss money matters. Not yet the end of the month. Though there are some new supplies from Jharsuguda that I can get you and Singh can't. Peanut butter, and pineapples, imported from Malaysia. You like to try....'

'Send me on the list as usual. And now Jhunjhun, what brings you here? Or rather what rings you here?'

I had made up that name that last evening at the club when the lights had failed. The flickering candle flames were caught in his variously coloured rings and he obliged us by playing on his rings, a favourite tune of his. Tapping, then hitting, even rubbing them against each other, with an almost hypnotic effect. Of course, after a while, all of us lost track of the tune but we didn't mind. The changing lights flickered past us, by turns a dazzling red, yellow, a glaring shade of green and even a soft gentle shade of turquoise, all glinting in the elastic darkness around us. At times, the moths butted their heads against his rings, some falling onto his silk shirt, felled by a fatal knock, but the music made us forget, and we hummed our own long-forgotten tunes.

He laughed heartily, and I joined in. Our laughter stretched like a carpet being flung hastily to cover up the dirt in a room. 'Sahib, you know this matter about the strike by the junior staff. I do know efforts are on to settle matters, to discuss things with them. But who do you think is instigating them?' His voice dropped to a whisper, and he gave the answer himself, 'It's Idris.'

I nodded, then shook my head. I was getting used to how the Indians stretched matters to include things that weren't in the remotest way connected. Ali's death was now being widely seen as murder, and to Das, it was all related to the scandal. Now here was Jhunjhun drawing lines between the motor mechanic Idris and the striking workers.

My attention wandered. Jhunjhun's two assistants, with thinner gold rings on their fingers, appeared painfully shy and nodded at every word the man said. Jhunjhunwalla was rumoured to be the richest man in the area. He had contacts with the government at Bhubaneshwar and Calcutta, but his Marwari connections reached deep into the villages of Rajasthan and as far afield as Malaysia and Indonesia. I wished I could have taken a photo of the three of them in my room. All looking the same and carrying the same musty smell of money on them, of soiled paper currency.

My reverie broke when his matter of fact, guttural voice broke over me.

'The temporary workers... I could get you some in place of the strikers, and you could pay me a token amount. I know how difficult it is for you now. But I believe you have already engaged a receptionist.'

'Yes,' I said, remembering Patricia. I must have smiled for I saw a sly gleam pass the Marwari's eyes before he was all serious.

'I can see sahib, you are happy with her. Very difficult to get someone of your liking. At least these Anglo-Indians speak English well.'

I nodded. She could be easily distracted though. And every afternoon, she spent too long talking on the phone. It had to be a man. She was by turns gossipy, shrewish, and petulant. I would not want to get on her wrong side. I would, the thought struck me in a sudden, panic-stricken moment, also need to keep my diary safe from her.

'Very good, very good. We shall not propose anyone as an assistant. But I could get you new workers. But there is one thing I am worried about. '

He went on, as I looked steadily at him, my curiosity aroused. He turned to his assistants in turn, his head moving first left, then right. 'Those men I'd mentioned,' he asked, 'what are their names?'

His assistants supplied the names eagerly, trying to outdo each other in alacrity. 'Ahmed Ali, Idris Mian.'

'Idris Mohammed.' He corrected, without even looking at the errant assistant, who subsided in his chair, looking mortified.

'And the other man's dead, isn't he?' I pointed out.

They looked at each other startled. 'Yes, that's true,' Jhunjhun laughed nervously, his ring catching the light as he lifted it to his throat. But soon, he had fixed his glasses more firmly on his nose and turned to me.

'Yes, dead or alive, their kind is known to stir up trouble, god knows how. Now they are getting together in some movement or the other and are even writing to the government about it. You see how matters worsened in the club the other day. Such a simple debate. There you were, sahib, trying to keep order and see what it descended to. Almost a boxing match....'

The assistants laughed weakly. Jhunjhun looked around, and his voice dropped significantly. 'They are troublemakers, Hans sahib. Only you can keep them in hand. Idris listens to you, otherwise that man is a troublemaker.'

'What do you think he could do?'

'Nothing, and everything. After all, they are not god-fearing Hindus like me or most people here, but they are Pakistanis. Don't know why they don't go there. You never know Idris Mian with all this new campaign of restoring Centrehood to Raurkela....'

He must have seen the confusion on my face and hastened to reassure me. 'Of course, sahib, I am not trying to scare you, just to make you aware. They have no common ground of course. The new people, the workers we will bring in, are all Hindus but then they, the Muslims are known to stir up trouble. I ask you, sir. If they have been given a separate country of their own to go to, why can't they go there? They can go to Pakistan! Live there in peace!'

Jhunjhunwalla was very worked up now. He had turned red in the face and his fingers trembled, the light flashing crazily through the multi-coloured stones. The assistant who had been corrected earlier dropped his register, and Jhunjhunwalla turned a shade redder.

'Can't you be less clumsy? How can you handle my daughter if you let things slip out of your hands, you dolt? He is my son-in-law, sahib; must teach him the basics,' he laughed shakily.

'That's good,' I replied absently, 'you keep it in the family.'

'If I am allowed. But these two men, they are not giving me a moment's peace. Hans sahib, do exercise your good offices.'

He had been so insistent that I had to respond, but I must have sounded bewildered, 'Two men?' But he didn't mean his assistants, surely.

Jhunjhunwalla looked startled, his two assistants frightened, as if they had seen a ghost somewhere. 'Oh yes, yes, I forgot. One of them is dead but his spirit still seems to be driving Idris Mian....' He laughed nervously, the veins in his neck throbbed uncontrollably. 'Can't believe one is dead. It just seems the other day we saw him.'

I went on, trying to soothe him, 'I am sure the movement is only a pet scheme of his. Idris, I mean. He is worried that the government might ignore this place.'

'Ignore..?' the other man shrieked, 'with a steel plant, and a dam coming up here. I tell you, sahib, we are special beneficiaries. Now all the big countries—England, Russia and your own are in competition with each other, fighting it out in our country. And you have especially blessed us here. Otherwise this was all jungle, all tribal country, full of tigers and elephants.'

I shifted in my seat. Somehow the allusions of another competition between the countries that had been at war so recently made me uneasy.

'This campaign, or movement, whatever, will draw unnecessary attention,' he went on, 'making Raurkela the centre again. Of what, and what would be the point?'

'Nothing, I don't know. I guess he is concerned. After all his family came here a long time back.'

Jhunjhun looked at me with the utmost commiseration. He knew I had been deluded. 'My god, sahib, what are you saying? Do you think then that gives him a right? That history justifies everything. He came here to kill and conquer. Bhaktiar Khilji, one thousand years ago came and burnt up the great library, Nalanda, and Ghazni destroyed so many temples... all monster rulers. They have a history of violence.'

'He is just waging a peaceful campaign,' I said, 'I think you are getting too worked up.' I stood up, it was nine, and I could hear Pat in the office, making herself busy. The phone had already rung twice.

They left not a moment too soon. I saw how the old Marwari leered at Pat as he passed. And she stared defiantly back almost making me grin in admiration. As for his two assistants, after their first glance at her, they averted their faces, blushed in embarrassment and slunk quietly past. It was already hot outside, the sunlight ricocheted off the asbestos roofs of the outhouses and sheds with great force, the leaves moved with a tired energy and everyone was already slouched over their chairs, wondering how the hours would pass. No wonder it was getting so easy to churn people's emotions up, things just festered if left inside for too long.

15

THE TRAIN CAME TO A STOP

Two days after this, I found myself at Mrs Hutchins's only to be told a fascinating story by her husband. To Mrs Hutchins's relief, Mr Hutchins had finally turned up, though a day later than his usual time. The train he was driving, he said, had run into some problems, and had delayed things, even his return.

I came by on the pretext of dropping Pat home. With her husband's arrival, Mrs Hutchins was already running around like a flustered hen. Lisa was there too for her English class, but Mrs Hutchins excused her from class, flapping her hands around and gesturing at Lisa as she said this. At this moment, Mrs Hutchins looked much like Pat, without Pat's self-confidence and swagger.

'Today, you can have a gift holiday, Lisa my dear.' She nodded toward the Daimler, and then invited me in as I made to leave. 'Do stay for a bit, for cake and tea. Tom has come home. I was so worried when he didn't come yesterday.' She said that pointedly, as if she knew about Tom's ways and of Tilo's plans to write to the government about the whimsical way trains seemed to run. Benny Ambrose smiled at me as I came in, blinking as my eyes adjusted to take in the dimly lit room, with its faded curtains and cane chairs strewn around a round glass-topped wooden table. I nodded, wanting to add something about meeting unexpectedly again, but Mrs Hutchins was everywhere, talking to all of us, doing too many things at once. The table swivelled as she placed a tray in its centre.

On the way to the Hutchins's, my intentions were to coach Pat on what to tell Das, if he ever called her in for questioning. We joked about Das's obsession with the billiards table, but I was in for several surprises.

'But he is trying to solve things. A man was killed, and...,' Pat sounded very serious, as if she was reading something rehearsed, 'so all loose ends must be tied.'

I knew then Das had got to her already.

I caught a glimpse of Lisa, and tried hard not to look her way. She stood by a glass-fronted wooden cupboard that had all of Mrs Hutchins's fancy cutlery. Her face was all flushed, and I rubbed my face, feeling the blood rush in as well. Next to me, Pat gave a whoop of joy and rushed past me to get to Benny Ambrose.

Her path crossed Lisa's who stood up. The other girl brushed past her roughly, her braid swinging past, leaving—as it had on me as she sat next to me in the car—a hot and furry feel on Lisa's bare arm, and she dropped her books. Benny who was closer reached Lisa faster. I was altogether too clumsy, finding too many things—Pat's dropped scarf, an awkwardly placed chair —in my way. Benny bent down, picked up her books, then looking up at Lisa, asked her with that crinkly smile of his, 'Are you hurt too?'

Pat's brusque interruption came as quite a jolt.

'Couldn't you see?'

'It was an accident, Pat,' said Benny lightly, 'don't take it so seriously.'

Pat tossed her braids again, she ran now to greet her father. Her father put his cup down and enveloped Pat in a warm bear hug and we heard the smacking kisses he gave her on both cheeks. Benny watched her, a wry smile on his face. He had switched on the porch light for me, thinking I'd leave soon, and it was

Mrs Hutchins who gestured me toward one of those cane chairs. There was tea and cake for everyone, she insisted again. Benny walked out onto the small porch, leaned against the chipped stone balustrade, and lit up a cigarette. When he looked back at us, his smoke wreathed face made him look quite spectral. Lisa remained standing too. It was then Mrs Hutchins rushed out from the kitchen again, looking even more flabbergasted. 'Oh dear, no one is sitting down. Lisa of course, you must stay on for a bit. I'm sure the rickshaw can wait.'

It was then I noticed the rickshaw standing by the tree. It had its orange awning up, and some words painted in black along its sides. The rickshaw puller lounged against the cycle, waiting.

Where was the raja sahib's Austin, and why was she in a rickshaw? But Lisa reading my thoughts answered. 'Abdullah was sick, so it's in the garage, and I didn't want to miss a class.' She smiled at me impishly, like of old, 'So I just walked out on the main road and got myself a rickshaw.'

'I will drop you home.' I told her firmly before brushing my too-long hair away from my face and smiling at Mrs Hutchins as she held out a cup for me. Lisa took the chance to walk up to me. She whispered the almost angry question at me. 'Why should I, and why aren't you with Das?'

I stirred the sugar in, and looked at her, instantly angry at her supposition. 'You can see I am not with Das.'

Mr Hutchins was made on the same plump, big lines as Mrs Hutchins. He had a red face, wreathed perpetually in laughter lines, pale blue eyes and a hearty laugh that sounded much like the thunder rolling in from behind the forest. His laughter began slowly, as if gathering force before it burst right out, zapping everyone with unexpected force. Now we heard it begin low and rumbling around us, as Mrs Hutchins busied herself in non-teacherly occupations.

'Something kept niggling away at me,' she said almost petulant as her husband rolled his eyes skyward, 'that was why I asked Benny repeatedly for any news about Tom and his train. Your recent delays have been just a bit unusual...even though now you can afford to laugh it away.

'Nothing I couldn't handle.' He laughed, pulled out a chair, gestured to Pat to sit down by him, and I knew a story was about to begin. He rubbed his thighs, his face reddening with pleasure at the audience now gathered around him. Lisa sat next to Mrs Hutchins, where she helped pass the cake around.

'This time the delay happened in Calcutta itself,' Mr Hutchins began. 'They had called a big protest in Calcutta,' he said, smiling his thanks at Lisa for the plate she held out for him, 'tens of thousands of people demanding proper compensation for the refugees. You know, the riot refugees from East Pakistan. They were spilling over into the railway tracks and our policemen were just looking on. They might have just fired in the air. This is the state of the police in our country. Totally lost. Now if some other country invades, China or even Pakistan, we will still be standing with our hands raised....'

Pat hooted in laughter, Mrs Hutchins sniffled, and we smiled. Lisa stared at the fancy China teacup that Mrs Hutchins had placed before her.

'Some tea, my dear? Tom got it especially from Assam. It really has a heavenly fragrance, and there is some of that strawberry cake you love too, darling.'

Lisa did not look up from her cup, until it rattled on its saucer on a new burst of laughter from Mr Hutchins. 'You are embarrassing the poor girl, Clara, with the attention. She will run away any minute.'

The revelation of her first name made Mrs Hutchins blush. She did not look like a Clara. An old-fashioned name that usually belonged to spinsters or governesses. There was a short silence at the table. Mr Hutchins winked at his wife who busied herself making her own tea before he returned to the subject, in a quieter tone.

'Something strange happened to me though as I passed through the forest the last time. I've been thinking about it.'

'What, Daddy, tell us?' Pat flicked his arm with her braid, and he laughed at Pat's impatience. 'Strange because they were people I had never seen before.'

I gasped, and almost dropped my cup before I managed to turn it into a cough.

Benny asked solicitously, 'Everything all right?' And I nodded, having missed Mr Hutchins's next words.

'The train had left Chakradharpur on time, and everything seemed on course. There was nothing to indicate that the train would be delayed and then, you know, the train came to an unexpected stop right in the middle of the forest, and in the dead of the night. I felt something pulling at my wheels, like something getting stuck in thick glue, and so while I tried to press ahead, tugging at my throttle repeatedly, the train jerked, swayed, first this way and that,' —Mr Hutchins shifted in his chair to give us a graphic demonstration—, 'and then it came to a stop. An agonizing metallic scream that shattered the darkness.'

'Yes, I heard it too...,' said Benny who had come back in, 'I thought something was up at the steel plant. It sounded quite animal-like.'

'You should have heard the scare it set off among the birds,' Hutchins went on, 'the trees shivered and trembled. Like a person who has got malaria, and the birds rose into the sky, shrieking and cawing. That was what first sent a funny feeling through my bones. The guardsman, Ranbir, was right at the other end, I could see his lamp in the distance. And I could see his lamp bobbing and shaking, like one of those jack-o-lanterns, then I heard his whistle, the thrash of his stick on the trees as he advanced towards me. Then suddenly, his lamp flickered and burnt out. We were plunged into darkness. The last I heard, as we sank into this silence, was his shout, "Hutchins sahib, it is very dark. I am going back."

'His cry echoed through the darkness, setting off fresh cries among the birds. Overhead the clouds moved at a fast pace, as if mocking us below, standing with a stationary train. But someone still advanced, slowly, and I knew it wasn't Ranbir moving along the tracks. He was back inside his cabin at the very end. It was funny because the tracks clearly curved, and he was diagonally opposite me, not behind me in a straight line.'

Mrs Hutchins took a chair, she was fanning herself, laughing breathlessly. Her small bun had come undone over one ear, and her thin nose, now red in excitement, twitched. She crossed herself as if her finding thrill in a story of this kind was a sin, 'Jesus, Tom,' she whispered, 'you are giving us all a fright.'

Tom went on, 'Imagine then how I felt, sitting there in the darkness, with the wretched cries of the birds all around me. And that man Ranbir, with his lamp snuffed out, waiting there in his cabin in that darkness. He must have been terrified. Singh don't come out. I roared. Louder than I had ever before. Hutchins sahib, I cannot see a thing, he shouted back, almost shrieking. Just stay where you are, don't move, I ordered. Everything echoed strangely in the darkness. But someone still came along. I could feel it, in the stillness, while the birds settled down and were quiet in moments.

'I was scared. That stillness seemed only to be a pause. All those stories I had heard, suddenly they seemed very real. The hordes of rogue elephants stampeding down the forest. If they barged into my stationary engine room what chance did I have? And the snakes? The eerie whistling noise in the forest, the shrieking of the birds that was quiet now and the crackle of twigs as someone still advanced, everything seemed magnified.

'Who's there?' I said once.

'In that darkness, Ranbir and I kept shouting to each other, trying to keep our spirits up. And whoever it was on the tracks, had gone silent. The train wasn't moving. Some spirit of the forest had perhaps possessed it, as the Adivasis believed.

'It was blasphemous, but he and I were now shouting to every god we knew. Radha Krishna, I heard him say and thought he was referring to the vice president; then Baba Fakir, Pir Mohammed, and I did too.' Mr Hutchins laughed embarrassedly, wiping his pink face with a dirty, checked handkerchief he produced from his pocket. Mrs Hutchins was sitting in the armchair, her hand on her mouth, unable to decide on a reaction. Benny lounged against the window, looking out.

'Then we heard a third voice, not from down the tracks but on a path that led to the edge of the forest. Someone singing carelessly, with abandon. A man. But the wind turned the other way and sometimes his voice was lost. It seemed ghostly. That broken cut-up voice singing some film song. That movie....' He broke off to hum a few lines, tunelessly tapping his thigh.

'Devdas,' said Lisa automatically. We did not look at each other. It must have been the same night. Our last night out together when we returned to the palace late, only to find that the raja sahib was late too, and he—I knew it now—had often hummed that song.

But Mr Hutchins was impatient to get on. 'Yes, yes. I called out, who's there? Turn back, Singh, if it's you.

'I don't know why I was warning him. I felt I had to. But there were too many strange presences. It seemed crowded, but no one was there. And the man we heard. Well, he was singing without a care in the world. As if he was possessed.

'It was then the skies cleared, or it could be that the last birds had returned, tired out. The clouds passed, and the moon gave us enough light to see by. I saw Singh, looking purple in the moonlight, wave with his snuffed-out lantern back into the darkness. The guard's cabin was many metres away and I shouted to him, don't move into the forest. Singh stay there. Then the moon vanished again, and I could see nothing except the grey edges of the trees. My voice echoed, there was no other sound. And then there were the footsteps, not moving away, but coming closer and they were clearly different.'

Pat shrieked. 'Those men of the forest, it must have been them.'

'I turned and then I saw them, there could not have been many of them, two or three. They were just standing there, looking at me, just watching. Eyes unblinking, expressionless in the dark, large in their dark, scarred faces, not moving. Some had on those loose shawls, but I was too startled, the fear came later, to even think whether they had a gun, or a knife hidden there. I just waited there. So did they. It must not have been long, for some moments later I heard Singh's relieved shout, I feel safe now sahib, safe. I heard him laugh, heard his door open and then snap shut. I hoped he wasn't going to come. Later he told me he was only locking himself up, alone in his cabin, with a rifle for protection. Then in that silence, we heard a shot. I thought it was them firing, but it was Singh who had raised his own gun and fired. Once, maybe twice.

'That idiot. The rules are he had no need to fire without being threatened. Now we would have to file a report.'

'But he might have been killed, who knows?' said Benny.

'True, but the government works in strange ways. I heard the rustling of steps and as the light came on from Singh's cabin again and spread itself out in slow circles, and they just melted away into the darkness.'

'You mean they just went away?'

'We could not see them anymore,' Mr Hutchins said, testily, playing with his cup. He noticed Lisa, sitting to his right, very still and pale, and managed a bluff, over-hearty smile, 'So my dear, I haven't scared you with my story, have I?'

'Oh, she's a brave girl...,' replied Benny Ambrose instead, 'but didn't you ask Singh about them? He had seen them too, so what did he think?'

Mr Hutchins turned a shade redder, averted his eyes, his cup fell over on the table, but it was empty, so nothing spilled. What unravelled was his embarrassment. 'We didn't speak about it. Once the train started, and we picked up speed very fast, it seemed fanciful. That voice, those men. Something out of our imagination. Sometimes the forests play strange tricks on the eyes. We didn't want to take it seriously.'

'You might have told the police about it?' Ventured his wife tentatively.

'Oh woman,' he thumped on the table, 'you are now making a big issue out of it. They could have been the Adivasis, or the forest people. They were not doing anything, just watching us. Taking it to the police would have made us look very foolish. And I didn't want to file a report. And Ranbir has gone to his village home. So even if we do, we must wait.'

Clara Hutchins persisted. 'If they were who you think they were, and mind you I am not saying anything, it's you who are vouching for who they could be, there is every reason to go to the police. You would not know, but there has been some trouble in this town....'

'There was a body found there too, wasn't there,' Benny said, and there was a long silence.

'The train didn't run over him. We'd have felt it.'

'No Tom.' Mrs Hutchins looked tearful, and then I had to break in. 'Just how many shots did you hear?'

Mr Hutchins's cup was halfway to his lips and now he paused. 'Now... two, actually. I was angry with Singh, thinking he had fired twice. But there had been two shots, and I checked his rifle.'

I said nothing, I stared at the cuff of my shoe, and outside a bus went by noisily. I saw the sky had darkened and it'd soon be time to leave. I had not heard one or two, but more, perhaps three. I had held a gun, and my breath had caught in my chest. It was my turn to put my cup down with a clatter. Lisa glanced my way, everyone else still looked on at Mr Hutchins.

'You forget the forests are huge, someone may have gone hunting,' said Mr Hutchins.

Lisa's hands shook, and I said, 'It was too dark, and you mentioned the birds shrieking. That might have....'

'Yes,' Benny Ambrose was nodding in full agreement, 'that could be it. But things have been strange...,' his eyes flitted towards Mr Hutchins, and then me, for a second before he went on, 'strange reports, something I don't understand. All that talk of the riot refugees coming in, seeking land in the forests, no one knows the truth of that.'

'In Calcutta, there have been big demonstrations by the refugees. They keep making demands of the government...but the government has its hands full.... But they seem to think it is a matter of right to have land where they want it,' Mr Hutchins looked thoughtful. The conversation meandered off then. Mrs Hutchins mentioned noncommittally that Tom must mention it to the police then moved on to talk of the shops on Park Street and Chowringhee. She sounded petulant for amid all this, he had not got her the yeast and raisins and other things that she had wanted. I saw Lisa gathering her books. Pat and Ben had stood up too. Everyone wanted to forget the story as quickly as they could.

'Are you getting late, my dear?' asked Mrs Hutchins looking at the clock, bustling around with another cup of tea for her husband. A fat, frumpy woman, she was now all flighty and nervous in the presence of her husband—a bluff, blustering man who had spent a nervous night locked in his own engine room.

'I will drive her,' I said, smiling stiffly at Mrs Hutchins, and at Lisa. 'It's all right,' when she made to protest, 'it really is too dark. Do be sensible.'

I followed her outside, hiding my disappointment that I hadn't been able to get to the Austin yet. After this story, somehow the gun took on some urgency. I had to get the gun back, to prove the story to Das. The raja sahib could not have killed him, simply because the gun hadn't been with him. Then there was the matter of Tom Hutchins hearing someone sing. That could only have been the raja sahib, who had been drunk that night, as even his palace servants knew. And the raja sahib loved that song. A song calling for one's love to stay in one's heart. *Balam, aayo baso mere mann mein.*

Lisa sat next to me and I drove quickly, my mind on the story, still thinking over what Mr Hutchins had said. There was the matter of the shots that still created confusion. How many shots had there really been? One or two, and had I then heard the third? What explained the gun that I had found? And how long was the raja sahib there too? I took a sharp turn at that thought and Lisa knocked against me, rather abruptly.

'I am sorry.'

She said nothing. For we could see the lights on in one section of the palace already. I drove slowly now, the last few minutes of the drive, glad not to look at her, ruing the fact that I could not look at her. But the matter of the gunshots bothered me. Had I missed something? Or was Hutchins being evasive.

'Did you hear the shots he mentioned?' Lisa asked me.

I looked away, wondering what I should say.

'I....'

She interrupted, 'That night, it woke us all up. We came out, me from my room, and Biswal from his room below, and I heard the guard up too, he said he had heard two. I did think it could be father.... Don't tell anyone I said this.'

I patted her hand, 'No. I promise. It wasn't your father, Lisa.'

'He had been out. Don't you remember he came back very late? And I wondered if he was the one singing.'

We were through the gates. The guard, now fully sober, opened it, looking at us with his bulbous eyes. I was suddenly glad my Daimler hadn't let me down. 'I will get off then,' she said quietly. With her other hand, she reached for the door handle and I tugged at her hand still in mine. 'I promise.'

'What?' Her eyes were on mine.

'Not to tell anyone.'

I lifted her hand to my lips and just then the porch lights came on and I had to let go. I got out of the car and watched her run in. All I would think of was how red her face had turned, my lips on her skin, her bony fingers on my chin, for that fraction of a second. I stood for a few moments, my chin on the Daimler's hot roof. It hurt soon enough, bringing me back to reality. The past, it would always haunt my present.

16

THE LOST DIARY

For a week, I had been looking for my diary but to no avail. I had even made the two temporary workers help look for it. I rummaged through every part of the cottage, hunting for it, evading Rao's curious, hurt questions. He was upset I didn't tell him about it; instead I tried to look casual every time he was around. Giving away any little fact about the diary and its importance would only make him more curious. If he found it, he might want to look in it himself first.

I rifled through the papers on Pat's table when she was not there. I even braced myself and asked her about it when she came, and watched her round-eyed, injured look of innocence.

'What makes you think I have taken something?'

'It's something you might have seen...just something I misplaced.'

Still she persisted. 'So you think I would have taken and kept it?'

'There could have been a mistake. Everyone makes mistakes.'

'I am not an idiot. You order me around all the time and then accuse me.'

So it was I who ended up saying sorry. Pat did that to you with her air of clueless hauteur. It threw me off track, her imagined hurt, and the protests outside over the engaging of temporary workers didn't help my mood one bit. I had had little sleep as well, for I had been up late trying to rewrite some of my notes, redraw at least some of the maps that I had painstakingly sketched out in my diary.

The introduction of temporary workers had made matters worse. More people appeared to have thrown in their lot with the earlier batch of strikers. I had had to clean my shoes myself, brush off some of the elephant dung that I must have picked up from the forest the other night. It took me a good while to brush off the thick hard brown flakes encrusted on the leather. The shoes, now hanging out in the sun, gave off quite a stench. The workers too remained in the sun, at their makeshift pandal and I read the posters, clear and unambiguous.

We demand our jobs back, Mr Hans.

We will not be insulted.

I turned away dismissively and heard them hooting behind me. But I had other concerns. My car had begun giving me trouble again. It was wheezing like an old woman and it was getting hotter by the day. I had this irrational longing to get away, go to the forest and sit under the old banyan tree right in the heart of it and rewrite my diary.

That afternoon, when I reached home, I found flowers, two yellow roses, and a note. A small bit of paper folded several times and left on the table in the lobby. The roses made me smile. The note, by the time I unfolded it, had turned black and damp from the sweat on my fingers. I read the two words in black pencil, printed painstakingly in a perfectly straight line, with the exact same gap between every letter, Thank you. She had not left her name. So how was I to thank her now? I sat down on the old lounge chair, pressing a glass of cold lime against my perspiring head.

How had they forced Eichmann to confess? How would they now extract all that evil knowledge he possessed? And was it even worth it? Losing my diary had almost made me lose my mind. The flowers would soon droop, the petals will fall off and I had no diary to save them in.

That evening, when I sat in my study trying to reproduce yet another map from my past, I had two visitors. The phone rang a few times, but by the time I got to the instrument, it had stopped. I did not think much about this at that time, for it was hard to recollect details as I tried to redraw a map from memory. Every time I realized that I had forgotten some important detail, I would get up and again search through my table and its drawers in desperation, hoping the diary I'd lost would turn up miraculously, but to no avail. Then I perforce had to sit down and begin my drawings again. This time, it was of the route Eichmann had followed in Buenos Aires, almost as a matter of habit, from home to his place of work in a Mercedes Benz showroom. I worked for a long time, finally happy and absorbed, playing a game with myself, throwing myself several challenges.

I was interrupted first by Singh, and Das soon followed in his wake. Singh was laughing in his usual, blustery way as his eyes darted to every corner of my room, hoping to catch sight of another new consignment of photography magazines. But my table was strewn with my rough sketches that I hastily turned over to avoid attention.

'What are you doing?' He asked in unabashed curiosity.

'Just a hobby,' and then asked, trying to dissuade him from following that line of conversation, if he wanted a drink.

I got out the glasses and poured out some beer. Singh took a long draught, leaned back against his chair, his eyes closed, so I didn't have the heart to warn him to go slow with the drink. We waited out a few minutes of silence. He looked tired and I knew it was all the preparations for his daughter's wedding. They had found a good boy, just the kind Singh wanted, a scientist in Canada. To all those who said it was too far, Singh had only said, Life far away from here is the best life. Now I saw there were more lines on his face, and his hands had become gnarled like an old man's.

'Are these your latest plans?' I looked up startled, he was gesturing to the table with my papers strewn untidily.

I nodded, not really understanding what he meant. Then he went on, 'Things are changing fast. The Adivasis are leaving in large numbers. They seem to have got a huge sum of money and even job offers. You know, Hans sahib,' he said leaning forward, the light flashing off the glass and into his eyes, 'now you can move around in peace.'

He had a pleased look on his face as he leant back in his chair, looked up at the ceiling, and said, 'It seems even our raja sahib's days in the forest are over. He can't just simply go in and claim the forests. It's government land, to do with as the government pleases. The old days too are gone....'

When I didn't ask him to elaborate, he looked disappointed and went on, 'Things are not really working for him. I hear his wife is planning to move away. And he is trying to stop inquiries and all that. The people in the government want too many bribes. And raja sahib doesn't have much or doesn't want to spend much even to get Das transferred. Still he's trying. And that is why he is spending more and more time in Bhubaneshwar....'

I had still not spoken, for I was irritated, trying now to redraw in my mind the route that showed all the twists and turns the secret service guys had taken when tracking down Eichmann, or as he called himself in Argentina, Richard Klement. Or had it all been deliberate on Eichmann's part? Where had the slip-up happened and who had given him away?

'You look upset, Hans sahib? Anything the matter?' He was so persistent, and I was so desperate to be alone that I had to tell him about the loss of the diary.

He looked appropriately shocked, though it took him several seconds to school his features. 'That is terrible, it must indeed have very important information. You must make a complaint about it to the police straightaway. Das must come to know of this. No, I insist, I will come with you to the station, the complaint must be registered.'

I was only half-hearted in my protests, 'The police, but they must be neck-deep in work. And it's a small thing for them....'

'Nonsense, they are starved for work. They make a big deal about nothing,' said Singh. 'Haven't you seen through Das yet? He's...how do you say it, barking at every dog?'

I had to laugh then, 'Barking up the wrong tree, you mean.'

'Nothing that you do is ever too small,' he said more fulsomely and kept reassuring me about the diary as we drove to the police station. I had hoped to get him away before he saw too much in my sketches. But there was little I could do to get away from him. In a small town, every small life was thrown together. I saw the lights still on at raja sahib's house. And since Singh was being so helpful, I decided to make conversation. 'He must be back...the lights are still on....'

The road to the police station led past the forest, and we had to follow the highway for a bit before we turned in to the city again. But as luck would have it, we were delayed by the rabbits that strayed onto our path. I swerved first to avoid driving over one and then when another pair came in front of my headlights, I screeched to a halt. I found my irritation close to giving way. 'There are simply too many of them.' The Daimler lurched ahead for a few metres and I stopped, reversed slowly by a few metres, then reached over and snatched the rifle from the back seat.

'You are going shooting now,' Singh asked nervously.

'The rabbits.' I said shortly, 'it would not be a good idea to let them go.' I could tell he was nervous about the rifle, his tongue kept wriggling out to lick his dry lips. The loss of the diary, this drive to the police station, Singh by me; suddenly everything felt oppressive. I wanted to step out of myself, even for a bit. And so I grinned deliberately sardonic, 'Come on, Singh, it's not that you have never fancied rabbit meat....'

It took only two minutes. The last of the rabbits running in a line across the road was startled into immobility by my headlights and came to a frozen halt. When I saw the twin points of my car headlights clot into dots in its black-brown eyes, I hesitated, willing the trembling in my hands to stop, to hold myself still for a fraction of a second. It took just one shot and it rang out in the stillness of the air. We stood quietly, hearing the shot shatter the stillness, moving like ripples through the empty air. And in some moments, from somewhere far away, the shot struck the hills and came back. It was strange, but we heard that shot. The second one that was almost an echo and sounded several minutes later. So this was what had happened that other night as well. There had been two shots first, one of which had been an echo. And I was some distance away, at a different spot, and so had heard it clearly.

The quiet returned like waves covering up an exposed beach. We drove all the way to the police station, without a word. The rabbit in the seat behind us still throbbed as I drove with breakneck speed, life ebbing away with every beat of its tiny heart. It was hard to take a life and I hated myself. I knew then I could never have fired that shot at Eichmann, even if I wanted to.

At the police station, the sub-inspector was standing on the porch, evidently about to stride out somewhere. He rubbed his nose, wiped his hand on the stone column nearest him, and looked none too pleased at our appearance.

'Is it something urgent?' And seeing my face, he made another effort. 'You came to register a complaint.'

'We would hardly come here to buy provisions, would we, my man?' I said. Singh was quiet next to me. I was relieved. That single gunshot had taken away his power of speech in one fell swoop. I should have had the idea before.

The sub-inspector laughed, 'heh heh...,' and now wiped his hands on a red and white checked towel that a constable held out.

'So is this about a murder too?' He became somewhat conversational as he led us in toward his table and indicated the two chairs lined with dirty white cushions that faced his own. He clicked his fingers at the constable asking him to get water for us. 'I heard the gunshot some minutes ago. Ever since that murder, people have been turning up, saying they heard gunshots. And not just on one day but every other day. Now it feels like I have been hearing gunshots all my life.'

Singh started again in some nervousness. He still had not said a word. I placed my hand on his shoulder in reassurance. 'No, this is clearer but more complicated. A matter of some precious documents.'

The sub-inspector rocked ponderously back on his chair, flipped open the pages of his file. 'A document.... Land deed or something?'

Singh laughed nervously. He was returning in degrees to his old garrulous self, I needed to hurry up and get this over with. 'It's important. A diary that has a lot of precious information.'

'But a diary still....' Now the policeman looked at me speculatively, and I held his gaze. 'I mean,' he cleared his throat, 'just as a human body is just a human body but the importance attached to it would differ. You understand.'

I didn't, but I gestured towards the blank paper in front of him. 'The details.'

'Yes, the details...height, weight, all relevant specifications.'

The man choked on his laughter and I held onto my anger. He

was greatly amused by his own wit. And I endeavoured to get in every detail. Blue, cloth covered, the word Krupp on it. 'Six by five inches,' I said, indicating with my fingers, 'and about this thick. And it has important diagrams and information...in German.'

He put all this down, never once lifting his eyes towards me. I made him repeat the details. He did and then closed his book with finality. 'Good. We will follow up, it should be easy. Not as complicated as solving a murder.'

He got up and moved with deliberation towards the door. We could not turn our heads a full circle to keep up with him and were forced to get up too. 'Can't tell you how long it will take.' He said instead with great relish. 'If you have any suspects, just turn them over. We have ways of getting the truth out.'

He turned towards us, indicating with a hand the scooter that waited outside. 'I must go, will keep you posted. Though for matters like this, it is difficult. Looking for a needle in a big bundle of hay...I must go, there has been a murder.'

The constable on reserve duty told us more, soon after the sub-inspector rode away in a flurry of importance.

'The diary may take some time,' he said apologetically, getting us water from the clay pitcher. His fingers made two oily stains on the glass, like a firm stamped-on seal. 'There has been a murder so all of us are on duty. The superintendent sahib wants it to be resolved quickly. We all have to look for some Very Important Evidence,' he cleared his throat officiously. 'It's very secret.'

'You mean the Ali...case?'

I thought now about telling Das about the discrepancy in the number of bullets. He'd ask in turn why I had taken so long. But it was only now that I had a possible reason to account for the difference in what people had heard.

The constable nodded, then shook his head in commiseration. 'It's a real mystery. The government schoolteacher Ahmed Ali was shot at when he was on his way back from the club debate.'

'Shot at?' I asked, raising my eyebrows.

He looked horrified. 'Please don't tell on me. But it seems clear it was planned. Someone placed his body on the tracks.'

'With all the elephants around?' I must have said that aloud. Hutchins would have heard more than what he had revealed the other evening then.

But the constable was babbling now. 'We are going to solve it. No one knows the motives or who could have done it. But we have suspects and his opinions at the debate were heard by many. He made many enemies....'

He saw the disbelief on my face and found himself forced to elaborate. 'You know, there is that lonely stretch of road between the back of the school and his house, bordered by the forest. It was the road that led to the highway and crossed the railway tracks.'

Then he clapped his hand over his mouth. 'Don't tell the superintendent sahib or the sub-inspector I said this. It's my theory only.'

As with the gunshots and how he was killed, there seemed to be many opinions now as to where Ahmed Ali had met his unfortunate end. Singh looked around and shuffled closer to me. 'It must be difficult to look for clues at night...' I told him now as we walked out, repeating myself when the sound of the passing train drowned out everything else.

Singh was still nervous, he asked me to drive fast as we returned from the station. His eyebrows twitched and his window was rolled right up, even though it had got stuffy inside the car with the stench of the dead rabbit. He would look nervously at my rolled-down window, peering through the passing darkness as if he expected someone to come charging through it.

'Relax, Singh, whoever killed Ahmed is unlikely to be roaming around free on the main highway.'

He laughed, it sounded like a yelp and died away with a weak, bobbing sound.

'And you can be sure the policemen will be everywhere. In fact, today we are safer than ever before.'

Strangely, it made the man more nervous. He clasped his hands, unclasped them, shook his head and shuddered. 'Who would have guessed it?' He said now, 'That he would do things to invite death.'

I braked hard as something about that second shot struck me. The shot that had followed the one Hutchins had described in detail. The one that appeared to be an echo but perhaps it wasn't quite one. Perhaps whoever had pulled the second trigger had waited for the moment of the echo to synchronize his own shot. He had known what to do. That could still mean four shots. Or three? No there were three. I was confusing myself. I shook the hair and the sweat off my eyes.

'Hans, Sir, Mr Gerder.? Why have you stopped? Please drive on.'

His high-pitched voice penetrated dimly through me, and I revved up again with a start. The car had stopped of its own accord. A bad place for the car to give way. I needed to give Idris a piece of my mind. I still managed to get Singh home, much to his relief, but then couldn't get the car started up again. He saw me through an upstairs window trying to push the car and then joined me in the effort. When it revved up, I ran in frantically and we were both laughing together, and genuinely for a change. I found myself thinking of the laughter as I drove home. It was, after my drives out with Lisa, the most companionable moment I'd ever experienced.

Hours later, as I sat alone in my study, painstakingly trying to re-recreate another of Eichmann's routes, the phone rang. I remembered those events from 15 years ago clearly enough. All that I had heard then, the rest I had tried to read up when I worked as a shelf assistant in that genteel, decrepit Durban library. After the war ended, in 1945, Eichmann had just walked out, hiding among some civilians captured by the Allies. Hanging next to a woman and her old mother and affecting a forced limp as he walked past the check post. No one questioned him or gave him a second look. His nondescript looks were a blessing. The ringing stopped and picked up again, quick and insistent. I looked at the jangling black instrument. These weren't the long-drawn, slow rings of a trunk call, nor could I bring myself to answer it. An easy, expressionless 'hello' seemed beyond me then. It could have been Singh, embarrassed about his fears or hoping to check on me. The phone stopped after a while but resumed ringing once again. Finally, I could ignore it no longer and had to answer it.

It was Das, and he sounded startled when I said my hello. He had called to apologize. On several counts. For the late hour (no I stay up late, I replied), for his not being there when I had come to make a complaint (that's all right) and for his subordinate's behaviour (yes, that was strange but all right).

Das appeared inclined to make further conversation.

'I came to know that you were there, with Singh. Panda the sub-inspector told me about your complaint. He found it funny. I had to make him understand. You see, Gerder, these people are very uncultured. They may be brahmins, but they really don't know much. It all stems from false pride. He is a Panda, his fathers were priests, and his son found the family occupation too poor.' Das laughed. A rumbling laughter that rolled over the phone, jostling me out of my reverie. Who was he talking of and about what?

There was a pause. Then I was forced to say something. 'Yes, he did dally in recording my complaint. That death had shaken him. It was the first time anything like this had happened.'

'What death?' Asked Das and then supplied the answer himself, 'oh the murder. No they take place all the time. We are as busy as the Calcutta police. But this is a very sensitive time and place now. The Muslims are saying that they are being targeted. That man who runs the motor shop....'

'Idris...?'

'Yes, yes, he says several of them have received threatening letters telling them to go to Pakistan. And now they stand the risk of being killed, if the letter writers take their own threats seriously. Ahmed Ali was just the beginning. Idris had the audacity to suggest we were chasing the wrong target.' I was about to say I agreed with that, but Das went on. 'I slapped him, really hard, for casting aspersions.'

I couldn't get over what Das had just said. Idris, for all his braggadocio and loquacity was a man of peaceful intent. I felt a rising tide of indignation. 'Perhaps you should not have....'

I wanted to tell him to take Idris's concerns seriously. I knew now that the men watching me had not been the native people of the forest, but others. People whom Jhunjhunwalla had mentioned. Who were now being resettled on forest land. How else had he gotten so many temporary workers in such a short span of time?

'Did you say something?'

'Yes, what Idris said, is that true? He isn't the one to spread rumours,' I found my voice was hoarse. I looked out of the window, it was all darkness outside. Was it a restless bird I heard calling outside, who could not sleep like me or something else altogether? I thought of the men, hooded and cloaked, their eyes bloodshot and staring? Were they the culprits? There was a light far away. Narrowing my eyes, I worked out that it was in the palace. But a different room. Was the raja sahib back? What was happening with him now?

I missed Das's words again. He was still talking of Panda and how insensitive he had been about the diary. 'A diary can often be a record of civilization. Panda doesn't know much, and I had to explain it to him later. About Samuel Pepys, who kept a record of 17th century London life.'

I laughed, and that was my undoing. For Das had simply meandered to get under my skin. 'Funny you've never mentioned that you kept a diary, Hans? That'd have helped us keep track of the dates, and whatever happened.'

'What do you mean?'

His voice sounded far too calm and collected against my ear. 'Your diary, if I had known about it, would have helped us solve it. The dates. Now people are confused. I must chase clues all on my own. I know for sure I am onto something. Oh Mr Hutchins came to me, he mentioned shots, he seemed certain there were two. But reports suggest more, maybe three or four. We must investigate that.'

'Let me explain.'

But he would not let me, for he was now in full flow. I heard the clear intent in Das's voice. 'No matter how long it takes, justice will come.'

His words filled me with dread. I strove hard to be casual.

'Yes,' I said lamely. The light shifted in the palace, or was it the breeze? It dimmed and then grew stronger again. Someone was playing with the curtains. Someone was looking out in the dark. 'We shall do our best,' Das said. 'By the way, old chap, can you check if your gun is there?'

'It is.' I looked across at my mantelpiece. The rifle lay there, cleaned up now, and shining like a cold hard piece of steel. I could almost hear Das's exultation, as if I had answered just as he expected me to. 'And I think the guardsman Ranbir had a rifle—a Lee Enfield model,' he said.

'Sure, I have a rifle.'

'Ah yes, of course.'

There was an odd silence between us. As if we were sizing each other up, hoping the other would give in first. The light was still on at the palace. I leaned fully toward the window, drew the curtains apart, and heard him say. 'Must ask the raja sahib when he's back. I think he has a .30 revolver, I remember, very proud he was of it too.'

'He does?' I asked, hoping my voice did not give me away. It was still in the glove compartment of that Austin. 'Isn't he in Bhubaneshwar?'

'Yes, he is. I placed a trunk call, and he said it had been missing for a few months.'

'Missing....'

A silence followed again. My mind was crowded with different thoughts, struggling to shape themselves into a pattern. But none emerged. Finally, I said, 'All right Das, good night and sorry for making you ring so many times.'

'No, no...,' he sounded surprised and very aggrieved, 'it's me who should be sorry for disturbing you. And I called just once. Not many times.'

Who had it been? Had it been someone trying to reach me about something else? I had no answers. The lights had finally gone off everywhere. I felt relieved. No matter how late, someone still looked out for me from the palace. It was a sweet delusion to fall asleep with.

17

RECIFE 1950

It was only ten years ago, and I still remember most things clearly. What happened before and after on the night of my failed attempt on Eichmann. It was just some days I had left Sète, the port in southern France, secreted away on the SS Giovanni, to accomplish a secret mission, all on my own. My failure too was all mine, a cross I had to bear on my own. It was a night on a ship I couldn't wait to get away from. As morning broke through, the SS Giovanni docked at Recife in east Brazil.

There were children playing hopscotch when I quietly disembarked. The Indian sailors were getting off at Recife and I joined them on the supply boats. It was one of those things that one prepares for well and then just as suddenly realizes it is not necessary. No one on the SS Giovanni appeared bothered; it seemed some were now fatigued by their nights-long vigil on deck, watching over a man who was marked in many ways.

It was warm, even early in the morning. The fog had moved away from the harbour and a quiet warmth was gathering over the docks and pier. I felt it through the thin soles of my shoes, but it did little to ease the trembling of my hands. Any moment I expected to be called, for one of the guards to stretch his hand out and stop me but nothing of the kind happened. There were children playing on the docks and everywhere it was the flag, with its yellowish diamond on green that caught my eye. Crumpled and all rolled up like a sleeping porcupine. In that stillness, I could even hear a military band playing. My hands trembled even more when I saw the soldiers everywhere. They stood in groups, talking amongst themselves, scanning the deserted roads.

The Indians were quiet and subdued, the way they always were. I looked at my scruffy shoes, the shirt I had deliberately dirtied, and my disembarkation pass. The guards did not look my way, just waved us on. Only one of them spat and shouted something nasty. 'Don't make a scene,' for he knew as well as we did that the pubs were open, as were the brothels.

It was downtown that I saw the posters and read of the dictator Getulio Vargas's visit to the city. The Indians stopped too, gazing curiously, and one of them giggled before he was hushed up by the others. It was a strike notice put up by the port workers and that explained the deserted look of the port and the children playing there. Their voices resounded in my ears till I reached the corner and took a turn, where for the first time I slackened my pace, wriggled my hands, hot from being inside my pockets for too long, and allowed myself a big sigh of relief. The stillness did not dissipate, the military band could no longer be heard.

The palm trees swayed tiredly towards each other. I sat on the bench and smoked, the puffs lingering in the air around me for a long time in the sullen heat. A gunshot washed away my temporary somnolence. The leaves shook violently, and gulls flew in the air. Next, I heard piercing police whistles and more gunshots fired at random for no certain purpose. Everything was now awash with noise. I heard the rumbling tank and before it turned the corner and came up the street, I walked calmly up to the ladder placed against the lamp post and walked off with it. As the soldiers fanned out in every direction, I walked with the ladder stretched out on my shoulder, calm in every way, studying the squares on the pavement.

'Hoy, hoy, you there....'

I did not listen, instead I merely walked on, the ladder now heavy on my shoulders.

There were running footsteps behind me, landing hard on the sidewalk. Any moment I expected to find a bullet in me. But there were gunshots elsewhere and then the footsteps behind me stopped. There was a pause in which I was only aware of the sound of my own footsteps on the hard, square tiles. On one, I could make out the shape of a heart, a sign of love marked in chalk. Then the footsteps started up again, but they were moving away, away from behind me. My sigh of relief mixed with the breeze that returned, brushing the leaves up and down. The afternoon returned to its state of somnolence and I walked on, unsure, uncertain now of the ladder on my shoulder, wading deeper into the heart of the city.

I did not know where I was headed. The ladder gave me a kind of security. Then I heard someone shout. Where I was now, no one bothered to give me a second look. There were those carrying all kinds of things on their shoulders. Metal pots and pans, ropes, someone played the banjo, a mournful tune that I had heard somewhere in the mountains during my time up north.

'Hoy, you there....'

All the vendors on the road looked up, twirled their heads in the direction of the sound. Then the man in front of me, carrying bird cages that bobbed up and down on his shoulder, broke out in a perfectly lecherous smile. Then he pointed in my direction, nodded and signalled me to look up.

There was a girl at the window, who spoke in a very excited tone and gesticulated freely, as she leaned almost half out of the frame. 'My cat, can you get it for me...?'

And the street vendor turned and spoke to me in clear English. I remembered this detail much later and thought of my rescuers always on my trail.

'She wants you to get her cat off the roof.'

For the next five hours, I was the focus of intense attention. But the strangest thing was that I did not get killed, did not see any movement in the trees or in the houses nearby, or even in the docks farther away. I saw a ship move away and could not care less if it was the SS Giovanni finally moving away from port. I breathed again freely. That meant that nothing was amiss, even if I had been noticed as missing, no one would do a thing for fear of raising attention. And though I had failed in killing Eichmann—you might even call it a deliberate mistake, or that I had not even made the attempt— they would let me alone now. Perhaps I could learn to live again.

My rescue attempt was in several papers the next day. Even as reports of the assassination attempt made on the Brazilian president Getulio Vargas made it to all the front pages. There was the pleasing picture of me that Dora showed me later, and the caption read, 'Hero to the rescue on an otherwise tragic day.' Somewhere else I read, 'There are heroes still left in our country.'

The brothel girls crowded around me, and somehow I found myself placed in charge of Garcia, the rescued cat. 'You are our cat man,' the girls said. But of course, it was Dora who had first claim on me. Garcia was her cat after all.

I spent a year in Recife in Dora's company. In the brothel I was the general handyman, doing things for them, helping in every way. That was how I learned the many ways of doing up a woman's hair, the kinds of hairbands and lipsticks that suited different skin types, and I made myself popular by taking their photos.

Sometimes when it all got a bit too much, I would take a walk along the pier, playing with the coloured tiles, and watching the changing colours of the sea. I was well aware that Lüderitz, the only home I had known so far, was a night's journey way. Ships came and docked and went their own ways, and I was tempted. It was so easy to just walk away, but there were things that held me back. Dora of course, who coached me in the ways of love, and I was like a starved man. She would always pull away from me at the most passionate moments, laughing. Why are you always in such a hurry? She never waited for an answer, as if knowing the truth her question held.

That photo of me on the roof would be my undoing only a few months later. I did receive messages—delivered by a handyman or sailor—and I knew it was from the Nazi hunters, from the colonel himself perhaps. But these notes, typed in block letters, were all unsigned. *They will be on your trail.*

The men on my trail must have seen me time and time again. Every time I climbed onto the roof to fix a broken water pipe or when I was asked by one of the other girls to spy on the madam and her brother, who had set himself up as a real estate broker on that road. Dora always said he was a spy trying to pass himself off as a broker. The latter had returned from jail a good three months after I found myself in Recife. He had been arrested, like many others, on charges of conspiring in the assassination attempt on Vargas. The crackdown on my third day in Recife had been drastic and rough, when the secret police and the soldiers came and detained many people; anyone hanging around on the road, or who had been spotted in the vicinity. Marias had been one of them. When he returned, he was teased by the girls, who found him sullen, more taciturn than before, and suspicious. When he tried to ask too many questions, the girls would take me away. 'Oh keep off him, Marias. He's no harm.'

They treated me much like a stray dog that had somehow gambolled in. Marias kept an eye on me and followed me around, trying to catch me alone. He always made me nervous, skulking around corners, appearing under my ladder or on the roof the time I was cementing a hole so the rainwater couldn't pour in.

When I escaped, leaving in a trader's van and reaching the port in an hour's time, it was not a day too soon. I had seen Marias pointing my room out to a man who was clearly a plainclothes policeman. I did not want to be picked up on false charges. I did not want a return to my old life. Instead I found myself in Durban where the next five years of my life would go by in a haze.

18

A WEDDING AND A GETAWAY

The first newspaper I read that had news of the Eichmann capture in Buenos Aires came five days later. At the club, the Germans I came across did not even know about it. Or they studiously pretended ignorance. Fifteen years is not such a long time after all. For me it was an eternity, having crossed four continents and half the world's seas. But everyone wanted to forget it, erase the last two decades from their lives. Just rolling a blanket over their memories, playing a game of hopscotch so that the past was just a few squares to be jumped over.

I read the news over, several times. They had managed to get Eichmann. In Buenos Aires, Argentina, where he thought he had secreted himself away for good. I thought of Mama and pitied her. Poor Mama, she must have thought he had managed to erase everything. But they would not let him. First the Nazi Hunters, and then the Mossad, had kept watch on him.

Mama. It was odd I should think of her now, but given her mental state, would she even know what had happened? But all the news I'd received seemed to direct me to Mama, and I knew I could not put off going to Berlin any more. I had to see her.

Two months, I thought as I read the papers, for two months the secret agents of the Mossad had followed Eichmann, noting his every move, talking to each other with their wireless sets as they made their plans. How had Eichmann not realized it? Every day he took the same road to work at an automobile workshop, where he did all the paperwork. Like he had always done. Making notes, writing his observations on the margins, clearing away the paperwork, as he had done day after day in his life as a Nazi officer. Never asking questions. Yet it must have bothered him. All that he had done, without question. He had made his plans so efficiently, so quietly, but the past had caught up with him.

They will catch them one by one, I remembered the anger in Mama's voice during that last conversation we had. She meant that Germany would never be defeated. All the opponents—Churchill, Roosevelt, Stalin, everyone would be caught, just like every small fry had been. I had written to her from Berlin and she had decided to take the last flight in. By the time she must have reached, the Allied armies were close, and there was no way she could have found me. What she saw must have devastated her, driven her even faster to insanity. She must have wept when she saw Berlin fall, the city of her childhood, whose memories had carried her through life, through her unhappiness. She knew nothing of the city, having left it when she was five, yet she had carried it with her wherever she had gone, treasuring it deep within as life dealt its harsh blows on her.

I had to travel to the consulate in Calcutta to get my passport updated. I never knew, never wanted to acknowledge that I might be seeing Lisa for the last time at Singh's daughter's wedding. I didn't want to tell her either. I feared it would all get a bit dramatic. Didn't she know of the separations, tumultuous and heart-breaking, that had happened just over a decade ago? What the Nazis had done? And what had happened in her own country?

Lisa was dressed in her best for Meenakshi's wedding. A finely woven yellow and gold silk sari made specially by the weavers of

Sambalpur, where her mother came from, and Tilo's turquoise necklace. She also had on a heavy gold tikli with the royal elephant insignia on it that was handed down by the chief wives of her father's family.

The turquoise jewellery set was also a family heirloom. The tiny diamonds danced in the light like distant stars. 'It's far more precious now,' Tilo explained to Lisa and me when we met at the wedding. 'You know the miner who went deep into the mines to get it was the best one in the Holkars' royal domains. He had somehow come across this treasure trove, probably belonging to a troll who had lived down there for centuries. When he went down a second time, he never came back. It seems the troll kept him prisoner.'

I was glad for Tilo's chatter. She never caught on to what was going on. She never let me really feel the heartbreak and for that, I was grateful.

'It's true,' said Tilo laughing as she caught Lisa's bewildered expression and my own amazement. The stones changed colour every time Lisa moved, and her face looked different each time. She was, it seemed to me, not someone I knew; she took on a new mystery at every turn. 'The miners in the coal mines in my father's kingdom in Dantewada, they would sometimes find fire as they dug deep into the earth. They would say it was the caretakers of the earth, those trolls, who were breathing fire, trying to scare them away,' Tilo went on, gushing about her past.

Tilo went on to tell me how the driver Abdullah had taken his time reaching the wedding venue. Not only was the lane already packed with cars, but he drove badly, lurching from one side to the other. 'I had to be sharp with him too. I told him that if I didn't know you well and how religious you were, I would have thought you were drunk.'

Abdullah had touched his ears at the sheer horror of this thought. Lisa could not bring herself to tell her mother that the stones had dazzled him too, it made him blink and flinch each time they flashed in the rear-view mirror over his head.

The next three hours would prove to be the longest in my life. I had to remember everything that happened. To save it for later. There was no way I could tell her my plans, and there was no way, it was clear, Lisa would let me. I had no time alone with her. Singh's smile was more nervous and embarrassed than usual as he welcomed everyone. His harried wife took the women to an inner room to meet and bless the bride. I saw for myself the envious venom-filled look some of the women directed Lisa's way, the silence as Lisa and Tilo returned to the sitting area, where space was made for them and yet no one spoke, everyone appeared intent on listening to the sonorous tones of the shehnai.

I had driven to Singh's house, but my Daimler was wheezing now. I hoped it would get me to the station though. And I needed a railway ticket to Calcutta urgently. Perhaps I could then take a flight out, one directly to Berlin. Only Jhunjhunwalla had the contacts, the necessary wherewithal to get me a ticket in a day's time.

I looked around for Jhunjhunwalla and found him whispering to Singh, his ringed hand on Singh's shoulder as the other guests milled around. Surely they couldn't be talking about work now?

Then I felt someone's eyes on me and looked back to see Lisa and Tilo staring at a burqa-clad lady who was walking through the gathering crowd, past the servers with their trays, who appeared to be heading straight toward us. We were in an alcove, with a brocade sofa and a pedestal fan on either side. From time to time, the other guests would dip in, make small talk with Tilo in a suitably deferential way, compliment Lisa while surreptitiously looking her all over, and then leave.

But this woman was different. She was covered all over in black, and she moved quickly, like an ant burrowing its way through things. Tilo looked at her and then glanced away again with a twist of her lips. But the woman came right up to Tilo, pulled her by the arm, and thrust a piece of paper almost at her. Tilo's bangles jangled in response, and Lisa and I both caught a glimpse of the woman's eyes through the thin silken slit where the burqa covered her face. Her voice, when we heard it, appeared to come from deep within her, 'Read it, don't throw it away. If you really want peace.'

'What did she say...?' asked Lisa, as her mother stood still, with a smile on her face, her brow uncluttered as she made to open the gold clasp of her bag to thrust the scrap of paper inside. Tilo shook her head. 'She could not have spoken in English. I couldn't follow her.'

'You didn't hear her?'

'No, I just could not understand....' Then Tilo laughed in relief. 'Crazy things they do. I am sure it was someone from Idris's movement asking for support for that campaign they are running.... That's so foolish.'

She threw the paper away then, and I saw it roll away before catching against the leg of a cloth-covered armchair.

Lisa noticed too, but her jewellery, heavy and expensive, bore her down. She could not bend down to retrieve it. 'Tilo, forget it,' I told her, leading her to the sofa. She needed to sit down, catch her breath over a drink. My hand brushed hers as she sat, and I reached down quickly to pick up the rolled-up, discarded missive. I glanced around, catching a server's eye as he swayed among the guests holding welcome glasses of roohafza and sherbet in his tray, ice cubes floating languorously amidst the maroon and pink translucence.

I walked out for a cigarette, and the cool darkness hit me. I had no place here, and I had to get out quickly. Somehow, I had to find out more about the man who had been so much a part of my childhood, and my youth. The man I had been forced to impersonate, and to protect, and whom I had failed to kill. The man, finally nabbed, and for whom there was no escape.

Tilo and Lisa were laughing when I left them, as if they wished to forget the strange incident that had just occurred. Now the booming, over-hearty voice that came from somewhere behind caught them by surprise. I heard Das, as I walked back inside, and it made Tilo even more nervous.

'I could not recognize her,' I heard Das, and saw him nod his head towards Lisa, 'my god, what a transformation.'

She smiled, blushed, it was the first compliment she had received that day. For a minute Das redeemed himself in her eyes. The very next minute he had raised her hand to his lips and kissed it. The moment stood still in my memory for a long time. How her sari had rustled almost in instinctive protest as his slender, clumsy hand reached for her, his cold, clammy touch on her skin, the feel of his hot, frog-like lips, Lisa moving her hand away as quickly as she could, with a firm jangle of her bangles, the many seconds her hand had hung limply in the air as if his sudden gesture had robbed it of life, the silence and the emptiness all around, the imprint of his lips, round and wet on her skin, which she could do little to wipe away.

Lisa pressed her hands tight against herself in case he repeated the gesture. She saw the flicker of his eyes, the bare shift in expression and then he had turned his attention to her mother. 'She looks like Devika Rani,' he said again, 'really, it's amazing.' Then he fumbled, looked at me as I looked around for Jhunjhunwalla, and then he began again, almost apologetically. 'I need to ask some urgent questions. Sorry to put them to you here. I understand your husband has a certain kind of …revolver.' I saw Das dig his hand into his pocket and there was that piece of paper with the details on it. It was a show, for knowing Das, he knew these details by heart.

'A what…?'

'A Smith and Wesson Model 30 revolver,' he said, more confident.

Lisa had been looking around, luxuriating in the stunned look that came over people's faces as they turned to her, the desperate effort they made to hide their envy, even appreciation, to keep their faces carefully blank. She could only hear snatches of this conversation interspersed with the remarks around her. But she heard Das's question and her mother's faint murmur in return.

'The shooting, ma'am. There's a possibility....'

Das did not finish. Lisa saw the blood drain from her mother's face and reached for her. Das noted Tilo's face with a certain satisfaction before he rushed to explain more, 'We do need to check this...this is as far as our preliminary investigations go, of course. But the matter relating to Ali is truly very political. The movement for Centrehood has had few takers...but we are trying to find out who his enemies were, who could have been against him....'

'You're upsetting her, Das,' I said finally. What was he doing? Trying to trap the family for some no-good purpose of his own. Was Ali really shot in the first place? He could just as well have run into the path of the elephants. He might have been run over by the train, an accident for all of Mr Hutchins's protestations to the contrary.

Das took his time to reply, and when he did he enunciated every word clearly, 'His body was mangled so badly that we could not tell. But we are not discounting any possibility.'

Lisa saw her mother's painful nods, as she vainly tried to keep up with Das's arguments. Not for anything would she make her distress evident. Lisa bit her lips, one hand bunched into a fist as she held her mother's hands with the other, and there was the polite smile fixed on her face. Her daughter's support seemed to give Tilo some strength. 'My husband, as you are aware,' we heard Tilo say stiffly, with her head held high, 'is away in Bhubaneshwar. I fail to understand what you are getting at?'

'Madam, madam,' Das was suddenly very earnest, almost pleading. 'I also want an amicable resolution. It is clear the

Movement has been drawing too many enemies. But we still need to be resolute in our inquiries. Otherwise, it will appear we are biased and unfair in our investigations.'

Something flashed in my eye, it was Jhunjhunwalla's rings that had caught the light. I saw him vanishing into the crowd at the other end of the hall. He had been talking with Singh and now he was intent on leaving. I had to get to him urgently. I strained my eyes, but I could not see his long red gold tasselled turban anywhere. There were at least three men wearing similar turbans. It could be that he had gone to the bathroom. And I shifted my vantage, hoping to catch him as he reappeared, hurriedly zipping up his trousers. It was this that made me miss several parts of the conversation that had continued between Das and the two women. For when I turned back, unfulfilled in my search for Jhunjhunwalla, I could sense a change in the atmosphere, a certain shift in the exchange. What had happened?

When I looked back, Lisa was looking at me, her shyness all gone. In its place was a hard, steely glint, and her mother and Das were laughing shakily but in a strangely companionable way. At some point he must have gestured to her mother, pointing to Lisa.

'I noticed things about her I never had.'

Then Tilo had directed her laughter toward me, 'Is it true, Hans? My daughter is growing and we must set an example.'

My eyes widened, and I felt an odd pain in my heart. I had to go then, and I would never see Lisa again.

It was around ten that they decided to leave. Das saw them walking out first, for we were on the porch, having a last smoke. Das blew away his smoke and I tossed my cigarette into a bin. 'Are you leaving?' I asked them. 'Isn't it early?'

Tilo smiled, 'It's late for us, Hans....'

Das was staring at Lisa in a way that made me want to hit him. 'Is the car with you, rani sahiba?' he asked, much too solicitously, 'otherwise it's not safe. Too much jewellery....'

'I have lived here for many years now,' Tilo replied, her nose rising regally.

We looked at each other, and then I quickly wiped my lips with a napkin. 'You have a car, come then I will follow you....'

Tilo laughed, a tinny, fragile and very young sound, 'That is really kind of you and unnecessary, I daresay. You might be late for dinner.'

'Not hungry,' I forced a smile, waving my hand at Das, 'he will eat for both of us. He has been working much too hard anyway.'

Das shrugged, his tall black outline framed in the darkness, 'What to do, the matter is under investigation. We are looking into the reasons, and murder has not been ruled out.' He seemed to recite that monotonously, almost subconsciously. As Tilo and Lisa exchanged uneasy looks again, I heard Das laugh. 'You look as if you'd seen a ghost. I am sure there will be resolution soon very soon.'

My hand was inside my pocket where I had balled it up into a fist. Damn Das, I was thinking, but now my hand closed around that crunched up bit of paper that the strange burqa-clad woman had thrust into Tilo's hand and that she had thrown away. As my hand tightened around the paper, I knew suddenly who the woman had been. Samineh, my former secretary. I was suddenly filled with more resolve. 'It's all right, Ranjay, I didn't want to stay too long anyway.'

Das looked put out but he smiled, and in the half-darkness of the portico, I caught a glimpse of his teeth in the darkness, 'Hans wants to play the gallant knight. Though your eagerness to rush away makes me suspicious, Hans. Hope you are not plotting a rendezvous of your own....'

I turned back to face him then. 'Really? How come I don't have an inkling of this?'

He shrugged, and I stood, hands in my pockets, looking up at the stars. The shehnai strains had stopped and the buzz of the night insects had taken on a greater urgency. Das looked away quickly from me to turn to Tilo. 'I don't know that. Not that it matters. But that matter of the gun, you see. Please don't worry, anyway. I shall drop by to see you tomorrow. Good night.'

Abdullah the driver was slumped forward on the wheel of the green Austin. Lisa leaned forward and called his name, and then I nudged her away and tried to shake him awake, at first gently and then more roughly. 'Come on man, wake up,' and I recognized the hoarse edge in my own voice. When he jerked up, Abdullah had a bewildered glazed look. His eyes took in the three of us, before he lowered his gaze and looked apologetic, even sheepish. Lisa managed a nervous giggle, and I sensed her panic.

'There is no way he can drive you home safely,' I told them, still looking at Abdullah, who hiccupped, giggled and insisted with folded hands that he would do his duty.

'It's no use,' I shook my head, 'I must drive you home.'

'No sahib,' Abdullah rushed out of the car and fell at my feet. 'I will lose my job.'

I was embarrassed, and exchanged a quick smile with Lisa, while Tilo, clutching her neck, and staring at the sky, declared. 'Oh god, such drama. No one will fire you. Just get us home.'

There were people emerging on the porch, curious about what was transpiring. I saw Singh again as he hurtled down the stairs and ran up, a hand on his chest. 'Is something the matter?'

'No, no,' We turned simultaneously, and I assured him, 'please return to your guests. I will take the rani sahiba and her daughter home.'

Singh was panting, but it was my breath that caught by the time I finished speaking. Lisa and I looked at each other again. Then I jerked Abdullah roughly against the car. 'Are you listening? If you want to keep your job, drive the car back safely. And follow my instructions, understand?'

The man nodded, his hands still folded. The green Austin

gleamed in the wedding lights strung on the roof and in the bushes, and I felt an urgency. I had to get the gun out. I hoped it was still where I had left it. 'You go ahead, get it. Go ahead in that car, and I will follow to make sure you don't veer off.'

'You are very gallant, Hans,' Tilo said stretching luxuriously in the Daimler's back seat, as the Austin's headlights shed a steady golden stream of light in front of us. Lisa threw her head back, and in the mirror I caught sight of her long turquoise-encased neck and it wasn't Abdullah who drove erratically this time. Tilo's chatter, her gasping laughter as she recounted Abdullah's behaviour, helped. My hands steadied on the wheel, and I listened to her, smiled occasionally and looked straight ahead. The lights from the car ahead and the Daimler lit up the surroundings in a half-dark, spectral way. The road was a purple ribbon. The trees came up, lit in patches, and the light caught some creatures of the forest by surprise too, their eyes turning a slow blue. Past the main road, the district high school, the shops now asleep, and then the turn toward the tree-lined old road that led to the palace. The car headlights shone on the leaf fronds that came in the way, the swing of a lamppost and the stretch of light across patches of darkness, in fixed repeated motions, was like a violinist drawing his bow across shadowy strings.

The journey was short and rendered shorter because the gate was already open. The portico was occupied by another car, and out of the shadows a man stepped out. The raja sahib was back.

I pressed the brakes hard to muffled gasps and the clang of bangles. I got out shakily and turned to help Tilo. She and Lisa could barely look at me, for they were both looking at the man who stood half in darkness, his arms folded across his chest, looking down at us. We remembered Das's menace-filled words. And the death of the schoolteacher, killed, as Das was now determined to suspect, by her father's gun, loomed suddenly close.

I held Tilo's hand, and Lisa straightened her sari and ran up the stairs, bunching up her sari pleats in one hand as she stumbled once. 'Father, you're back.'

'Switch off the headlights, Hans,' her father said at last. He stepped out into the light cautiously, his feet crunching over the gravel.

'Why are you here?' Tilo asked, and then she asked again, as the three of them stood together, and I stood by my car, uncertain, 'are things all right?'

He didn't answer, for now I heard footsteps coming down toward me. Raja sahib touched me on the elbow, and only I heard the pleading note in his whisper, 'Not a word of this, Hans. I will go back tomorrow. Do not tell anyone you saw me here today, tonight.... Okay? I just had to check on something.'

I nodded quickly, now afraid to look up again. Das had called him, as he had told me, and the raja sahib must have returned to check on his gun. Of course it was missing, and now I had to get it back, to keep it safe, away from Das and his many-tentacled insinuations.

'Things appear to be missing, so many things, Hans,' he was speaking to all of us now, his voice reaching his wife and daughter standing at the head of the portico steps. 'I have had to dismiss Ghana. I came back unexpectedly and caught Ghana riffling through the antiques cabinet.'

He looked at me, 'I can trust you, Hans, right?' For he must have seen my face, as the blood receded. So, those were the antiquities Ghana kept bringing for me, and I'd been paying him too.

'Yes, you can.' I grasped his hands and then whispered. 'I haven't told them, but I am leaving. Something urgent in Berlin.'

A look of shock spread on his face, and I continued. 'You must go now, go on.' I added, as if he was a particularly recalcitrant child. 'I will take the car to the garage.'

Abdullah had fallen asleep again, relieved that he had reached the palace safely in perfect accordance with my orders. I shook him awake, pulled him out and jumped in, taking a quick glance at the glove compartment by the passenger side. In the garage, it'd just take me a couple of minutes to get the gun away.

I breathed in the lost fragrance of the shawl, and when my hands finally closed over the piece of cold metal, I heaved a sigh of relief. I took off my coat, hid the gun in it securely and only then did I return to my Blue Daimler.

'Sahib,' it was Biswal the butler who came running down just then, 'they want you to come in.'

Tilo appeared behind him. 'For a bit only, come in, Hans.'

They were sitting in the study and I felt a bit of an intruder. But Lisa, and she had now taken off her jewellery and her loosened hair fell around her face, fetched tea, and they talked of the deterioration in the household.

'Things are missing. Too many to count,' said the raja sahib.

He looked from mother to daughter, and Lisa put her cup down calmly and said, 'That's because of all the problems. Both of you were arguing all the time and never had time to notice.'

'Yes,' he ran his fingers through his black and grey hair, the waves stood up, 'but Lisa...there are some things you don't understand.'

He tried to catch my eye, and this time I put my cup firmly down and said I must go. 'Hans, are you leaving?'

'For home, yes,' I smiled at Tilo and at Lisa. Suddenly I felt very tired and very old.

'Didn't you say something more?' said the raja sahib looking puzzled. He looked as tired as I did, but always handsome. He wore a neat kurta, and tight shalwars, and his hair was brushed back elegantly. Even when he ran his fingers through it, his hair settled back in its original waves.

'Yes,' I told him, 'but you need to be here now. I will explain it all later. Goodbye.' And this time I was careful not to look at Lisa. As I walked through the door, I heard the raja sahib speak up again. 'He can keep asking over and over again. I last saw the gun many years ago and now it's just missing.'

Once in my room, I got the gun out. It'd go right in my suitcase at the very bottom. I'd make sure it wasn't lost. Samineh's note fell out when I took the gun out. In it was written in evenly spaced letters: *your husband, raja sahib, my friend too. He is in danger.*

The more I looked at it, it did not seem a warning, in the way one expected. It held concern, and admonition. I realized I was imputing meanings it might not have. It had been written out in block letters, and there had been something in the way she had moved...Samineh. I was now certain it was her. I tossed the paper from one hand to the other, and finally let it drop onto the table. Deciphering this letter was a complication I could do without.

I sat in the darkness. There were no lights on in Lisa's room and that filled me with an emptiness too. Then to gather myself, I thought again of the events of that night; the night of Ahmed Ali's death. The elephant herds had passed. Had that happened later when I had driven out with Lisa? Or perhaps the elephants hadn't really gone. I knew also that I had taken the car out alone, and fallen asleep in the forest road, and seen those men. They had melted away at the first shot. The train, as Mr Hutchins had described it, must have stopped before that. Then the man running. It must have been Ghana, running with the gun that he had stolen. He had fired in fear, and then dropped the gun. The poor man, already nervous, already under great strain, Ahmed Ali must have met his end right then, perhaps felled by one of the shots. The train, the elephant herds had run over him. And the raja sahib must have been in his hunting lodge, listening to his music.

It seemed so simple yet convoluted. But there had been an unfortunate death and a terrible, quite senseless plan in it all. I thought over the first time I had met Ahmed Ali and understood that I too had had a role in it.

Now I could think through quite calmly of what had happened on the ship: the SS Giovanni, me, and the man who was my quarry. We were on calm seas one moment and the next moment, the ship was shaking, the waves high. Just a whale, I told myself. No one had thought about this possibility. The unsteadiness of the ship, the beauty of that whale moving along by himself, oblivious to the world around.

My hands shook. I had left my childhood world behind, the memory of the whale on Skeleton Bay was long gone, and here I was, on the ship, about to make a new memory of myself as a killer. For it was at this moment, Eichmann took a turn around the deck and it would have been the easiest thing in the world to kill him. Except that I didn't. Our paths crossed, I neared, my hands in my pocket, and there were the figures who half-rose in their deck chairs. From under the awning, someone lit a match. As I approached him, Eichmann slipped on the cold wetness of the deck and I lost my nerve. His minders ran to him, thinking I had shot him, with a gun fitted with a silencer. I ran, down the stairs, past several flights, to the engine room, and the deck hold. I found the Indian sailors and joined in their card games. I knew I had to get off the ship the very next morning, else I'd end up at the bottom of the ocean.

I sighed as I thought through every memory of that dark night on the ship, sitting here in my room in Raurkela. One demon at least had been laid to rest.

I decided to go to the dark room where I developed my photos for one last search for the diary. I turned over everything in that room one last time. Old albums, film roll covers, camera stands, old magazines that Rao had arranged in a corner, but the diary, with its blue velvet cover and the string tied around it, still eluded me. Things clattered over as I searched, sounding a hollow laughter at my incompetence. As I let my perspiration run, wallowing in my failure, I heard a soft tapping on the door.

By the time I rose out of my lounge chair and pushed away the curtains that led to the main room, she was already inside.

For a moment, I could not place her. Thinking of what had happened on the ship and my last desperate search for the diary had totally consumed me. I had to blink repeatedly to adjust to the sudden brightness she had brought into the room. *Lisa.*

I saw her face, lit up by the porch light that was always switched on at night. She was, I realized to my surprise, very worried, and shy. She looked at me in that half-darkness, and then I wondered at my own surprise.

'Is something wrong?'

'No.... No.... My mother,' she was hesitating, kept stopping and starting again like my Daimler in its bad moods, 'I had to say something.'

'About not seeing your father. I promised that....'

'No, no.'

She gulped, held onto a chair. 'Das came, he came to visit.'

'What do you mean? Lisa you must sit.'

'My father told you about Ghana did he not?'

I pointed to some things on the shelves. 'He got me some stuff, some of it obviously stolen. He said it was from his village.'

Her eyes widened and she managed a faint laugh. 'At least we won't have to go far to look for the missing things.'

Lisa played with her fingers, her hands ran over the table, and then she went on to tell me that she had stopped Ghana from being fired. She knew at once that Das would suspect him of the murder. 'He would think that father had sent Ghana off with the gun, so I worked it out this way. I told Ghana he could come back after a month when things had calmed down. He would go to his village and wait out for some days. I'd explain it all to father.'

Her voice was expressionless as she told me how Ghana's eyes had filled with tears. He had wrung his hands in his relief and gratitude. 'There is no need for all this, Ghana, we are now an independent country.' She felt independent and that was why she used the word.

She had then heard a car downstairs, a jeep, and voices. Das had arrived too soon. Her father had not been warned. I heard the despair now in her voice and felt it too. 'He asked if my parents were going to get me married and then he asked for my hand.'

Lisa.

I felt shocked and breathless. She went on, 'He won't stop otherwise. And I know why the butler paid the servants less, and why the servants stole. Father is being cheated out of his land. He's not smart enough. All the lawyers... agents are making him sign. There is no way out.'

The drama of the young, I thought. They do believe their heroism can save the world. I had looked out for my father, staring out of the highest window to wait for him. He never did return. And mama would come out of the porch to wait too, except that she waited for her letters. Then I had to leave, not just to get away, but to make mama think about something else. No matter how much one hides from such thoughts, our earliest attachments linger, some bonds remain hard to shake off, and sometimes these can be as steely as love itself.

'There was no need, Lisa.'

'But....'

She stood there, like a distraught princess, and the porch light flickered in through the window, leaving changing shadows on her face. I gazed at her eyes, her lips, and her face blurred and vanished while I looked on, as the light shifted and dimmed behind us.

'Things will be okay between my parents now.'

'How...?'

But I did not complete my question. When one is young, one does have all the power to change things, and often it does work.

'Do you think it's all right?' she asked.

'But Lisa, you've already done it.'

Her hands found the paper on the table, the one I had thrown away. She held it up to the porch light and then she shrugged and threw it away.

'Yes, but if you.'

'I can't....'

But I stopped too, and then she looked at me, 'You are leaving....'

'I think you need to leave too,' I said, my jaws clenched. I stared at the clock, pretended to stare at it with a deep concentration.

'I will see you through the forest path.' She said nothing to this. Her face was turned away in profile and she was lost in thought.

'Are you really leaving?' she asked.

'I will see you home, Lisa,' I said again.

'No. You think you're being gallant.'

'Don't be silly, Lisa,' I told her in the end. 'Your parents could be looking for you. It isn't like those times.'

We walked through the path that led away from the back door. I followed her. My footsteps in rhythm with hers, keeping close to her, whispering to her to be careful. 'There could be snakes around, just trample down the old cycle path.'

At one point, midway between the palace and my cottage, we stopped. I had left the light on, and from where we were, we could see the twin lights—the other lights from the palace now visible—shine like friends signalling each other. We stood against a tree, her arms brushed mine and then I kissed her.

She put her arms around my neck. And I held her close. The elephants could have trampled us for all I cared then. *Lisa*. My hands were on her waist, and I felt her soft skin, I felt her tongue on my neck, the pulse there beating fast.

We broke apart when we heard the rustling of feet nearby. In that darkness, a deer's blue eyes came close and then it ran away.

'You must go.' I thought for one dark wild moment that there might be another dead body. We held hands and she looked up, staring at me. She was trying to say something but didn't have the words. So in a foolish and gallant sort of way, I tried to stem the silence with my words. We both wanted to avoid the more painful things. 'You looked lovely today. I am sorry I didn't tell you that.'

'There was that man before you who took photos,' she said suddenly. 'He took a lot of photos too, the one before you.'

I went still as I realized something, and forced myself to stay calm, 'What did he look like?

'He had a certain stoop. Hazel eyes, and a head like a ball.'

I drew in a sharp breath. Keith Rawson was Colonel Oakshott. Of course. He had looked out for me. Given me safe haven here, of all places in the world.

I stared at Lisa but could not kiss her anymore. I kissed her hand instead, hoping it would erase the mark Das had left there once and for all.

19

LEAVING

For all my plans, I did not venture out the whole next day, or the day after. For what Lisa had said last kept niggling at me.

I checked Keith's handwriting. But that would never help. The colonel rarely wrote anything. And I had never heard Keith's voice. The only thing they seemed to share was a fondness for explaining things and photography. My thoughts chased each other in circles. It irritated me that what I wanted to remember was nothing compared to what I had to figure out. If they were indeed the same person and if he was hiding out precisely to avoid detection, why hadn't he reached out? Should I go to Berlin to see my mother or was going to find Keith more important?

I spent the day cleaning my cameras, pottering around the dark room and even taking a few photos. The leaves shimmered golden, and then moved through varying shades of yellow and green as the light bounced and slid off the trees. The streaks of orange splattering the sky appeared as a sudden rush of blood. I felt in turns guilty and exhilarated, it was like being with an old mistress again, who made you forget the immediate, worrisome present. I could not help telling this to Das when he came over towards late afternoon.

He listened to me for several minutes, his eyes roaming around the room, looking at the photos I had hung up and the leopard skin that had been dressed up by a friend of Rao's. It occupied one entire portion of the wall over the fireplace, its eyes still a watchful, lively red. Das's own eyes were unnaturally bright, and I caught the forced loudness in his words.

'Are you leaving?' He didn't wait for me to reply. 'I did hear something, and it's best you get out fast.'

He proceeded to tell me about the intelligence information he had. That the Muslims would create trouble. 'For the still unresolved mystery. But I tell you all this takes time, and we've been looking.'

He looked a bit lost. Now that he was engaged—and I could not give it away without revealing Lisa's presence the other night—the investigative zeal seemed to have fizzled out of him. I was certain he had never had an iota of proof. That all he wanted was to rid himself of his past, to climb the social and career ladder. What better way than to solve a case and marry someone from a well-established family?

I felt a surge of murderous fury but then stopped abruptly; wasn't I too trying to rid myself of my past? I had no idea I had spoken some of this aloud. But my directness caught him by surprise. He laughed his loud laugh again and cast a dramatic and nervous look at the rifle. 'Aren't you going to miss the shooting?'

'It's not so easy, Das. It's not so easy, shooting. Easier by far to blame someone, easier by far to just give orders.'

'What did you mean by that?' He advanced. I had not wanted to say all that I did, except that it had been on my mind. How easy it had been to plot murder, to make assassins of the most ordinary of men, simply because they had strayed, or found themselves on the wrong side of history, or on no side really.

'Don't come near me, Das.'

'It is clear the raja sahib was in trouble. You think....'

'Don't obfuscate the matter anymore, Das.'

'I thought we were friends.'

'Congratulations, Das.' I said coldly. I knew then I was glad to be leaving this place.

When I finally received the telegram from the consulate office, I made haste in rushing to the station. If I was lucky, I could get a ticket that very day on the overnight train. But things did not begin auspiciously. The Daimler was at Idris's, but the mechanic's office was closed. The beggar who sat outside the garage every day, as a self-appointed and unpaid gatekeeper, waved me away, and there was only one sullen assistant, polishing the hub caps of an Ambassador so meticulously that the smell of the varnish hung around him like an invisible halo. My car was again missing, it was not in its usual corner.

The boy barely looked up when he replied. He poured the liquid generously on his already soaked cloth, spitting on the part he was to polish before he rubbed it with the varnish-freshened cloth. 'Idris bhai has gone out. Out of town.'

'But where is everyone else? All of them have gone out of town?' My sarcasm like the heat was unflagging.

'The police sahib came. Asking for Idris bhai. When he wasn't there, he said the others had to go to the thana. I was not allowed.'

'They left you behind to make their excuses.'

Then I saw the limp as he dragged his leg and felt ashamed of what I said. The boy evidently did not understand for he bent his head down to rub at the car in a concentrated manner. I knew he could still see me, my distorted, convoluted self, as I appeared on the shiny visor of the hub cap.

I kicked around a few stones, but they were listless too. He spoke up then. Perhaps he did not think I would leave soon or maybe he felt the unwavering heat, his lone presence in the garage among the silent cars, the cats sleeping on the walls, their eyes tight over their whiskers. 'The police searched bhai's office and put their lock on it too.'

Behind us, the door creaked plaintively in the wind. It looked unassuming and bare, but I saw the heavy brass lock that hadn't been there before. Bits of paper were caught against the door, stamped into the ground with the imprint of someone's foot. The boy might have been polishing the hub caps for an eternity, as if he was impaled to the spot. Polished hub caps, and those still needing attention were arranged on either side of him, like Ravana's heads.

'Bhai will be back.' He nodded matter-of-factly, spitting on one shiny end of a cap, and rubbing it again with greater vigour. A stray dog came in through the half-open gate and he threw the hub cap at it. The peace was broken by the hollow clank of metal as the cap landed on the ground, emitting a thick cloud of dust, the yelping of an injured dog and the beggar's shrill laughter. 'The police said he'd better come along and not try to hide. They would give him a fitting farewell before sending him to Pakistan. I don't know. What will happen to this garage?'

These were observations I could little match with my own. The heat was overwhelming, and the garage with the lone boy in it, and cars in various stages of repair, appeared like a scene out of a dystopian landscape. I retraced my steps and walked to the gate that stayed open, like an old man's mouth left slackened by age and despair.

The beggar looked up as I emerged. He laughed, shaking his head at me, nothing happened, did it, sahib. No bribes were required, and no corpse was taken out. He shook his head, laughed to himself. The dog came up and sniffed him companionably.

I took Rao's cycle to the station, my suitcase strapped to the back, feeling the heat rise with my ponderous pedalling. It helped me to not think, or to feel the sudden sadness. I had no idea I'd miss saying goodbye to Lisa and not meet Tilo. But I was glad when I could finally disappear into the cooler confines of the station, among its disembodied clamour and the drift of anonymous bodies.

I could see the van from the steel plant parked among the other vehicles in the parking lot, and then the police vehicles.

The policemen were all inside the station, ubiquitous in every manner—under the terribly overweight fans swirling overhead, at the water cooler or occupying most of the available benches. Das was sprawled in one of these, his arms stretched wide to cover its backrest, barking orders to his men. One of them pointed me out to him, and Das turned around, fixed his cap, and his frown changed in a matter of seconds to a broad smile.

'The train will be delayed. I hope you do not need to reach Calcutta on time.'

One of his subordinates, having planted himself very near to be able to overhear our exchange and intervene at will, chose to do so now, smiling ingratiatingly, 'Nothing happens on time here, sir. Nothing at all.'

'Sit, sit, Hans, why are you standing?' And Das wriggled away from the centre of the bench to make space for me. The round orb of his sweat-filled armpit moved along with him. 'But you never said why you were going to Calcutta?'

'I did mention I am going home.' That statement came very easily to me at that moment. I felt an indulgence in the way they looked at me, and Das's understanding smile. It was something they all understood. Home was not where you went every evening, but it was a place where you could be yourself, the self you wanted to be, and there was no need for pretensions. It was where everyone held dear precious secrets, where nothing changed, where time itself stood still, where no one stood in judgement.

'Germany...it's not so hot there,' said the other policeman.

'Might take you a long time to get there.'

'I suppose so. I am making as quick a start as possible and now you tell me the train will be delayed.'

The two policemen looked at each other. 'Just some routine checking. We have been told to be on our guard.'

'Someone important arriving?' I asked, nonchalant.

Again the looks were exchanged. Then Das shrugged, 'It's to do with the recent spate of troubles here. It looks like a very political thing. In fact it is.' He mulled things over in his head before he rushed to explain it all to me. 'These Muslims and the Centrehood people have called in people to protest at the slow pace of investigations, and so we are arresting them. To keep the peace. The Muslims are not happy, they never are.' With his men around him, Das was now more voluble.

'All that talk of being at the centre of things, of instituting a political party, is a facade. They are really a group of murderous men. They will retaliate at the murder of Ahmed Ali. The Centrehood dream is in tatters. He was one of their thinkers. Still, you cannot take the law into your own hands. We believe that the mastermind of the movement is arriving this very night. Hence these arrangements.'

His finger swept around the platform, and I noted the policemen I had missed before. They were everywhere, fitting themselves into every aspect of life on the platform. Around the tea stall, the book stand, some still dozing under the fan where I had first seen them and a few at the palm reader's stall right near the ticket booth.

The train arrived from Vizag two hours later than usual and the policemen then made things difficult. They scrambled around the exit doors, cursing, beating at the sides of the compartment with their batons, giving rise to a tinny clamour that stilled everything else. We watched with increasing bemusement as Das led the policemen into one compartment, then another, their voices rising and falling, khaki-uniformed figures flitting about in light and shadow. Their increasing vociferousness was matched by the growing incomprehension writ large on the faces of the onlookers.

In this melee I spotted Singh and he and I shook hands perfunctorily and watched, our suitcases carefully placed by our sides, wondering when it would all be over and we could find our way to our respective seats. He looked sad, though he was his usual loquacious self. He was going to Calcutta to negotiate with the suppliers. But he missed his daughter. 'I miss her. I was so much involved in her wedding that I never realized....'

'You are going to Calcutta too?' Singh asked after a few minutes over the din. He cupped his hands over his mouth but before he could ask again, I nodded my reply. I felt raw and exposed in the crowded station.

In the train, Singh managed to find his way to my compartment. And having tried unsuccessfully to worm anything more out of me, and about my unexplained reasons for going home, he now offered to trade secrets.

'There are rumours the raja sahib came back and tried to reach a settlement. The superintendent knows something about it, he's a smart one, that officer.'

But I wasn't listening. Lisa had tried to protect her parents. I thought of our last conversation. I had had no idea till then that Keith and Oakshott had been the same man. I wondered if I should go northward to seek him out. And yet I felt this knowledge was all very new. It gave me more things to think about.

I looked out of the window. The sal trees brushed close by my window, and a raw sweet smell mixed with the rottenness of the decaying and dying leaves filled the compartment. A stray leaf detached itself and found its way into our compartment. Singh stretched out his toe and smashed it, and a strain of slimy green appeared on the shiny, silver floor. I rose and stayed away for nearly two hours, taking the vestibule to the other compartments. The genteel silence in first class ate up the scrunch of my shoes on the carpet and was only broken by the raised voice of a terribly excited woman. When it was really quite dark, I saw the train had stopped somewhere. *Chaibasa*. I read, and the boy came running down the platform, beating his stick across the windows. Chai. Chai.

I got down, where he held out a clay cup for me. He poured tea from the kettle he carried, almost half his size. I stood on the platform, feeling the heat from the cup course through me. The boy was making small talk with the other passengers. I wondered why Singh too had not clambered down, like he usually did at these stations with long stops. He would rush for the magazine stand, looking for the stuff he liked. But the magazine shop had its shutters down, a lone dog had curled up near it, his tail flicking occasionally as he dreamed of his past lives. It was two in the morning.

'You go up, sahib, train will start.' The guard had come up.

'Is the driver ready?'

'That Anglo? Today he is in a hurry, god knows why. Must have seen a ghost on the tracks, it makes him go very fast.'

I smiled thinly. He could be talking about Hutchins. But I yanked the door open and re-entered my own compartment. When I awoke next, we were already in Calcutta. I felt it, in the way the train slowed, then kept slowing, like a heart whose beat was about to stop forever.

As a swamp of coolies entered the compartment, Singh and I became strangers. The coolies jostled around me, calling out for the luggage, and Singh stood helpless and forlorn, trying to exchange last minute notes with me, and getting the coolies' attention. He had two large suitcases that he looked very embarrassed about. They were all patched up, belted tight and over-labelled. 'My wife packed them. For our daughter,' he said, 'pickles and things like that.' He kicked at the suitcase with his shoe, 'I myself don't take much. Like you, one small suitcase.'

I left him there, he was haggling with the coolies, trying to bring down the price. I did not know that that was the last time I would see him alive. All I knew was that I had to head for the consulate.

20

DHARMSHALA 1976

In the end, I did not go to Berlin. Instead, I went up north to Dharmshala, where late one afternoon, sixteen years later, the past came back with a knock on the door.

'Hans, Hans.'

When Karma Dorje called in so insistently, it could only mean the police. They had come around once again to ask me about someone new in the area, someone who didn't fit in. People who, so the police thought, would invariably come by my photo studio. Why would they want to incriminate themselves, I always asked myself, by having a picture taken?

There were all kinds of people in Dharamshala now. The trickle of people from across the border that had begun with the Dalai Lama's arrival had never stopped. Besides the refugees, there were the tourists, eloping couples, students, and in their wake, the police. Now it was summer, the silly tourist season had just begun. With students who had slipped away for a furtive weekend, from the fancy boarding schools in the hills east of the town. Middle-class government employees with their families came up every summer, packing themselves and their noisy children into tinny, stuffy buses, their roofs stuffed with their middle-class baggage.

Late summer mornings, they would walk down the Mall, pass by my studio. For I had my hours—from ten to six, almost every day, with a mid-afternoon break. I'd hear them playing their token prayer bells, their silly chatter and then the request for a studio photo, choosing between the few backdrops I offered: sunflower fields, the snow-capped mountains or a palace in Rajasthan.

'Hans,' Karma called again, and I flitted from a slow awakening to an abrupt dream. 'Hans, wake up. Post!'

My bleary eyes saw the green barred window, the wrought iron balcony rails of the guesthouse that abutted my studio shed, and outside, the sky that turned a dull blue right on my face. Soon the square below would fill up with much-in-love couples and students bargaining with the vendors over their colourful wares, the monks bowing and sidling past them. The buzz of the portable lighters would echo the moths and remain till the last tourists had dwindled to a trickle, then the vendors would have a last smoke before they too drifted away, like the evanescent soft clouds that lingered over the mountains every morning and vanished in a few hours.

'Hans, Hans a special post for you. From Delhi.'

I pulled the door open, flinching at the sharp buzz of other voices. The bus that was to take the group of American students to Shimla was several hours late, and there they were, clamped to the guesthouse steps outside. Karma tapping his feet outside, jerked his head toward the door and he smiled a silly toothy smile. 'Special post from Calcutta. Shorry. Not Delhi.'

The man who waited where the steps ended was not the usual postal guy who came by in the afternoons and before every festival time, asking for baksheesh. This was someone from Shimla perhaps, and the brown packet he now held up against the sun, squinting to look up at me, looked to be a government document with its red seal.

I waited, deliberately, for the man to come up, glancing quickly at my old front office, the clammy registers full of receipts and bills unclaimed, the photos of tourists on the boards and others hoarded up in boxes. The keys of my old blue Daimler thrown carelessly on the table, and the weak light from the table lamp that Karma Dorje never turned off. The light helped him see the dust better, he always said. The late afternoon sun made lines on the floor as it pushed its way through the curtain ends, yellow and orange.

'Hans Gerder?'

He had a low, brusque voice, and came up the last few steps, holding out the package. Its brown, frayed edges told me it had travelled long, in place and time. 'Registered Post from Calcutta. You must sign this slip. And this other one for the government.' He pulled another piece of paper out from his pants, stumbling on a step as he held it out.

Two slips of paper. That meant it couldn't be a summons or a government document. But it was something important, for a tracking slip to be signed twice. He was a square and short man. His left shoulder, raised an inch or two higher than the other, gave him a somewhat tilted look. He pressed a finger to his nose to ensure his glasses stayed on, then thrust out that dirty brown packet. Placing a stubby yellow-nailed finger over the two dirty, dog-eared pieces of government paper, he asked me to sign. The paper was familiar with its musty smell and dirty white look, something pulled out from an old perforated pad of government forms.

I asked, as uncurious and brusque as his voice. A voice I've learnt to use over time, one that demanded and gave away nothing. 'Why? What's in this?'

'I don't know, from Calcutta, says so in the form.'

He tapped below the packet, pointing again to the taped square piece of paper, 'If you have any questions, call her. She said it's a personal document. And important.' My throat had gone dry, I looked to where the man had indicated, and signed in my usual inscrutable way. The man took the slips I held out and ran down with speed to the waiting scooter.

Ignoring the question in Karma's eyes, I walked to my room and shut the door behind me. My hands seemed numb as I tore the package open. I lifted the diary, smelling of mothballs and age, flipped the pages over and saw my past reappear. I picked up the envelope I had carelessly torn.

My name. In her writing.

Mr Hans. It was the way she had called me always.

I took the envelope and the diary to the window; the faint light only enhanced its age. The writing appeared startlingly clear, my fingers moved over every word. I forgot the questions I had, such as how she had found my address, and managed to send me this. I smelt my younger self in the diary's pages. Now its return only elicited a wry twist of my lips. Memory does this to us; for all our determination, our most precious mementos only come grudgingly to life.

Other things though, memory preserves in its entirety. Like the handwriting on the letter. I saw it again, against the light, a small, square sheet, folded in two, the clip holding it, glinting faintly. The writing was hers, the words spaced out, distinct and thoughtful. She had taken her time. All this time of sixteen years since I had last seen her.

Lisa, she wrote at the end. Not Lipsa.

For that was the name I had called her by. It came to me, in a hushed tone: *Lisa.* I quickly looked over my shoulder, but the door was secured. Karma was not eavesdropping. I remembered Lisa, that first time I saw her, peering over the banister, her plaits bouncing, and her toes curled below her long, frilly skirt.

I hope you are well. I got this diary from Mrs Hutchins, my old tutor. She is leaving finally for Australia. She wished to return it to you, and I am writing for her.

I looked out at the fading afternoon, listened to someone tuning his guitar. There was one evening she had come upon me as I traced a new map in that same diary. I read on:

It is very strange that you should be in Dharamshala. I saw a photo of you ~~with~~ and the Dalai Lama, and looked for your address. I hope you are happy to get your diary back again after all these years.
Lisa

Her crossing out a word indicated an uncertainty, or something else. It was an old diary I no longer cared much about. Still she had looked for my address. I walked toward the board and looked at the photo pinned to the very top. There was Lisa, her face turned away. A day in June 1960. With my old Pentax, I had shot the three of them one late evening. Lisa, to the left of the photo, standing self-consciously, holding on to her scarf. And that young English teacher, who had been in love with her, and Pat next to him. Holding on to him, her fat arm around his like a club. The man's features were blurred, his crinkled-up smile almost a grimace. Pat had the same smug defiant look she had when I asked her if she had seen my diary. She had looked as if it was a thing she had never seen; and as I learnt now, sixteen years later, she had had it with her all this while.

I saw in the diary again, the lines I had drawn, the routes I had taken, moving halfway across the world, moving up and down an entire ocean once and then across it as well. The places I had marked on a map. All my hasty scribbled notes, deliberately made cryptic, for fear of the diary falling into the wrong hands. But I had lost it, and the diary had become something missing in my life for these many years. The monks at the monastery had once told me that a thing sometimes returned of its own accord, if it wanted to, and if I wanted it so. Wanted it, with a heart that held only love.

21

CALCUTTA 1976

There really aren't many people called Hutchins in Calcutta; the telephone directory, I noted, listed just two. I called the number listed for TP Hutchins and after an unexpectedly joyous exchange with Mrs Hutchins, I arranged to go over.

Clara, I still remembered her incongruous first name. 'Clara here', is how she had answered the phone.

After she served me tea, she walked slowly away, to methodically rearrange again the pictures on the mantelpiece. Where I sat, I could make out Tom Hutchins—now the late Mr Hutchins—his walrus moustache twirled up in the air, the hint of laughter on his face. That was his most effective weapon. Was it that famous laugh that had scared away the elephants as he drove his train through the forests? I could not ask her these questions, not now, not ever.

For there is a time when memories become just like the accumulated baggage one has stored away in an upstairs attic; knowing it's there gives you the assurance that you have lived. But take it all down, and you are amazed at what you have acquired over the years. The stuff that was once yours has taken up too much space, even in your head. And looking at it will not tell you anything about the person you were, but rather the person you would rather not have been.

I asked her instead about her children. The girl, for a minute, I floundered for her name. The girl with the hearty laugh, and booming voice. *Pat. Pat.* I suddenly recollect.

'In Australia now,' she says walking back toward me with a framed photo. It had one of those stylized frames, spiralling roses at the corners with notches in it to give it that old-style look. 'This is one she took with her youngest.'

The youngest was a baby who scowled at me in the photo, and Pat looked much the same, the smile bursting out of her flushed cheeks

'In Australia...,' I said.

'Perth. She moved there in 1971..'

1971, I was in Dharmshala by then. It wasn't a very definitive year for me. There were, I realized, no particularly defining years for me. Except for that month at sea in 1950, when I almost became a murderer. That didn't change me the way I feared it would; now I know that those events had simply forced me into a course of action I had no option but to take. But I might have let myself love a bit more fully.

I had looked for Keith Rawson in those initial years of living north, and then over time considered that it might have all been a coincidence: the two men being the same person. After all, my life itself had been shaped by a coincidence. That I had happened to look like someone, and that had taken my life down certain routes.

Pat had stepped out in 1971, from the town she had grown up in, the little excitement it offered. She had moved out that year, to another country altogether and it had seemingly left her so untouched in life.

'She has four children. Tim and Vera, Clara whom she named after me, and then Bill,' Mrs Hutchins smiled at me as I took the photo.

'Does Pat come back here often?'

'No, she was last here at the time of Tom's nephew's wedding. Now he too has moved there. And anyway, as families grow bigger, and bigger, those on the sides will get forgotten.'

She meandered from one thought to the other, giving me time to look over the photos on the mantelpiece, and those she had pinned up on boards all over the small room. There were too many of them. I remembered her house in the old times. All those impressionist prints that lined one wall of her corridor. I stopped when I recognized one of my own photos. There was Pat and the young man who was always hanging around at Mrs Hutchins's house those days.

'I remember him. This was the English teacher, wasn't he?'

I knew the answer even before she turned around slowly, almost watching the unwilling swell of memories that rose tide-like in her mind, 'Benny. Benny...,' and she crossed herself. I sat down, in the cushioned chair, aware of the dust emanating from it, sealing me, even if momentarily into that old world.

'So many years now. I can't say....'

'What happened?'

He had that same indecisiveness on his features, even his crinkly smile seemed overdone. I remembered how I had been surprised at first when I learnt that he was a teacher. Perhaps he didn't look strict enough to be one.

'He went swimming off Puri beach and never came back.'

'Drowned,' I must have said that to fill the silence.

'But his body was never found. You know Pat kept going around to the police station, until they got fed up of her and pushed her away. Such a silly idealistic girl, once she had an idea in her head, nothing could dissuade her. And I told her to give it up. What is the use? Even if he had gone away, vanished because he was tired of her chasing him, she was spoiling her own life. And Allan would not wait for her.'

My eyes darted back to the photos. The most unlikely people are chosen for death, I thought, looking again and again at that photo. It was strange how the two of us never became friends. Yes, I saw him occasionally at the club, and more frequently once Pat was there, but he wasn't a regular. Once the raja sahib had teased him loudly in everyone's hearing, in the unthinking careless way the raja sahib had, and Benny had been embarrassed by everyone's eyes on him. Other men made him feel inferior but with the women, he came into his own. I remembered him with Pat, there had been an intimacy between the two of them long before she had told me, half-angrily, and sadly, that he was her fiancé and she had watched my face for a reaction. And what reaction could I have had but of profound amusement? Marriage was too big a deal, a whole new baggage that was, as I felt then, quite unnecessary to take on.

'Dear God, such a long time ago it was.' Mrs Hutchins had returned and was now dragging the table fan near me before she realized there was no power. 'Oh dear, I keep forgetting...,' she looked at the clock on the old fireplace, hand on her mouth. 'Thirty minutes more. Perhaps you would use this.' She handed me a bamboo hand fan. It gave off a whiff of powder as I waved it. Mrs Hutchins' face appeared and reappeared in shifts like an old silent movie. 'And Pat really liked him. It happened so long ago. Benny kept getting dragged into things he wasn't concerned with. Do you remember that police officer? We didn't realize till it happened,' she looked away from the window, 'how much he wanted to marry the Mishra girl, the raja's daughter?'

'Who?' I asked deliberately, putting the fan down, the sudden cold had turned the sweat around my forehead to a welcome dampness.

'That Das, the superintendent, he was terrible, remains so. They said even then he had engineered everything..., that it was all cooked up. That matter of that Mohammedan teacher whose body was found in the forest? Das even pressed Tom to change his statement that one time, kept saying there was more than he was letting on. Tom always told me that it didn't help much, his going to the police. And so many of those Mohammedans, including the mechanic Idris, were picked up and thrown into jail. They had started some trouble in the town and were blamed for it. And the teacher's death was all forgotten. Ali, I think his name was.'

For her age, I was amazed she seemed to remember everything so clearly from a certain time. After she had finished, Mrs Hutchins sat looking down with a fixed expression at the fireplace, like a shaman expecting secret messages from the fire spirit.

'Nothing like that, I told Tom. But that man would not rest till he had driven the family apart. Lisa was always a nice girl, too kind.'

I rose to pick the photo up again from the mantelpiece. It was the second picture I'd taken of them, just to be sure. Lisa standing next to Pat and Benny, the English teacher. This time she stood a bit more to the side and did not appear part of the photo.

'Did you get the diary back?'

My diary with all my Eichmann notes. In blue velvet with the ribbon around it, silk and frayed with age. I nodded embarrassedly, thinking the diary was like a lover one no longer wishes to acknowledge.

'Yes, you left rather abruptly. That year there were so many weddings. That Singh's daughter.' Mrs Hutchins laughed, almost like a teenager. 'Then Lisa's...I keep calling her that, you know. Then some years later there was Pat's in Calcutta. It was a small affair in comparison.'

I walked back, taking a long detour, stopping by the Maidan, and it was late when I reached my hotel. There was just so much to think over. For a day or two I dithered. I wondered if I should look for Lisa. Mrs Hutchins of course knew where she was; they might already have spoken about my visit. My heart thumped faster at that thought. For Lisa had written to me after all these years. She had seen my photo in the papers. And she had sent the diary back to me. That could mean something.

Letters, cryptic and short, had always meant something to me. Keith's notes, those short letters of advice he had left behind, had helped me so much. That time, in Calcutta, many years ago, I had waited for a response from him. Then I had called up the post office at Dharmshala, as Keith had said. Someone called Karma Dorje had answered, only to tell me that Keith had gone over the border to Tibet. In search of peace. Karma laughed the way he still does.

Keith never came back of course. The border between the two countries became contentious and there was the war in 1962. But I stayed on, moving to other places at times, other towns around Dharmshala. Once I did go up to Kailash, and even toward Tibet, before I was stopped by the Chinese police. Somewhere during that journey, I lost the revolver. The one I had hidden away. I never did go back to Berlin. I always had the Daimler though. I returned from Calcutta one last time to claim it. I left without meeting anyone, or even letting anyone know. Finding the blue Daimler in Idris's abandoned workshop had given me immense comfort.

22

LISA

The blue Daimler had held up all through my long journey from Dharmshala to Calcutta. It broke down only once when I drove within the city, somewhere on the stretch between Alipur and Lord Sinha Road. For a day, I had toyed with the idea of calling on her. Then I had put on my best British accent when I called her. Colonel Oakshott had, after all, never failed me. A man with a wispy voice asked, and I answered, 'From Shimla. And it's important.' When she came to the phone, my voice was a hoarse whisper.

Lisa.

Lisa, it's Hans.

I'd always remember how the little we said bridged the long gap between us. Less than fifteen words for the many years in between.

I did go to meet her then. In an old government house in the Port Trust building, with its high ceiling and dark wooden floors. My shoes knocked against each other. She had her hair in a net and looked elegant and poised. She had something of her father in her. We smiled and could not look away. I must have turned red.

'You didn't give an address in the letter. And I went to Mrs Hutchins.'

'You came to thank me, Mr Hans. All the way here?'

Then I plucked up my courage, when I saw the look in her eyes, 'Well, that wasn't the only reason.'

I did kiss her then clumsily, and the blue Daimler amused her no end. She told me then that I was the kind who found it hard to give up on things. The sturdy old car did take in her two suitcases though. As we drove back up north together, she told me what had happened in the days I had been away in Calcutta. It was a long drive, and we spent long leisurely hours stopping at places before we moved on. She had much to say. I had a lot to listen to.

'I did not know what had happened to Idris's shop. I was in Bhubaneshwar, to attend a wedding. The minister's daughter.' Lisa told me of the dissolution of her parents' marriage. 'It just happens. They were kind of friendly and yet indifferent to each other. Father, he lived with Samineh for some years, and my mother remained in the palace, where there's now a school for girls on the ground floor.'

Of the riots that time, she had little direct knowledge. Idris's shop had burnt down to the ground. 'Someone had been smoking near the leaking petrol tanks. I am glad your Daimler was saved.'

'My mother returned from Bhubaneshwar a few days later. She looked so very different. The other women said she looked better than ever. Their eyes scoured her face carefully, looking for possible giveaways. But my mother held herself straight and firm. She was her ever-smiling, cheerful self.

'There were the photos of the new plot of land she had bought at Shahid Nagar. It would be a cultural centre, Ma said, a centre where all the traditional cultural forms of Orissa would be developed and exposed. There was a small mention of her work in the *Hindustan Standard*, a Calcutta paper as well. Rani Tilottama, it said, would now devote herself to promoting culture. It was very different from all that she had done so far.'

'And the servant?' I asked.

'Yes, Ghana. He had gone home to his village for a month. But he was found dead in the forest, the tiger claws were visible on his neck and back. We do not know what he was doing in the forest. His family said he had gone looking for something.'

One day I would tell her about the missing gun. The gun that Ghana must have gone looking for. The gun he had dropped when he, and I too, had been in the forest that night.

'The truth,' Lisa said, 'was that we had not noticed that the gun had gone missing from father's study. Father had already lost interest in his guns. It was from the time an elephant hunt had gone horribly wrong, and two villages along the river paid a heavy price. The elephants destroyed everything. And father blamed himself for having organized it all.

'Ma too remembered this story about the gun, before she died. She said, I don't think your father used it any more, after that day. I don't even think he cared for it. Though it had been a very expensive model. He had had to take special permission from the minister Patel to get it from Belgium. But I think that incident with the elephant put him off it.

'After one of their own had been killed, the elephants descended on the villages, on either side of the river Koel, their grief driving them beyond madness. For all the preparations the villagers had made, with their bamboo barricades and their flaming torches, they could only offer flimsy resistance against fifty or more elephants. Tossing houses aside, trampling over anything that came in the way, it was as if a marauding army from the past had returned. "We have lived with them for so long," the people said later, "the elephants would not have harmed us, if the raja had not upset them."

'And father listened to them, said he would do something. Two villages, two banana groves, even the old temple to the forest Devi. That in sum was the damage incurred, the repentance he paid for the dead elephant, and just for one night of elephant hunting. But events had moved far beyond by then. It wasn't simply a matter of an elephant hunt gone very wrong. It was the newness of the times. In the space of a few years, things had changed, utterly, and totally.

'You know the rest. Can't you see how it all fits together? Father had no problem giving up land for the refugees. But the factory coming up had other ideas. A symbol of modern things, and father was not able to match it action for action. The strike happened, there was so much confusion, and then the strange death of the teacher, Idris's shop destroyed. Things had never been this way. It was how things were meant to be.'

She shrugged, laughed and stood up. There was something still of the abruptness of her youth.

Lisa, she still had her smile, it gave her a glow and I felt the sadness in her eyes. I reached for her fashionably styled bun and asked if she remembered the time I had undone her hair. 'Your hair feels the same. Things haven't changed, have they?'

My fingers lingered on her hand, her arm. I remembered the photo of Das in her Calcutta living room. Now I remembered a conversation with him, in the beginning of our friendship. 'You have seen all the sights here, old chap?' he had asked then.

I told him about the beach at Konark, the temples, the animal sanctuaries, especially the crocodile that I had seen basking in the sun. The creature had so terrified me that I could not move, until the village forest official told me that it was tied up, it was a pet of the local maharaja.

'Are you sure it was a crocodile?' Das had asked. 'It was perhaps a seal. They develop warts there because of the heat.'

Das had made me laugh then, one could never take him seriously. So, when he told me about his intention to marry the most beauteous thing ever, I never thought he meant it.

'Which makes you still an idiot, Hans.'

I agreed, and she leaned up to kiss me, and left a trail of lipstick on my chin. She made to rub it off, and I held her hand. I heard myself murmur against her ear. *Let it be, Lisa, let love stay this time.*

I'd tell her in time the rest of my story, or what I felt was important. Keith had already crossed the border. Perhaps he had indeed wanted to disappear before I caught onto his identity.

We drove around the country in our blue Daimler. I did take photos. And after some years the Daimler really couldn't run anymore. But it was all right, the two of us were in Dharamshala. I would always love her, and sometimes I really didn't need to say it. Sometime toward the end of 1989, we saw images of the Berlin Wall falling on television. I told Lisa then that I was ready to go back.

ACKNOWLEDGEMENTS

I am grateful to Arpita Das for having faith in my manuscript when I first emailed it to her and my thanks to my marvellous Yoda editors, Ishita Gupta and Tanya Singh. I would also like to thank my family for being there always, when it mattered: Ajay, Devyani, my mother, Uma Chakrabarty, and my father, Chinmay Chakrabarty, whom I lost in 2017 but whose stories linger on in my life, in small and big ways.

www.ingramcontent.com/pod-product-compliance
Lightning Source LLC
Chambersburg PA
CBHW021843130726
47989CB00009B/3063